Anna Ferrara

**THE WOMAN
WHO MADE ME
FEEL STRANGE**

This is a work of fiction. Names, characters, places, and incidents either are the product of the author's imagination or are used fictitiously. Any resemblance to actual persons, living or dead, business establishments, events, or locales is entirely coincidental.

Copyright © 2017 by Anna Ferrara.

First published December 2017.

First print edition. v1.4

ISBN: 9781976878183

Cover design by Anna Ferrara.

All rights reserved.

No part of this book may be reproduced, scanned, or distributed in any printed or electronic form without permission.

To acquire the rights to reproduce this book, contact Anna Ferrara via annaferrarabooks.com

Books by Anna Ferrara

Snow White and Her Queen

The Woman Who Made Me Feel Strange

The Woman Who Pretended To Love Men

The Woman Who Tried To Be Normal

Coming Soon

Eritis Mea

More information available at

annaferrarabooks.com

CONTENTS

The Woman Who Made Me Feel Strange

(33 Chapters)

About the Author

Other Books by Anna Ferrara

To those who've been criticised for not being normal.

CHAPTER 1
5 MAY 2030

The night of the falling incident began normal. A regular Sunday just like any other Sunday. I left work at eleven, got catcalled by the punks loitering about my apartment building's piss-covered corridors just after midnight and triple-locked the door to my apartment exactly two minutes after that.

Everything was as it always was until perfumed flesh fell over my eyes and made my world go dark.

"Guess who?"

The voice vibrated down my spine and made me visualise us standing in one of those black and white arthouse films, her breasts pressed up against my back, her lips next to my ear. She smelled very elegant, like roses, vanilla and a hint of champagne.

My mouth curled upwards at the ends. I didn't have to guess. There was no one else but her in my life back then. She was the one my mind was preoccupied with. The only one I thought of in quiet moments.

"Hmm. Lina? Marion? Or Sally?" I laughed.

"I am better than any of those girls, Lane," she said to

my bones. "Never forget that."

How could I? Her face was practically everywhere I went—on buildings, in magazines, on screens, sometimes even on moving vehicles. Nobody could ever be better than her. I didn't get to say so though because her lips ran over my mouth and for a good while kept me preoccupied.

The kiss we shared that night, I would never forget. It was the type of kiss you used to define all other kisses. The type you kept fresh in your mind and cheered yourself up with during low moments.

I could have kissed her forever but her lips left mine. I opened my eyes.

Arden Villeneuve stood in my apartment in an overwashed, oversized, hooded tracksuit that night. With her height—two-thirds of a head taller than I was—she would have looked somewhat like a malnourished male drug addict if not for that stunning face perfected by glossy, nude-tone makeup and that blonde bun so tightly gelled back, it looked almost like plastic over her skull.

Electricity coursed through my veins when my eyes met her legendary brown ones but I managed to smile as if unaffected. "How did you get in?"

"Easy. Found out your boss was your landlord, told him I wanted to leave you a surprise and he lent me a key."

I nodded despite the overwhelming urge to wish my boss death for having done so. Right next to the majestic Arden Villeneuve was my half-bathroom which hadn't enough space for a sink and my compact kitchenette that hadn't enough space for a normal-sized fridge. Behind her, a ratty single mattress on the floor lay snugly between three grubby walls—two made of brick, one false—under a mess of clothes and shoes dangling from a rusty rack. This side of me, she was never supposed to know of, much less see with her very own eyes.

"It's a temporary living arrangement," I mumbled and felt my cheeks burn. I could hear every vulgarity the couple next door yelled at each other and see vibration on the false wall every time they threw objects around. Somewhere in the distance, a baby wailed. Some punks laughed. A dog barked. Normally, I barely noticed those sounds but on that particular night, with Arden Villeneuve in my room, they nettled me to no end. "Why the surprise?" I said. Loudly.

Arden Villeneuve reached down and picked up the giant bouquet of roses lying by her feet. They had been there the whole time yet somehow, I never noticed. She presented them to me.

"I want to spend a night with you. Have a night we can both think fondly of for the rest of our lives."

A rush shot through my body when she said those words. The roses were the expensive sort—huge, long-stemmed, bright red, with tiny droplets of water glistening on their petals—but what was most exciting was the look on her face when she offered them to me.

"Will you come with me?"

I said yes. You would have done so too, I'm sure. She drove us out of Far Rockaway in a beat-up 90s car—a vehicle she borrowed because my neighbourhood was way too dangerous for her Porsche. I took a good look at the loners lurking by the shuttered 99-cent stores and homeless people sitting in rusty fast food joints and decided she made the right choice.

We ended up in some part of Manhattan I had never been to, in front of a squarish mass of creeping plants shaped like a single-storey building squashed between two skyscrapers.

Part of the mass of green rose and folded into itself when Arden Villeneuve picked up her phone and did a facial scan with its camera when we were in front of it. It was a hidden garage door she unlocked.

She drove us into the plant-covered single-storey building and switched off the car's noisy engine. The inside was exactly like the outside. Walls of creeping plants. A ceiling of plants. More plants than I had ever seen in one place in New York. The garage door closed behind us and engulfed us in absolute silence. More silence than I had ever experienced before.

"You'll love it, I promise," Arden Villeneuve said and winked. She stepped out of the car just as the wall of green within folded itself upwards and revealed a cemetery surrounded by black walls, lit by theatrical lighting fixtures that seemed to mimic the faint glow of a moonlit night.

Holy mother of Christ, I thought as I got out of the car myself.

It wasn't just any cemetery that was before us. It was the sort with larger than life sculptures of humans in dramatic poses and mausoleums the size of subway entrances. It was so huge, I couldn't see the end of it from where I stood.

"Have you ever been to a cemetery before?"

"No." Of course not. In 2021, just months after the fever of city-cemetery collecting came upon the top 1%, the last public cemetery in New York had been privately acquired. After that day, those without the right connections, nobodies like me, simply had to contend with photographs. "Who owns this one? Some old money friend of yours?"

"No, me." Arden Villeneuve peeled off her tracksuit, dropped it to the ground and revealed the glossy latex bodice she had been wearing underneath all this time. It had a shiny silver zip running all the way up the front that seemed to be screaming to be pulled down and I couldn't help but think she looked very much like a dominatrix from a state-of-the-art Sci-fi universe. She smiled when she saw the look in my eyes and told me to follow her.

My heart pounded in my ears as we walked down the mossy brick path that ran right through the middle of the cemetery but I did my best to look calm. There was an unusual chill in the enclosed space and there was the smell of dirt and grass in the air. I felt as if we were outdoors even though it was obvious we really weren't.

"This is a piece of history." Arden Villeneuve pointed out the dates carved into the tombstones we passed; many were over a hundred years old. "The final resting place of prominent individuals. Billionaires. Politicians. Celebrities. I too will be buried here. Some day."

Awesome choice, in death, but I wasn't sure I felt the same about us being in the cemetery before that. It was too quiet. Every step we made sounded too loud. I didn't like the idea of corpses being that close to us. "There are cameras," I said.

"That only I have access to. Don't worry."

"Graveyard workers?"

"They come only once a month and they're not here now."

"Paranormal seekers? Visitors of the dead? Plus, isn't this a little... disrespectful?"

Arden Villeneuve laughed and turned to face me. I saw a naughty twinkle in her eyes, one I understood all too well. "Are you scared, Lane? Nervous?" She pushed her body up against mine and I heard the deafening sound of latex cackling right next to my ears.

A collection of nerves churned in the pits of my stomach and my skin began to tingle. Because of the dead or Arden Villeneuve's perfume, I did not know but I did nod. Slowly.

She leaned into my ear and whispered, "That's what's going to make tonight wonderful."

That shiny silver zip between her bosom found its way right to the front of my face. I found myself pulling it all the way down towards her crotch without a second thought.

We fucked stark naked on gravestones and raw dirt because Arden Villeneuve wanted to. She said she needed to experience what it was really like in case she ever had to act a situation like it at some point. I went along for the ride because hey, she *was* Arden Villeneuve.

She came five times in total that night. Twice while seated on gravestones, once while standing next to a statue of a semi-naked woman with a pained expression, once while lying on a coffin-shaped marble slab in the ground and finally on a bed of shrubs, crying out into the dim darkness like nobody would ever hear.

I managed to come three times myself despite not really loving the environment. My final orgasm was the best of the three. I lost all restraint and screamed like Arden Villeneuve had been doing all night long and finally got why she thought sex in a cemetery would actually be a fun idea.

In that very moment, I remember thinking that gorgeous Arden Villeneuve—iconic and world famous Arden Villeneuve—was possibly the only woman I could see myself making love to for the rest of my life.

We sat with our naked backs against the headstone of a once famous technopreneur and kept our arms close for warmth once satiated. I lit her a cigarette—as I always did after every sexual occasion—and thought the sizzle of paper and tobacco catching fire sounded as if it had been put through a loudspeaker.

"You have a gift," she said while watching me light a cigarette for myself. "You really get how to bring a woman pleasure."

I laughed and was about to repay the compliment when I noticed something unusual. Arden Villeneuve was looking right at me, scanning every inch of my face, as if trying to commit all my features into memory.

She never did that before. All I usually got after sex was a sleepy contented smile followed by a lazy 'I'll-see-you-next-week' goodbye. But not that night.

On the night of the falling incident, I had Arden Villeneuve's full attention.

"I'll miss you," she said, in a voice so low, it sounded almost like a whisper.

The solemnness of her expression as she said those words made the happy relaxation I had been feeling disappear. My fingers tightened their grip of the cigarette between them but I made sure my face did not reveal my concern. "Why?" I asked.

"I've been proposed to. I said yes."

Oh. I peeled my eyes from hers and dragged at my cigarette in a manner that would suggest the revelation hardly bothered me at all. I blew out a thick cloud of smoke in front of my face before I said, "And that means?"

"He's religious."

My heart tripped. My cheeks stiffened. *Oh.*

"This ends tonight."

Great. Of all the people in the world to marry, Arden Villeneuve, one of the hottest women in the world, had to go marry a religious man. *How perfect.* I nodded and took another drag of my smoke before flicking the ashes over some dead person's unseen body. "In that case, I wish you love." I made myself look her right in the eyes. I pulled my lips upwards into a smile as if all were well.

Arden Villeneuve took one look at my face and frowned. "Will you miss me?"

"Should I?"

Those two words bothered her very much, to my delight. She looked away and crossed her arms. "No. I guess you shouldn't."

"It's late. We better go," I said and stubbed out my cigarette on the stone toes of a pained man with eyes on the sky and hands clasped together. I found myself thinking the man looked like a loser and deserved whatever fucked up pain he got.

A chill cloaked my unclothed skin as I stood up and

scoured the cemetery. I shuddered, despite wanting to look untouchable.

"Spend the night with me, Lane. It's our last together."

"No. I'm not sleeping with corpses." My bare feet went across cold dirt and scratchy weeds as I went in search of my clothes. The tombs no longer creeped me out. Rage was all I felt in that moment even though I made sure I didn't show any of it. Inside though, I couldn't help but wonder why, of all the millions of people in the world to marry, Arden Villeneuve had to pick someone religious.

"Why don't I drive us back to your apartment? We could sleep there," she said.

"No, you can't." I spotted my black jeans in front of a mausoleum, my grey singlet some distance away on the dirt, and went to put them on.

"Lane…"

I didn't bother saying a word.

"Lane!"

I turned only when I was fully dressed again, when my waist long hair had been pulled out of the back of my singlet, and I was no longer exposed and vulnerable.

Arden Villeneuve was too far away to see properly but I could feel her staring and expecting a reply.

I will miss you, Arden, I thought. *I will miss you with every inch of my soul, for as long as I live.* But to her, I said, in the most flippant manner I could muster, "Thanks for the memories."

After that, I turned and let myself out of the cemetery I knew I would never get to experience ever again.

A few hours later, the falling incident occurred.

CHAPTER 2
5 MAY 2033

Right after the falling incident, there was blackness. Huge blackness wrapped in silence. Endless silence like nothing was all there ever had been.

Eventually there was also softness. Under me. Holding on to me. Under my palms. Under my head. The softness made me notice how heavy I was. That I was a weight.

At some point, a sound appeared. A beep-beep-beep-beep-beeping sound that seemed to beep at precise intervals.

My body shivered in time with the beeps until something materialised over me. Over my chest. Over my arms. A strange prickly sensation ran under that something. Somewhat like a thousand needles pricking my skin. I knew there was a simple phrase to describe that sensation precisely but for the life of me could not remember what that phrase was.

I plunged downwards shortly after, like I had gone into free fall. I felt like I were on a roller coaster backwards. A really steep one. The kind you worry about being asked to ride on.

I was in the pits of despair, endlessly falling, trying to scream but not knowing how to, when my eyelids flipped upwards. All by themselves.

Just like that, I was no longer falling. The insanely bright world of white I was in was most definitely still. Patches of blues, greens and sand browns began to appear. I realised I was squinting.

Blue skies and green hills. That was what was in front of me. Blue skies with white fluffy clouds and green hills confronting me with their idle peace. It took me a long while to make sense of what I was seeing and an even longer while to realise the scene was but a mere painting.

Not real. There was no real sky where I was. Just a bare, white, concrete ceiling. No windows. Two more similar paintings on my left and right but no real trees anywhere. I was in a bedroom of sorts. A big one.

There was a large TV screen built seamlessly into the wall on my left. Next to it, two white armchairs sat around a side table in front of a floor-to-ceiling bookshelf full of books. One cushion on each armchair. One blue. One green. Their colours matched the paintings. How nice, I thought.

Towards the right, another bookshelf but one that had a connected bar table that went around the corner at a ninety-degree angle. A single barstool sat in front of the table. A green couch for two sat beside it.

There was light in the room; the warm, soothing sort of light you sometimes saw in luxury places. It came from seams in the edges of the ceiling. The monotony of the white paint all over the walls was broken up by light-coloured wood panelling behind the bar table and the bed I lay on. The floor was carpeted. Cream. The whole room was very soothing to look at.

Unlike my wrist. My wrist had a piece of metal stuck to it, a little like a sticker. Connected to the metal, a clear rubber tube.

I followed the tube past the edge of the bed and found a standing drip with a squarish black device above it. The black device was beeping.

I realised that was the very beeping I had been hearing from the time I had been stuck in that huge, infinite blackness. It sounded like a digital pulse and felt in tune with my physical one.

Damn. I jerked into a sitting position and looked all around again, this time with my mouth open.

Where was I? A hospital? Was the bed I lay on a hospital bed? It didn't look like it. The queen-sized bed I was on had no handles on its side; no buttons you could press to move it up or down. It was not on wheels but on a modernist wooden platform that matched the wall panels. Very chicly done. A high-end hospital? Or something else I hadn't realised existed?

How had I gotten here? I tried to think but there was nothing there. No memory, no recollection of anything other than that huge silent blackness. I got the feeling I might be better off mobile so I peeled off the piece of metal clinging onto my wrist.

The beeping I had been hearing changed into a persistent flat tone at once. Like someone in a hospital had died. It made my hairs stand.

Instinct told me to get away from the sound. I flipped the blue woollen blanket off the lower half of my body and dragged my legs off the bed. I could move my legs but they felt as heavy as lead. When I tried to put my weight on them, they buckled. I managed to grab hold of the side of the bed just in time to stop myself from crashing onto the ground and that was when I noticed my outfit—a light blue cotton gown. Short sleeves at the arms and a skirt that came to my knees. Pyjamas for hospital patients. *Christ.* This place was most likely a hospital after all, I realised.

There were two doors in front of me and a treadmill built into the floor. They were both made of the same light-coloured wood that made the wall panel and the bookshelves. Very subtle, very harmonious.

I chose to try the door on the left first—a purely random choice. I hobbled over to it with legs full of pins and needles and realised it was a phrase I could now form. *Pins and needles! That was the phrase I had been trying to find before!* My brain was beginning to work again.

I fell on the door's sleek metal handle but it would not go downwards, no matter how I jiggled. It was most definitely locked.

There was nothing else to do but try the door on the right. That metal handle turned 90 degrees easily and the door, when opened, revealed a bathroom. An ensuite bathroom that was almost completely white—white ceramic toilet, white ceramic sink, white tiles all around. The shower area was separated by a plate of clear glass and the white fluffy towels hanging just outside it looked very, very clean. The bathroom smelt like lilies in the summer and was six times bigger than the bathroom I was used to.

The bathroom I was used to? Which bathroom was that?

The half-bathroom that hadn't enough space for a sink. The bathroom I showered in for five whole years. My slummy micro-apartment with its worn mattress and claustrophobia-inducing walls came to mind. I remembered my home.

This place was not home! The exit had to be the other way. I made my way back to the door on the left by holding on to the wall because my legs still didn't quite work. Just as I reached it, the flat tone I had been trying to escape vanished and the very door I had been heading for opened all by itself.

A man walked in. A doctor, I presumed, because he wore a white lab coat, shirt and tie, thin-framed metal glasses and had a black tablet in his hand. He saw me, smiled, and shut the door behind him. I heard a lock within the door latch into place almost immediately, as if automatic.

THE WOMAN WHO MADE ME FEEL STRANGE

"Nice to see you awake, Miss Thompson," the man said.

Miss Thompson? He knew my name and all I knew how to do was gape at him.

"I'm Dr Clark, your psychiatrist." The man gave me a bigger, friendlier smile and stuck out his hand.

Psychiatrist? The man looked like a grown mummy's boy with his neatly pulled back light brown hair, freshly scrubbed, stubble-free face and gentle manner. I took his hand, shook it and let go almost at once. There was something about him that made me not dare to fully trust him. I had a feeling it had something to do with the fact that he looked extremely… kind? For some reason, I knew from the bottom of my gut it was not a good idea to trust anyone who looked too kind.

"Please, take a seat." He gestured at the two armchairs that were of a modern, squarish design. They looked pretty comfortable.

And—I found out when I did sit—they actually were.

The man took the other armchair across the side table. "How are you feeling, Miss Thompson?"

Confused. And awkward. There seemed to be a black hole where my memories used to be. And the scent of his very masculine cologne was making my head throb. "Where am I?" I said and found my voice hoarse. I cleared my throat. "How did I get here?"

The man smiled. Again. "You're safe, Miss Thompson. And healthy, it seems. The Wonderdrug Psychiatric Centre has been giving you the very best of care."

Had I not been seated, I might have collapsed. *Wasn't the Wonderdrug Psychiatric Centre one of the biggest mental hospital chains in the world? Did my being here mean I was… mentally ill?* My breath quickened at the thought and my fingers began to tremble.

The man noticed and got up to go to the bar table right away. He took a glass from the stack in the corner and put it under a metal tap that stuck out from the wall. Clear water poured into the glass without him having to touch anything and stopped pouring automatically when the glass was full.

He came back over, handed the glass to me and pulled out a clear plastic box from his coat pocket. It had multiple compartments, each with a different colour of pills.

He opened the compartment with pink pills and took out two of them.

"These will help you cope with your anxiety, Miss Thompson. If you take them three times a day, I promise you'll feel a lot better eventually."

The pills were the pink of cotton candy, cut like a slice of chalk, but scentless. I popped them into my mouth and downed the water, only to discover that the glass when empty was a lot lighter than I expected it to be.

Plastic, I realised, when I flicked the back of my nail against it. Plastic that looked just like glass.

The man was back in his armchair by the time I looked up. "Does it hurt anywhere?" he asked and fished out a modish stylus pen from his front pocket. "Any pain? Discomfort?"

I stretched my neck to the side and thought about it. "I can feel a headache coming on but... that's about it." Every other part of my body felt... okay. Normal. "Why am I here?"

The man scribbled furiously into his tablet. "No pain anywhere else?"

I checked. My skin looked fine. My limbs moved fine. "No. Should there be?"

He stopped scribbling and looked up. "You don't remember?"

Remember what? Apart from my half-bathroom and micro-apartment, I had no other memory. I knew things, like what the Wonderdrug Psychiatric Centre meant, what size the bed I lay on was, but I had no clue how I knew of them. I didn't even know my first name. I shook my head.

The man narrowed his piercing blue eyes and frowned.

"Miss Thompson, you attempted suicide three years ago."

My heart jolted to a stop then jumped right back into action at a million miles an hour. Suicide? Three years ago?!

"You overdosed on Zoleplax then jumped from the fifth floor of the apartment you lived in."

"What the hell is Zoleplax?" I whispered.

"Sleeping pills. You swallowed a whole bottle, remember?"

No, I did not remember. I remembered nothing. Only blackness, how my former home looked, random facts, nothing else.

"Hmm." The man scribbled another chunk of text into his tablet then looked up with concern all over his face. "Do you know who you are? Your name, for instance. Do you know what your name is?"

I shook my head then gave him a nod because my name came to mind in that very instant. "Lane. My name is Lane Thompson." *That was right. That was exactly what my name was.*

The man raised his eyebrows. "Do you remember how old you are?"

30 came to mind. I had no idea why. I just knew 30 was the answer the same way I just knew every object in the room we sat in was top of the line.

"That's partly right. You're now 33, to be precise. Do you remember what you used to do for a living?"

"I was a freelance masseuse at The Gentlemen's Dinner Club," I said and gasped. My memory *was* coming back, just very slowly, in random pieces, and for some strange reason, only when prompted.

"You gave wealthy men massages for a living?"

"No. I gave wealthy women massages for a living." *Because I loved women. Only women.* My hand flew over my mouth.

I remembered Arden Villeneuve. Beautiful, naked, with legs so long they nearly stuck out of the ends of the massage tables at The Gentlemen's Dinner Club. I remembered her!

"Are you sure? As far as I know, women aren't allowed into that establishment."

Really? I looked up at the man in the white coat and thought hard. Faint bolts of pain zapped my head as I did so. "No, some are," I said and winced. "The Gentlemen's Dinner Club invited a select group of women to become members in 2025." I had no idea how I knew that but I just knew from the bottom of my gut that that was most definitely true.

Arden Villeneuve had been one of those women. She and I shared many long kisses within the Club's dim massage suites. I was crazy about her.

"How about your parents?" the man interrupted. "What do you remember of them?"

My parents? An unpleasant sensation crawled over my skin and I soon realised why.

I had only one memory of my parents. In it, they were pale, purplish, with eyes rolled backwards and mouths wide open. They were on our living room's couch. Motionless. I was just a child when I found them and I screamed with every ounce of energy when I did—a bone-chilling scream that began to replay in my head.

"Nothing," I said quickly. Firmly. I pulled myself out of my thoughts. I didn't want to have to hear that scream a minute longer. It made me very uncomfortable.

The man adjusted his glasses thoughtfully and scribbled into his tablet again.

"What about your uncle? The husband of your father's sister? Uncle Tim?"

Uncle Tim? Another unpleasant sensation appeared on my skin so I shook my head quickly and stopped myself from thinking further about him.

"Hmm."

"When can I be discharged, Dr... Clark?"

"When you get better, of course. When you stop

wanting to kill yourself. When you stop having attacks of anxiety."

"I... don't think I want to kill myself anymore." I frowned. *Do I?* I thought doubly hard to make sure. The answer in my gut was definitive. "I really don't."

"Why did you jump before?"

Good question. Why *did* I jump? I tried to think of an answer but nothing came to mind this time. Just more zaps of pain in the head but no thoughts. My brain was just… blank.

"You don't remember?"

I took a deep breath and shook my head.

"We'll need to observe you further, Miss Thompson. We'll need to make sure your mind is working as it should be before we can let you go. It's just a precaution."

"How long will you take?"

The man put down his tablet and smiled. He looked like he truly cared about me. "We will take all the time we need."

I laughed because I suddenly remembered something else. "Thing is, I can't afford all this time. I doubt I'll ever be able to pay off the last three years as it is."

His smile never wavered. "You don't have to pay a cent, Miss Thompson. Wonderdrug has a scheme that covers all costs for needy patients like yourself. So, relax. Take all the time you need to heal."

Right after he said that, the panelled wall in front of the bar table groaned mechanically and rose a little. A drawer-like tray slid out and stopped in the middle of the table, right in front of the lone barstool. On it was a steaming bowl and a plate that held a fat roast beef sandwich. The smell of piping hot chicken soup filled the air and felt like the promise of warmth after a long, harsh winter.

My stomach growled. That man kept on smiling. "Life can be overwhelming, Miss Thompson. Needing a little professional assistance from time to time is perfectly normal. The experience doesn't have to be unpleasant."

Me, getting to stay in a place as nice as this and eat food as good-looking as that for free? For as long as I needed? Without having to work for it?

I stared at the perfectly-browned crust atop the fat roast beef sandwich and I felt as if I had won the lottery.

CHAPTER 3
6 MAY 2033

I dreamt about the falling incident the next time I fell asleep, except, I wasn't seated on the fifth floor like Dr Clark said but on a weather-worn roof, miles above ground.

I was there sometime before 5am. It was quiet. The sky overhead was dark and pinkish. I was all alone, surrounded by a jungle of low quality housing blocks in which I knew the working poor lay exhausted. My calves hung down the edge and the heels of my sneakers grazed the building's grimy facade. There was wind on my face and in my hair. Puffs of whiteish smoke from my mouth formed abstract swirling patterns right in front of my eyes.

I felt calm and in control. I felt no pain, no anger, no helplessness, no sadness. Nothing bothered me—

—until something soft landed on my back.

By the time I felt it there, it was already too late. The force it sent forth disrupted my centre of balance and propelled me and my cigarette forward. My head went beyond the edge of the building and dragged my body along with it.

The view changed right away. Instead of buildings, I saw cement and tarmac. Then, it was sky and buildings all over again. A head of a person stuck out from one of those buildings—the one closest to me, the one I had been sitting on. Man or woman I could not tell but he or she had short platinum blond hair and lips that looked as if they were covered in a bold red lipstick.

My eyes opened the moment my back hit the ground in my dream.

I found myself back on the queen-sized bed at the Wonderdrug Psychiatric Centre, all tucked in and safe. The lights were on now. They had been turned off before I went to bed, I remembered. I tried to sit but an excruciating pain in my left thigh made me collapse.

I looked down at my thigh and realised stains of blood were on the blanket right over it. I flipped the blanket over and saw, to my horror—

—a clump of flesh, shaped like a small but thick piece of steak, next to a matching hole in my thigh. The hole was so deep, I could see my own bone! Blood was all over the sheets like a murder situation had occurred. Whatever it was that took a bite out of me didn't swallow!

Once I saw the hole, I could feel it more and it stung more than anything I had ever experienced in my life. It was so bad I truly thought I might just die from the pain. I screamed till tears came gushing out of my eyes, till my lungs grew weak. I screamed till Dr Clark and a nurse barged in and injected me with something they said would calm me down.

I have no words to describe how grateful I was when whatever they injected me with knocked me out of my senses.

"Wake up, Miss Thompson. It's time for therapy."

The next time I opened my eyes, I found Dr Clark smiling at me with his hand on my shoulder. The lights in my ward seemed much brighter than before.

I found myself still on that queen-sized bed, minus the murder-like patches of blood. Somebody had changed the blanket and sheets. They were clean now. As was my left thigh. Somebody had wrapped it in a thick cream-coloured bandage. I couldn't see the wound or blood any longer and it no longer hurt.

"What happened to my leg?" I asked.

"You don't remember?" Dr Clark crossed his arms and watched my face carefully.

I frowned and thought hard.

I remembered my dream. Me, smoking on the rooftop of my apartment. I remembered walking away from Arden Villeneuve at a cemetery. And how we kissed. Her roses. My job. My rent. All the women I ever loved before. The day I moved out of Aunt Mary's apartment. The day I dropped out of high school. Uncle Tim! My parents' death!

My memory was back, I realised. "I didn't attempt suicide, Dr Clark," I said quickly. "Somebody pushed me. Somebody with short blond hair and lipstick. I remember now."

Dr Clark inhaled sharply and frowned. "Who?"

"I don't know. But I didn't fall from the fifth floor. I fell from the roof!"

He licked his lips and looked away. "Miss Thompson, the police checked all security cameras in your apartment's building after the falling incident. You were most definitely on the fifth floor and there was no evidence of any foul play."

"No. I was most definitely on the roof that night."

"The roof is fifty storeys above ground, Miss Thompson. There is no way you would have survived."

"But that's what I remember!"

I was on the roof telling myself to forget Arden Villeneuve. I was reminding myself that a nobody like me would never ever get to be with a person like her in the natural order of things and I had come to terms with that. I had accepted my lot in life on that very rooftop, on that very night, right before someone pushed me!

"The police told us about your financial situation and your lack of stable familial or romantic connections, Miss Thompson."

"Fine, I'm broke and live alone, yes, but—"

"We also know of your Hyperpro habit which could—"

"Who the hell doesn't have a Hyperpro habit? Everyone who works has a Hyperpro habit! It doesn't mean I would want to kill myself, does it? Come on!"

Dr Clark left my side without a word and came back with a glass of water from the tap in the wall. He reached into his coat pocket, took out his plastic box of pills and opened the compartment with the pink ones again. "Miss Thompson, I am not judging you. I just want to talk this through with you, to help you get better. Please." He offered me both the glass and pills.

Great. Just great. I sank back. I hated talking about my feelings. Talking always left me vulnerable and self-conscious, in a state that didn't fit the image I wanted to project to the world. I would have preferred never to talk about my feelings if it were up to me.

"Miss Thompson, when people fail to meet popular milestones or keep up with their peers, a sense of failure can sometimes set in."

"I did not—"

"Just let me finish, Miss Thompson. Please."

"Fine." I heaved in frustration and snatched the glass of water from him but left the pills behind. The water quenched my parched throat beautifully and made me feel that little bit better. "Say what you need to."

"Thank you." He took a deep breath and sat himself next to my legs. "Miss Thompson, we suspect your brain might have been affected by the overdose of Zoleplax and also the long duration of your coma. That would explain your persistent anxiety, agitation and confusion right now."

"What in the world is Zoleplax?"

"Sleeping pills. You ate a whole bottle before you jumped from the fifth floor, remember?"

Oh, that. But no, that was not what I remembered. Not at all. My memory was still of me falling off the roof. "So you're saying I've gone crazy?"

Dr Clark adjusted his glasses and smiled. Again. "We don't use that word here, Miss Thompson. We just think you might benefit from some help. Everyone here just wants to help you get better. To fix you up when you hurt yourself." His eyes darted to the bandage over my thigh and there was a ridiculous amount of sympathy on his face when he looked back at me.

I stared back at him for a really long time afterward and struggled to accept what his look truly meant.

Did I... really? But I had no recollection of doing anything as horrible as that to myself... Or did I?

"You seem to be blocking out the most unpleasant of memories," Dr Clark said. "Why?"

How the hell was I supposed to know? The smell of his cologne was starting to give me a headache again and my body felt heavier than usual. The sense of control I remembered having while on the roof in my dream was certainly not with me at Wonderdrug.

"That's okay. That's why you're here, isn't it? You just need a little help." He extended his pill box towards my face and jiggled it lightly.

Those cheery pink pills in the open compartment bounced around and looked very much like candy, even though I knew, from experience, that they weren't sweet-tasting at all.

"Medication can help you cope emotionally, Miss Thompson. You don't need to tough it out all by yourself. We can help you. We are here *just to* help you, in fact."

I took one look at his outfit and believed him.

CHAPTER 4
MAY-JUNE 2033

At age 33, I looked almost exactly as I did at age 30. My skin was still flawless and wrinkle-free, my jaw still sharp. My hair had gotten a great deal thinner, for some reason, but because there were prickly coin-sized sections of new hair growing out of various parts of my scalp, I wasn't all that worried about it.

My body was the only part of me I worried about. Despite my religious intake of pink pills, I didn't stop mutilating myself in my sleep. One morning, I woke and found sharp edges of bone sticking out of my right forearm like spears. The bones had been completely severed down the middle; my forearm broken into two. The week after that, my entire left arm turned black. It had been so banged up over the course of the night, not an inch of it was spared from bruises. Another time, I dug another thick clump of flesh right out of my right calf.

Good thing I was already in a hospital. They had injections to take away the pain and bandages to save me from having to look at my grotesque wounds. Dr Clark added two baby blue pills to the little plastic cup of two pink pills that came on the tray with every meal. Painkillers, he said they were. And indeed, they did the job. I ended up looking like the victim of a bad accident—three limbs fully wrapped in cloth bandages, one arm in a cast—but didn't feel one ounce of pain, thanks to his pills.

Dr Clark visited me twice every weekday. After breakfast, he would come in with a nurse to take my blood pressure, temperature, weight and height, and sometimes some blood or pee as well. After lunch, he would come in alone for an hour of therapy, during which he would run through the usual gamut of questions—*How are you feeling, Miss Thompson? How did you sleep? Do you feel like hurting yourself? Do you feel any pain or unusual sensations around your body?*—before jumping into a topic centred around my past—*Tell me about school? When did you first fall in love? What was your first job?* I no longer remember exactly what I told him during those sessions—my brain seemed to be shrouded in some kind of fog most afternoons when I was there—but I remember keeping it simple, making it sound as if all I ever did with women was peck them on the lips and hold their hands. I didn't mention Arden Villeneuve, of course. The first time we slept together, she made me swear never to tell another soul about us and I thought it right to honour my promise to her.

Three times a day, like clockwork, hot meals, pink and blue pills, and clean drinking glasses would come out of the wall above the bar table on that attached, immovable drawer-like tray. That tray would go back into the wall sometime after so you could put your used plates and glasses on it when you wanted to get them cleared.

The bed was also connected to the wall and some mechanism would remove it entirely from the ward the moment I opened the bathroom door in the morning and bring it back—fully made, with fresh sheets—the moment I opened the bathroom door after dinner. A fresh gown and fresh towels would always be on the bed in the evenings and I soon figured that leaving my used gown and towels on the bed in the morning was the way to get them out of the ward as well.

I thought the entire room was ingeniously designed and phenomenally hassle-free but its design wasn't what I loved most about it. The VRM entertainment system, which you could access by touching the built-in TV screen on the wall across the couch, was, hands down, what I loved *the* most. VRM contained over a *billion* movies, games, and music tracks—its loading screen always said—and came with a headset that allowed you to experience all its content in virtual reality. Virtual reality headsets were crazy expensive items I never could afford so I spent all my free time at Wonderdrug—late afternoons, evenings and whole weekends—with the VRM headset plastered over my eyes.

I watched all of Arden Villeneuve's movies multiple times, in a chronological fashion. I watched her grow from a cherubic toddler into a pretty kid, a charming lanky teenager into a worldly sex bomb, and then I did it all over again. And again. Many times.

With the headset on, she always looked as if she were right in front of me. So close, I sometimes imagined myself smelling her perfume again. I always found myself trying to touch her virtual face and body, longing to be close to her the way we used to be all those years ago, and I always found myself solemnly wistful afterwards, knowing she wasn't at all close to me any longer.

I didn't think I would ever be able to forget or even stop loving Arden Villeneuve. I really didn't think that would be possible.

CHAPTER 5
? JUNE 2033

"We need to talk about your uncle and aunt," Dr Clark said during therapy one afternoon.

I didn't reply. I simply peeled the tip of one of my fingernails away from its nail bed and kept my eyes on the carpet.

"Miss Thompson, talking about your past, however unpleasant, is the only way you're ever going to get better. Why not just get it over with now?"

Because thinking about my uncle always made me feel as if ants were going wild under my bandages and cast? Fidgeting wouldn't stop the crawly sensation, no. Not thinking about him was the only way. I refused to say a word.

"Alright. What if I gave you a special treat afterwards? Something you don't normally get? Cigarettes, maybe? And a chance to leave your ward?"

The cigarettes were of interest—God knows how much I had been craving the taste of nicotine in my lungs the whole time I had been there—but leaving the ward, not so much. "I just want the cigarettes. Super Menthols, and I want them permanently in the ward from now on."

"Deal. Now can we talk about what you were doing the night Uncle Tim died?"

I sighed for it felt as if the number of ants scampering underneath my bandages had tripled. "I was fast asleep on the living room couch. Didn't wake when he hit his head and fell. Didn't wake till Aunt Mary got home from her shift and found him on the kitchen floor."

Dr Clark nodded and scribbled into his tablet as he always did. "Why hadn't you gone to bed?"

"The couch *was* my bed. Aunt Mary's apartment had one bedroom only. None for me."

"I see. So, what happened to Uncle Tim?"

I shrugged. "The police said he tripped and hit his head on the kitchen counter. He was very drunk apparently."

"You believe that?"

"It's what the police said."

Dr Clark looked up at me. "But not what Aunt Mary thinks. She told the police you murdered her husband, didn't she?"

My heart skipped a beat. *How would Dr Clark have known about that? Were medical records fused with police records now?* "Well, that's untrue. I swear."

Dr Clark nodded and looked like he believed me. "Aunt Mary also told the police you might have been responsible for the gas leak that killed your parents. She said you were dangerous, probably not your father's daughter, and that you, I quote, 'should be kept locked up'. Why would she say all those things about you?"

Because the persecutory fat bitch hated me? Because her husband liked to ogle at my body way more than he did hers? She said it to get me out of her house and life for good, I bet. "I don't know. But I was five when my parents died so I doubt I would have known how to start a gas leak then. And I have no idea why I looked as ethnic as I do but legally, I am my father's daughter. I know of no other father."

"What were you doing the night your parents died then?"

I shrugged again. "Lost all memories when I saw them dead. Shock and PTSD, the investigating psychiatrist said. Even now, I remember nothing before the day they died. No birthdays. No family dinners. No childhood. Nothing. It's like I didn't even exist before that day."

That made his eyebrows go up. "Seriously?"

"Seriously."

There was only blackness and nothingness before my memory of the two purple dead bodies on the couch. I tried a million times and a million ways to see past the blackness but never once saw anything different.

"Hmm. How about you and I work on unlocking those memories next? What do you say?"

I said thank you.

CHAPTER 6
? JUNE 2033

Dr Clark arrived for therapy the next afternoon with one of his nurses who had a basket of all sorts of items—a bowl of potato chips, a bowl of gummy worms, a bottle of whisky, some glasses, some napkins, an ashtray, a box of Super Menthols, a lighter and a box that contained a board game—in her hands and what looked like a picnic mat under her arm. He and she were both all smiles.

"Ready for your treat?" he asked.

"Sure."

The nurse with the basket went to the empty space right in the middle of my ward—where the bed would be at night—and lay the mat over the carpet. She put the items in the basket on the picnic mat as if setting up for a picnic—the bowls of snacks, glasses, whiskey bottle and cigarettes all neatly laid out around the sides and the board game right in the middle.

"It comes with a surprise," he said.

"What sort?"

Dr Clark gestured at me to wait then opened the door he always entered from. There was a nurse outside. All smiles like the other two. Only when that nurse stepped in did I realise there was another woman behind her, clinging onto her arm and hiding behind her back. A woman who wore a blue gown just like mine, with feet that were just as bare. She looked about the same age as me, had a mess of curly red hair that travelled past her waist and wore no make up.

A fellow patient in the same bad state as me, I realised.

Her eyes were brown like Arden Villeneuve's but that was where the similarity ended. She had been staring at me as she entered but looked away and kept her face hidden behind the nurse in front of her the moment I stared back.

"Miss Thompson, meet Miss Paul Rafferty. Not Paula, just Paul." Dr Clark said. He sounded excited, for once.

A male name? Was she transsexual? I checked out her body and decided not. She didn't look like she had been born a man nor did she try to behave like one. She simply looked like a timid girl child who was scared of me and was trying her very best to keep out of my line of sight.

"Why?" I asked Dr Clark.

"Thought you both could benefit from some company, since neither of you get any visitors. A little socialising might be a welcome change."

No, it wasn't welcome at all. Not for me at least. What I wanted most at that point was to be seen by as few people as was humanly possible. I wasn't proud of my bandages or my lack of make up or where I was in life. I wasn't proud of who I had become. I didn't want to have to deal with the inevitable, loathsome second in which the redhead would glance down at my body and form a likely negative opinion about me. I had seen enough of that sort of reaction on the faces of the nurses who came in with Dr Clark on some mornings and even the nurses who came in on that day. They would always try to cover up their judgement with polite smiles but there would always be that flicker of a second during which I would catch sight of their honest opinion and *just know* it wasn't favourable.

Unfortunately, there was no escaping interaction with Paul at that point, was there? The introduction had already been made and mutual acknowledgement of each other's existence was already in order. I straightened out, put on confidence, extended my hand to the redhead and braced myself for that loathsome second.

To my surprise, the loathsome second never happened. The redhead kept her eyes on her toes, her head shrouded by the nurse's torso and simply refused to look at me no matter how much the nurse she hid behind tried to persuade her to. Eventually, the nurses sat her down on the picnic mat and left her there, alone and exposed, but even then she refused to look in my direction. She hugged her knees and rocked herself and looked way more awkward than I felt.

Dr Clark went up to her and crouched down so that their eyes were on the same level. "Paul, look! It's Snakes and Ladders!" He spoke slowly and in the sort of high-pitched manner one would only ever use when speaking to a child under the age of four. "Your favourite! And we found someone to play it with you! Isn't that great?"

The redhead apparently didn't think so. She pouted and pulled a ton of hair from the back of her head down towards the front so her face could no longer be seen.

I felt much better about having to hang out with her after that. Knowing she wasn't all that normal made me feel much better about myself. My facial muscles relaxed and my back sank into a more natural posture.

"We'll be back in two hours," Dr Clark said to me.

Without waiting for a reply, he left the room with the nurses.

The lock within the door latched into place right away.

Paul the woman emerged from behind her mop of hair only after I offered her a gummy worm. Since nobody ever served gummy worms with whisky, to my knowledge, I guessed the worms had been brought to the occasion specifically for her. And I was right.

Paul's eyes widened like an animal's would at the sight of a treat and she snatched the worm out of my hand shortly after. She stuffed one end of the worm into her mouth and sucked at it noisily while playfully flicking the end that stuck out of her mouth in the way only a preschool child would.

I couldn't help but wonder if she was intellectually slow and if that was also the reason she had no visitors. Had her parents given up on her because she was never going to be the perfect daughter? Or had they died, like mine had, because they were intellectually slow, as she was, and failed to thrive in the world?

Paul offered no answers. She behaved as if I didn't even exist.

I made up my mind to be nothing but nice to her. We were, after all, in the same boat, down in the dumps, with nobody to depend on but ourselves. Paul was now, possibly, the only person in the whole world with whom I could properly relate to, although unfortunately, she was probably never going to ever feel the same way about me.

"Would you like some whisky to go with your worm?" I asked on a whim. I knew it was probably a dumb idea to give a person like Paul alcohol, but then, I didn't want her to feel left out. She did have a grown up body after all and deserved the same privileges, I thought.

To answer my question, Paul shook her head till her face was shrouded by hair and swivelled around so that all I could see of her was her back.

After that, I decided she might actually be smarter than I previously thought. "I didn't know doctors could prescribe alcohol," I said as I poured myself a glass of whisky anyway. "Did you?"

Paul wouldn't say. She simply grabbed a fistful of gummy worms without turning around and brought it all towards her mouth.

Likewise, I downed the entire glass of whisky in one gulp. I felt the occasion called for it. Here I was in a mental hospital with no possessions, no lovers, no mission to speak of and the one person I could possibly be friends with wouldn't even look at me. I was at rock bottom and knew the time to embrace and celebrate it was there and then.

I poured myself another glass, drank more, then lit a cigarette and enjoyed many long, deep toxic breaths. By the time my stick and second glass were done, my limbs were warm and loose and I was feeling way more gregarious than usual.

"What are you in for, really?" I heard myself say.

Paul didn't answer, as expected, but I didn't even care.

"I'm here because I have anxiety, depression, self-mutilating tendencies and memory problems," I told her. "Multi-talented, don't you think?" I poured myself another glass and drank almost all of it right away.

I think I did spot Paul peek at me briefly but she looked away again the instant I met her eyes.

"I know, Paul, I know I look weird now, but do you know I wasn't always this weird? A long time ago, I was really hot. I was cool, daring, sexy, and I was definitely fun. Many, many, many women had crazy crushes on me. Because I was so fun." I sighed heavily and emptied what was left of my glass down my throat.

A pair of dice hit me square in the middle of my forehead the second I put my glass down. When I looked up, with a grimace on my face, I found Paul staring at me with the board game in front of her knees.

"Play!" she said in a voice that was as screechy as a child's. "Play now!"

I honestly didn't want to—my forehead smarted like a motherfucker and the board game looked boring as hell because it was the vintage sort without sound or lights—but I knew I didn't want to say 'no' to her. How often did Dr Clark 'find someone' to play it with her? I suspected practically never. I didn't want to be another one of those people who didn't give two hoots about her happiness—the world had enough of those as it was—so I said yes.

She squealed when I did, threw her arms around me and squeezed me so tightly, I found it hard to breathe. The fact that my bandages might be injuries that could hurt when jostled that way never occurred to her at all.

She grabbed both my cheeks with her sticky fingers and said, "I likey you. I likey you much."

Our eyes met in that moment and to my astonishment, a warmth charged up my torso, all the way to my face.

It felt like the kind of rush I sometimes encountered when a woman I was interested in getting to know more intimately felt likewise. The kind of rush I last felt in the presence of Arden Villeneuve.

Except, Paul wasn't Arden Villeneuve. Not at all. Five seconds after the rush began, Paul peeled her eyes away from mine and began throwing gummy worms towards my face.

"Snakes! Snakes! Snakes!" she shouted as she bounced back to the board game like a hairy kangaroo on a high. She shook her torso the way kids in sing-and-dance shows always did and flapped her arms as if she were trying to lift herself off the ground.

We played Snakes and Ladders nonstop for the rest of our time together and I kept myself entertained by getting to know that sweet, helpful bottle of whisky better.

CHAPTER 7
? JUNE 2033

I woke in my ward the next day with an awful pain piercing through my head and saw, through scrunched eyes, Dr Clark staring down at me with both hands on my shoulders. He was shaking me.

"Wake up, Miss Thompson…" His voice sounded muffled and far off even though I saw him close to my face. "It's time for therapy."

"Hi," I said and struggled to sit up. The bed seemed way too soft and the room spun ever so slightly every now and then. I felt nauseous and my mouth tasted foul. It must have also smelled bad because Dr Clark let go of my shoulders without a smile.

"How are you feeling?"

"Fine." I dragged myself to the bathroom because my stomach started to churn and I felt it would be dangerous staying on the bed where there were vulnerable white sheets.

I spotted a pastrami sandwich on the bar table on the way over. Lunch, probably. The bread looked drier and harder than usual, and not in the least appetising. The four pink and blue pills I took with every meal sat in their small plastic cup untouched.

"Were you an alcoholic?"

"No."

"Are you certain?"

"Yes." I closed the bathroom door between us. Had there been a lock, I would have used it too.

"Is something bothering you?"

"No." A wave of sickness came over me and I leaned over the toilet seat just one second before a bitter-tasting spew of pulp jostled out.

"Clean yourself up and we can talk about it."

The white toilet bowl was full of a brownish-yellow porridge-like mess by the time I was done. I flushed, grabbed the sides of the sink for support and rinsed my mouth out with tap water. When I stood up properly, I saw a female ghost with tangled black hair past her shoulders in the mirror. There was shock in her black eyes as her greenish caramel face stared back at me.

I looked away at once and cursed under my breath. *No woman would ever love me again if I kept this face up. I wouldn't even want to kiss me.* I closed my eyes, drenched my face with revivifying tap water and prayed I would feel less dizzy sooner rather than later.

"What do you think of Miss Rafferty?" Dr Clark asked from outside, oblivious to my turmoil.

Who? Oh, the redhead from yesterday? I had no opinion of her. I could barely even remember her face. She had one of those indistinctive plain faces, I thought. Nothing like Arden Villeneuve's. "She's alright," I said as I scrubbed my mouth out with toothpaste.

"Did you have anything in common?"

Did we? Oh, wait, yes we did. We both slid down a couple of snakes in the game that was life and ended up right at the bottom. Apart from that? "No."

I gargled and spat and felt my head throb when it tilted downward, as if something inside was trying to pound its way out. The smell of lilies began to get to me. I could tell I had to get out of the bathroom fast or the sweet fragrance of lilies would make me retch again.

When I emerged, I saw Dr Clark looking more concerned than usual. He even frowned. "I think we should leave the bed as it is today," he said. "You don't look too good."

I didn't feel good at all either.

Dr Clark duplicated himself and doubled in front of my eyes.

I felt as if I had to prop myself against the bathroom door just to remain standing.

"Do you have questions for me?" he asked when he merged back into one.

I shook my head and was surprised by how difficult it was to do so. My head felt way too heavy for small talk. Way to heavy to be held up for long periods of time.

"Anything you want to know about Paul?"

No. All I wanted to do then was sleep and hide my ugly self from the world. And retch. Hot fluid gushed up my throat and seeped into my mouth before I could stop it from doing so. I made it back into the bathroom just in the knick of time.

"You know, Paul's mother used to be a patient of ours too," Dr Clark said from the outside, over the sound of me gagging. "A paranoid schizophrenic. For years, we've been trying to find out if Paul inherited her disease but we've been failing because, as you might have noticed, Paul isn't exactly the most verbal of patients. So, I would love to hear what you think. Is Paul normal or is she… unusual in any way?"

"Normal," I said at once. *Or maybe she wasn't?* I didn't care either way, I just wanted him to stop talking to me. My thighs lost their strength and I found myself sinking onto the ground. Had the toilet seat not held my chin up, my head would have ended up where my thighs were.

Lucky for me, therapy hour ended right after that. Dr

Clark advised lots of sleep and water, wished me a good weekend then left. Thank motherfucking goodness, I thought when I heard the door shut and lock behind him.

I got on all fours and crawled towards the bed. After throwing myself face down onto its crisp sheets, I groaned like a bear. I knew I sounded hideous and a tad like a porn star but I didn't care. It felt so darned good doing so and I felt so much more relaxed afterward.

Who would have ever thought that falling from a building and losing my mind would actually be the best thing that ever happened to me? Before the falling incident, when I had to work for a living, I was allowed only one day of rest each week. If I chose not to go out, that day would be spent in a cramped room on months-old sheets with no entertainment other than what I could get for free on my phone. Housework had to be done or I would live in filth. Bills had to be paid or I would have to go without. At the wonderful Wonderdrug Psychiatric Centre however, I no longer had any of those problems. Food was served to my face, always. I never had to wash dishes. The ward made the bed. The ward did all the laundry. On top of all that, I was now living in a space bigger and more luxuriously equipped than any sort of space my sort of paycheck allowed me. And I didn't even have to pretend to be someone I wasn't to enjoy it.

I pulled a pillow under my head, nuzzled my face into its antiseptic fragrance and realised Dr Clark had been so right. Taking the time to heal in a psychiatric facility was not in the least unpleasant at all. Quite the contrary. It was way more pleasant than being fully recovered. For me, at least.

As my body sank into the heavenly-soft mattress and my eyelids closed down over my eyes like heavy curtains, I told myself to never get better. I decided never to take any more of those pink pills right before I felt myself defy gravity and float, in my self-created darkness, into the cosy embrace of an indulgent, worry-free sleep.

CHAPTER 8
? JUNE 2033

"Hello, Lane," a voice said.

My eyes shot open and I looked around at once for it sounded as if there was a woman right in front of me.

Only there wasn't. Not in front nor anywhere near. I was, as I remembered, all alone in my ward at Wonderdrug, on my queen-sized bed, with my cheek on the pillow. My ward was all dark now though. All the lights had been switched off, as they always were shortly after dinner. I checked the bar table.

There was pumpkin soup, potatoes and steamed vegetables on it. No pastrami sandwich. Lunch had been replaced by dinner. The usual plastic cup of four pills sat untouched.

"Hungry?" the same voice said.

I jumped out of bed at once. That voice sounded like it had been right next to me, yet there was nothing under the covers or anywhere else. "Who's that?" I shouted.

"Shh! Get back to bed and act like you're asleep! You don't have to speak with your mouth. Just think the words you want to say and I'll be able to hear you."

What in the fuck?! My eyes grew wider yet I never once saw nobody in my ward. I checked, double checked and triple checked and it was always only just me around.

"I'm not in your room. Just do as I say, Lane. The cameras are rolling. Hurry."

My mouth fell open. *Where the hell was that voice coming from?* It sounded very familiar too but I couldn't remember where I first heard it. The Club? Some woman I briefly dated? Something from a movie?

"Get back to bed and close your eyes now!"

The voice sounded angry so I thought it would be best to do as it said. I went back under the blanket and flipped my eyelids shut.

"Thank you," the voice said, as if it had seen me. "Now we can talk."

The hairs on my skin tried to dash to the ceiling. "What do you want?" I thought to the voice. I felt very weird doing so but at the same time realised thinking with my mind was actually easier to do than talking with my mouth. I hadn't had a drop to drink since I woke in the afternoon and my throat was suffering for it.

"I want to set you free," the voice said. "Get you out of here."

What in the...? "I'm good here," I thought quickly. "I want to stay. And heal."

"You're not even sick, Lane. Don't buy into their bullshit, and more importantly, don't eat the pink pills at dinner. The pink pills are tranquillisers. They keep you knocked out all night. That's why you've never seen all the things they've been doing to you while you sleep."

What?! My eyes shot open once again. I looked all around but saw absolutely nobody anywhere. The voice had been so close though. So close, it could only have been right in front of me or... *in my head!*

"No, you're not crazy," the voice said, to my absolute horror. Nothing in the room moved.

My fingers curled over the blanket on my body and

squeezed. Hard.

"They say you are because they want to keep you here. It's your body they really want—"

"Enough! I don't want to hear anymore," I thought. I ducked under my pillow and pushed its cottony-soft filling up against my face. The smell of antiseptic entered my nostrils, reminded me I was already in a hospital and made me feel that little bit better.

"You have to," the voice continued, to my dismay. "We have a chance to escape—tomorrow night, 3am. There'll be a system reboot during which the doors on this floor will be unlocked for five minutes. The cameras will be down so—"

"I'm not going anywhere," I thought. Fast.

"—it's the perfect opportunity. There's no knowing when you'll get to escape again if you miss the chance tomorrow."

"I'm not going!" I thought. I could hear my heart beating in my ears and thought it sounded like a war drum.

"You'd rather be a lab rat for the rest of your life? Have your every move recorded and dissected so that people who don't give a shit about you get to improve their lives?"

I had no idea what any of those words meant. "Shut up!" I shouted. Out loud. Into the pillow on my face. "Shut up!" I didn't know what else to do.

I heard only silence after that. Long buzzing silence. When enough silence had passed, I removed the pillow from my face and looked around.

My ward was still empty. Dinner and pills were still on the bar table, uneaten. Nothing had changed at all.

I heaved a sigh of relief and released my grip of the pillow. I thought all was good again, that all was well, until—

"Don't eat the pink pills at dinner tomorrow. At 3am, head out and meet me at the corridor. Don't scream now."

My legs jerked and my hand jumped over my mouth

just in time to stop the scream that almost came out of it.

"Do not say a word about this, Lane," the voice said in my head. "Not even to yourself. Trust me, you don't want them knowing. Okay?"

I did not answer and the voice did not speak again but the damage had already been done.

I spent the night with my eyes wide open as swirls of theories ran rampant in my mind. *Did the voice belong to a ghost? One I inadvertently offended when I mindlessly fucked in a cemetery all those years ago? Or was the voice part of a psychotic episode? Brought on by missing two consecutive doses of pink pills?*

When at last I recalled why the voice sounded so darned familiar, I found myself grappling with a whole new level of unease.

That voice hadn't come from the Club or a fling or a movie. No. *That voice* belonged to the woman I met only the day before. The Wonderdrug patient named Paul. The one with crazy hair like a cave-dwelling witch's. The daughter of a paranoid schizophrenic.

By the time the lights in my ward came on again, I was convinced not taking the pink pills was a terrible idea.

I dashed out of bed and swallowed the ones in the tiny plastic cup on the bar table without a second thought.

CHAPTER 9
? JUNE 2033

"Lane, wake up! It's 2:45!"

Shit. Where was I? I bolted upright and looked around. *Still at Wonderdrug? Check. Still on that super soft queen-sized bed? Check.* But the lights were no longer on. Why? I turned my eyes to the bar table.

The pumpkin soup, potatoes and steamed vegetables I last saw were gone. In their place, three flame-roasted chicken drumsticks and two cobs of corn sat on a plate next to that familiar plastic cup of four pills. It was the sort of dish Wonderdrug would only ever serve at dinner, which meant…

…I must have slept through breakfast and lunch. *Again? How in the world…? Sleep deprivation from being awake all night? I must have been exhausted.*

"Nope, it's the pink pills. Told you they're tranquillisers."

I jumped and swivelled around, but there was no one there.

No one I could see, at least.

No wonder I had been taken to a mental hospital. I shook my head, rubbed my eyes and said the Lord's Prayer in my head, in case those might help.

"You're *not* crazy and no, I am not a ghost. Go wait by the door, it's almost time."

Fuck. Why was this happening again? My stomach growled and all at once reminded me of the three doses of pink pills I missed while sleeping through the day. *That could be it! Maybe if I ate the pink pills now, the voice would stop?*

I thought it was worth a try. I jumped out of bed, tossed the cup of pills into my mouth and washed them all down with a glass of water. To make sure the pills stayed down, I grabbed a drumstick and sent huge greasy bites of chicken down after it.

"Lane, this is not the time to eat. 2:55!"

Shit. How long did the pills need to work? My stomach growled again so I quickly took in another five bites of chicken. They tasted cold and hurt the sides of my throat as they went down but I persisted because I was beginning to think hunger might have also been a trigger of psychosis. I had skipped two meals the day the voice started up, hadn't I?

"2:56!"

Fuck. How not hungry must I be to not hear things? I filled my mouth to the brim with more chicken and chewed as fast as I could. This time, the dry meat tickled my throat a tad too much and induced a massive coughing fit. Bits of chicken hurled past my lips and scattered all around the carpet.

"3am! Don't make me have to come get you!"

"Leave me alone!" I shouted into thin air, as loudly as I could. "I'm staying right here!" Right in the middle of the mess I just made on the carpet.

Nobody replied. I dropped the chicken bone that was between my fingers and looked around. Nothing in the room moved. I counted the seconds that passed. One, two, three, four...

When I hit 10, I heaved a sigh of relief and very slowly

relaxed my tight shoulders.

All this, I most definitely had to tell Dr Clark about, I decided. What was it? Schizophrenia? Was I a schizophrenic now? I never paid much attention to that disease before—I never thought it would ever happen to me—but clearly, I should have.

A loud bang startled me out of my thoughts. It came from the direction of the door Dr Clark always entered from but sounded far away. I tried to think of a place to hide myself but before I could even think of something, the handle of the door Dr Clark always entered from tilted downwards and the rest of the door swung open. Paul barged in.

At least, I think it was Paul. Her size and outfit was just as I remembered but her face and manner seemed different. All the awkwardness she possessed before was no longer apparent. Her thick, curly red hair was now completely out of her face, firmly tucked behind her ears. She had on a serious-looking frown that was pretty intense.

It was me who flinched when eye contact was made this time. The Paul that barged in looked so determined to do whatever it was she came in to do, I had no idea what to expect.

"We have to go. Now!" the new Paul said when her mouth was right in front of my face. Her voice sounded exactly like the voice I had been willing out of my head, only this time, it seemed to be coming out of a mouth—her mouth—that was moving in sync with the words right in front of my eyes.

My jaw dropped. I froze. I wondered if everything happening before my eyes was really nothing but an illusion.

The new Paul's hand—solid and heavy as if it were real—fell onto the plaster cast on my right arm and dragged my entire body towards the door.

I didn't resist because I was too stunned. I couldn't

decide what to think, much less what to do. It was all so weird and made absolutely no sense!

"Just move!" the new Paul said out loud as she opened the door effortlessly and led us into a small room with black painted walls. "We have only three minutes left, all because you hesitated!"

What the—? Why wasn't the door Dr Clark always used locked this time? I blinked many times but the sight of a fellow patient dragging me through a small room with black painted walls, towards the two doors at the end, never went away.

She opened the door on the right instead of the one on the left. Beyond that was a long, dark corridor full of black doors on both sides. Doors that looked just like the door we had come out from. Doors with metal squares and a decorative line of green light above their handles.

Was this really the rest of Wonderdrug? Or was this all just a dream?

Before I could answer myself, the green lights on the doors began blinking, as if grooving to the beat of music in a dance club. Red lights appeared above us and flickered. I looked up and realised they were coming from the many globed security cameras on the ceiling.

Maybe it was a better idea to just get back to bed, I thought. I turned and tried to go back through the door we had just come from—

—but its handle wouldn't budge. The line of green on its metal square was now red. The door was... locked?

I turned back to Paul just in time to witness the green light on the next door turning red. After it did, the door next to it turned red too. It seemed the redness was spreading towards all the doors, down the corridor in a chronological fashion, down towards...

... the door with a green exit sign sticking out from above it.

"We need to get to the exit! Run, Lane! Run!!!"

The new Paul broke into a sprint. Her hand was tightly

around my plaster cast so I had no choice but to run with her or be dragged to the ground. My legs struggled because of their injuries, stiff dressings and lack of use, yet she never slowed.

"The handle needs body heat to open! We need to get to it before it turns red and locks up! Move it!!!"

Why would an exit door lock itself up? Unless... this was all just a dream and... my dream's way of telling me how I could get out of this situation and wake up?

Why not find out? I picked up the pace and ran as fast as I could towards the exit, almost as fast as Paul was running, almost as fast as the lights were turning red. I shook off Paul's grasp eventually because I knew I could run even faster. I knew I could out run the lights. At least that was what I thought until I realised—

—the light on the exit door's metal square was next, and I was still two doors away.

"Fuck!" the new Paul screamed from behind.

Fuck, I agreed. There was no other option but to try the insane. I rammed my foot hard against the floor and propelled my entire bandaged body towards the exit door the way a long jump Olympian might. My body stretched and extended as it flew across the remaining ten feet or so until—

—the tip of my middle finger made it onto the exit door's cold metal handle and pushed down a mere second before the light on the exit door's metal square changed into red.

I crashed onto the cement floor right as the new Paul caught up and shoved the door open. She grabbed my arms, dragged me through and let the door close behind my feet.

I heard the familiar sound of a lock within the door click into place right after.

I did not wake up. Instead, I saw us both panting

frantically on the floor of what looked like a commercial building's stairwell. There were no windows in sight.

"That was too close," the new Paul said between large gulps of air. "A few seconds more and the alarm would have gone off."

She grinned, to my surprise, and looked, unexpectedly, a little pretty. Her features had not changed—they were as unremarkable as they had been before—but there seemed to be a new sparkle in her eyes that made all the difference.

She stared right into my eyes and her grin widened. She dragged me to my feet and told me to follow her in a manner that suggested she knew exactly where we were going.

I followed her only because I didn't know what else to do. What I really wanted to do was go back to my ward and go to sleep, but I had no idea how to get there.

We went down six flights of stairs, through windowless spaces, until at last, we got to a landing that actually had a window.

A window which could not be opened, I realised, when I got closer.

I peered through its plate of glass and saw a dark and isolated back alley far down below. It was night out there and there were good-quality skyscrapers all around the building we were in; skyscrapers that looked like they belonged to the Financial District.

"Stand back," the new Paul said. She pulled a showerhead—exactly like the one my ward's bathroom had—out from under her pyjamas. In one dramatic move, she swung the showerhead against the glass.

Glass shattered, onto us and through the window, and almost immediately, I felt fresh air hit me in the face like a splash of cold water on a humid summer's day. It was unexpectedly delightful.

"This is your jump," the new Paul said.

My delight vanished at once. *Jump? No way!* There was a long drop out that window and the red painted numeral on the stairwell wall read '10'. Ten storeys! Twice the amount I had fallen from before!

"You sit on the ledge, I sit on you, and we tilt backwards. That's how we're going to get out of here." Her brown eyes sparkled with excitement as she broke into a grin again.

"No." My eyes processed our distance from the alley below and my gut plunged. *Fucking hell no!* "It took me three whole years to wake up before. I'm not doing it ever again."

The new Paul laughed. "You were only out five days, darling. Like I said, don't believe their bullshit. The year's still 2030."

What? "That is not possible. My body was fully healed by the time I woke."

"Precisely why you're here. Look, turn around."

Before I could even decide if I wanted to, the new Paul swivelled me so that my back faced her and pushed my shirt up. Her fingers ran along my spine then pierced through my flesh like sharp, pointed claws.

"Oww!" I screamed and tried to run away from her but she jumped right in front of me and blocked my path.

"Don't worry, it's done," she said and showed me the little blood-covered stone in between her fingers. She had a strange device in her other hand. It had the shape of a fat syringe but with the foot of a sewing machine at its tip instead of a needle.

"Now you do mine." The new Paul shoved the strange device into my hand then turned and lifted her gown so that her pale back and bony spine was exposed right in front of my eyes.

"Look for a lump somewhere near the base of my spine. When you find it, put the Remover over it, press down, then let go."

It sounded so ridiculous, I couldn't resist the urge to see what would happen if I did exactly that. It turned out there was a lump, just like she said, and the lump came out with the 'remover' very easily.

The 'lump' I held in my palm afterwards turned out to be a tiny microchip with some blood on it. It looked exactly like the blood-covered stone the new Paul had been holding in between her fingers moments earlier.

The new Paul replaced her gown and grabbed the microchip from my hand. She held it up to the florescent light and looked very pleased when she saw it. "You're a fast learner."

Not what my teachers thought, unfortunately. "What are those things?"

"Trackers. Helps them find us if we ever run away." She tossed them over the balustrade and they fell out of sight. I didn't even hear them hit the ground.

"Now you need to jump," she said to me.

I took in the seriousness of her face and felt my heart begin to pound like it had gone crazy. I tried to will myself to wake up but no amount of wanting changed what was in front of me. "Can't we just use the stairs?" I said eventually.

"This window is the only way out. Believe me, I checked and checked and checked."

"But I don't even want to get out. I like it here. I'm… happy here."

The new Paul raised her eyebrows and moved closer. Now that her back was fully upright, I realised she was just about the same height I was, with eyes on the exact same level. She put both hands on my shoulders and gave me a look that made me think she might be very wise. "You're happy only because you're new and don't have a clue what's really going on."

The hell I didn't. I had been soundly asleep and then boom! This happened.

"So, sleepy head, just do as I say," the new Paul's voice said in my head.

She laughed when I gaped at her lips which hadn't moved.

"Yes," her voice said, although her lips still did not move. "Fact is, I can read *and* talk to your mind. You're not crazy and neither am I."

After she said that, I laughed. Here we were in the stairwell of a psychiatric centre, both in sad blue pyjamas, with bad hair and no make up, me wrapped up like the Michelin Man, she doing all sorts of bizarre things and insisting we weren't crazy? This was one helluva big leap from what I knew to be sanity that was for sure.

My laughter didn't faze her one bit. She grabbed my cast arm and, without warning, smashed it hard against the ledge of the window.

I screamed so she threw a hand against my mouth. She came so close to my face, I could even smell the soap on her body—the same soap I myself had been using for weeks. "Shh," she whispered as if we were in a romantic situation. "Look at your arm."

I shook my head and squeezed my eyes shut. I hadn't forgotten how my lower forearm looked the morning I woke up and found it broken—dangling at a right angle with bones and flesh exposed. I had no interest in seeing how it would cope without the plaster cast holding everything together.

I panicked when the new Paul grabbed my other hand and forced it over my broken forearm. I tried to push past her but she was stronger. Try as I might, I could not stop my hand from moving towards the site of injury.

"Stop, Paul. Please just stop!" My words came out muffled under the weight of her hand on my mouth.

"Just trust me."

Against my will, my hand fell onto my right forearm and rubbed against it thoroughly from top to bottom and then all over again.

My eyes shot open once that happened and I stopped resisting entirely.

My arm felt normal. In fact, it *looked* normal. It was a perfectly normal arm. No open wound, no visible bones or flesh. Not even a scar of any sort. *But... how?*

"Told you," the new Paul said with eyes that seemed to twinkle. She let go of my hand and mouth at last.

"But… Dr Clark said…"

"Dr Clark lied, get it?"

No. I did not get anything, but somewhere below, along the stairwell, a door opened. The sound made both of us turn.

Paul peeped over the balustrade then stepped away almost at once. "Uh oh," she whispered, very softly this time. "We really have to go."

She pushed me towards the window and shoved herself, backwards, against my chest. Her arms grabbed mine and pulled them across her body as if she wanted me to hold her.

"Here's what we're going to do," she whispered. "On the count of three, jump backwards. Don't let go of me, don't let me hit the ground. I don't have what you have and if I break anything or die, there'll be nobody to drag you away to safety. Do you understand?"

No. Not at all. How in the hell had I gone from being perfectly safe in the best psychiatric centre in the world to being in a situation as dangerous as this? Had I done something I shouldn't have? Or... what?

"One, two, three!"

Paul pushed all of her weight on me and I felt myself levitating in mid-air, into the pitch-blackness of night, with good-quality skyscrapers moving all around me.

All I could think of to do was pray. I prayed I would find myself back in my ward after the fall and see Dr Clark all ready to explain what was really going on, with breakfast hot on the table, ready to be eaten with pills.

CHAPTER 10
DATE UNKNOWN

Absolute black, that was next. A menacing sort of black; the sort you saw in horror films. The sort that made you want to check over your shoulder at least once every minute.

There was no beeping this time, only a foul smell; the sort you encountered in mouldy abandoned toilets; a mix of rot, excrement and other putrid liquids stirred together.

Seconds or perhaps hours later, something began growling right next to my head. It sounded like a wild beast that was determined to fight me and not ever back down.

I struggled to make contact with my eyes. *Open*, so we can see the foul-smelling beast and run from it. *Open!* My eyes did not open. All they could do was twitch and I soon realised there was also—

An intense, shooting pain behind my eyes. As if very sharp and very thin objects were piercing through my eyeballs. I tried to open my mouth to scream and realised my mouth already was open. In fact, there was nothing I could do to close it. I tried to use my hands but no longer seemed to have any, nor did I have legs, or a body.

It was utterly terrifying when, right after I realised all of those things, my eyes shot open, all by themselves.

I was horizontal. Some place dark. On a mattress, I think. My vision was blurry so there was no way of knowing for sure. The growling I had been hearing sounded further away now, as if the beast had gone a long distance away, but the foul smell was still most definitely in the air, close by.

Not my clean and quiet Wonderdrug ward, that was clear.

My next thought was of Paul. The jump. Ten storeys. *The new Paul! Where was she?*

I tried to call out to her but my vocal chords did not seem to work. I tried to sit up and turn my head and discovered I couldn't do that either. My brain seemed to be no longer in contact with my body—everything I wanted to do I no longer could—but that wasn't the worst of it.

The worst was the shooting pain that spread from my eyes down towards body parts I hadn't realised I had. Once it spread, it began to feel like a zillion spikes were pulling at and stapling my body together at a million clamps per minute. The pain never once ceased. I found there was no avoiding the discomfort of it, no relief at any moment. I screamed—not by choice—and could not stop.

My voice bounced all over me and blanketed me with its persistent presence. It was so loud, so shrill, my ears began to hurt. Yet nobody came. Nobody else seemed to hear me.

I stopped screaming only because I wore myself out. My head collapsed down onto my chest against my will and I then saw, right in front of my eyes...

Spears. All over my body. They had the texture and colour of teeth and a brown core in the middle. They stuck out from bloody holes; holes in my skin! Those spears were my own bones! All broken! And my limbs all looked very peculiar. They weren't angled in a logical fashion, like a normal person's would be, but instead were twisted into all sorts of unnatural poses, the sort only wooden artist mannequins could get into.

It was happening again. I had self-mutilated again! And there was nothing I could do then but scream.

I screamed again. I screamed for Dr Clark, for nurses, for anybody who could get me medical help. I screamed till my voice turned hoarse but not once did anyone appear. Not even Paul.

Where the hell was Paul?
Where the hell was I?
Where the hell was everybody? Anybody?

"Dr Clark?" I said when I finally found a way to use my vocal chords again. "Can you help me?"

Dr Clark never replied. Nobody replied. All I could hear was the growling of the beast overhead and nothing else.

I think I eventually cried myself to sleep.

"Wake up! Are you dead?"
Somebody shook me.
What? Was I? Dr Clark? My eyes opened.

Dr Clark was nowhere in sight but I did see Paul leaning over me. She looked different though. Her hair was no longer red or as long and messy as I remembered it to be. It was now brown, half the length it used to be and quite neat despite still being curly. An illusion of light? I realised there was light; a dim one, from an unknown source behind me. Paul smiled, put two fingers over my cheeks and turned my face from side to side as if she were checking a piece of meat at a supermarket.

"You okay?" she asked.

Was I okay? Hell no. I was in a fuck load of pain because my body was all messed up. Again! I opened my mouth to say so but closed it when I noticed I wasn't in any pain at all.

I felt... okay. I sat up and rubbed my eyes. The shooting pain that had been behind them was no longer present. Nothing hurt. Not my fingers, not my hands. My hands looked... fine. They felt fine and moved fine too. No different from normal hands.

My arms and legs were now normal too. They no longer looked peculiar. They were... healthy. And clean. Way cleaner than the thin, shabby-looking mattress they lay on. The mattress under me was greyish with faded patterns covered by huge dull maroon patches.

Dried blood, I realised when I took a closer look. *Gross.*

"Amazing, isn't it?"

The bed frame under me groaned when Paul threw herself down on the mattress, next to my arms. Her eyes were on my legs and she looked somewhat impressed.

"What the hell is going on?" I asked. My voice came out croaked. Again. As croaked as it had been when I first woke at the Wonderdrug Psychiatric Centre after the falling incident. *What was all this? A dream? Reality? Or just my mind playing tricks on me?*

Paul held up three fingers in front of my nose. "Three days. That's how long it took your body to recover."

What the hell did that mean? "Where were you before?"

"Getting food so we wouldn't die of hunger." She reached behind me then handed me the box of Chinese takeout and disposable wooden chopsticks she grabbed. "The canned ones here were all expired, unfortunately."

I had no idea what that meant either but I stopped caring because the sugary-sweet garlicky scent coming from the takeout box made my mouth water. *Had it really been three entire days since I last ate?* My stomach made a squelching noise as if to concur.

I ripped off the outer flaps of the takeout box and used the chopsticks to shove battered chicken, chilli peppers and sesame into my mouth.

Sweetness, saltiness and oiliness overwhelmed my

senses at once. I realised then how hungry I was so I poured the whole box into my mouth and chewed as fast as I could. I thought that box of takeout was absolutely the most delicious thing I had ever tasted until, very abruptly, it stopped being so.

What had gone down really fast came back up even faster. I leaned over and regurgitated every last mouthful onto the floor.

"Guess you aren't as cool and fun as you said you could be, huh."

When my head came up again, I saw Paul grinning at me with her arms crossed. Her bare shoulders drew my attention to her outfit—a simple white singlet and skinny blue jeans. That blue hospital gown was gone! And she had makeup on! Eyeliner, mascara and blush, the full works. She actually looked rather decent, like a well-adjusted member of society, not in the least mental.

I, on the other hand, was the exact opposite. Not only did I now have puke around the sides of my mouth, I was also still in that thin, blue hospital gown which was at that point also full of patches and specks of dried blood. *Whoever cleaned my limbs must have missed out the clothes.*

"I didn't want you to crumple your new ones," Paul said. She reached over to the broken canvas chair next to the bed and threw the grey t-shirt and black jeans on it over to me.

A simple grey t-shirt and skinny black jeans. Exactly my style. *Coincidence?*

"Comes with a leather jacket," she added and pointed to the two black jackets hanging on a circular rusted structure at a corner of the room we were in. It looked a little like a submarine's door.

I rubbed gunk out of my eyes and looked around.

Next to the submarine's door were floor-to-ceiling metal shelves full of canned food, glass bottles, tins, boxes of Kleenex, packets of Dixie cups and stacks of toilet paper—useful, considering there was a dated-looking toilet bowl and sink at the far end of the room. Behind the bed we sat on was a small table on which a stash of snacks, soft drinks and a vintage kerosene lantern—the sort you only ever got to see in movies about the 50s—lay.

Where in the hell were we?

"A fallout bunker," Paul said out loud.

For real?

"Yes, for real. An electrician at Wonderdrug who was big on urban exploration found it. He didn't tell anyone because he wanted to keep the place for himself. A rent-free housing option in case he lost his job or something."

"Yet he told you about it?"

"Of course not. I heard him thinking about it. He doesn't know I know."

Right. Because you can read minds. Okay.

"I know it's a lot to take in, Lane. But it is what it is."

I nodded and looked around. "Did the takeout come with fortune cookies?"

"Yes, but it tastes bad so I'm not recommending it."

"I'd like one. Please."

Paul observed my face and began to smile in amusement. "Sure. If it'll make you feel better." She dug around the table behind the bed and tossed a small, shiny silver packet onto my lap shortly after.

I ripped open the packet, broke open the cookie and read the strip of paper in it in silence.

'A good way to keep healthy is to eat more Chinese food,' the strip of paper read.

"A marketing gimmick," Paul said, without even looking at the strip of paper in my hands. "To get you to purchase more Chinese food, get it?"

Yes. Maybe. Or maybe... it was... a hint? If I ate more Chinese food, perhaps I'd find myself healthy again? Sane? Back in the world with laws I understood? Where people didn't get their minds read and end up in fallout bunkers after jumping out of stairwell windows?

"Lane, for the thousandth time, you are not crazy or stuck in some dream."

I shrugged and made up my mind to eat only Chinese food from then on anyway. "What did yours say?"

"'The one you love will never love you back.' Utterly rude, in my opinion." She snatched the fortune slip out of my fingers and tossed it carelessly onto the floor.

I watched her and wondered if she was simply a twin or relative of the worm-loving Paul I played Snakes and Ladders with. *Maybe they all had the same first name because it was a family tradition? Like Paul the third and Paul the fourth—*

"You know what," Paul suddenly said. "I think we better get you some fresh air."

I didn't know what to say to that so I said okay.

CHAPTER 11
DATE UNKNOWN

Paul turned the circular, wheel-like structure our jackets had been resting on and opened the fallout bunker's circular door. Beyond it was a pitch-black, water-filled tunnel that smelled like death.

"Avoid things that float," she said with a knowing smile and invited me to step out before her.

I did as she said and realised we were in the sewers—some place I'd always known of but never thought I'd ever end up standing in with a backpack full of snacks and sugary drinks on my back. I also had galoshes on my feet and a torch in my hand, thanks to Paul, which was great since brown water came to my ankles and the ground underfoot felt slick. The circular door creaked and shut with a dull thud after Paul made her way out and shut it behind her.

"This way," Paul said. With a backpack, galoshes and a torch of her own, she led us through the tunnel, moving as if she had been through the route a thousand times. She was not in the least concerned about the slime or bad smells that seemed to be everywhere.

"Is it safe?" I asked and tried to keep up without splashing brown water onto my new clothes. We were the only things making sound. The vast expanse of quiet made me very uneasy, for some reason.

"Safer than it is above ground. Nobody will ever mug you here. Anyway, pay attention." Paul turned and shined her torch back at the fork in the tunnel behind us. "We came from the right. Remember that. If we ever lose each other, find your way back to the fallout bunker. I'll meet you there."

"Why would we lose each other?" I asked.

"You never know. Look, you can use visual markers like these." She shined her torch at a patch of blue graffiti on the damp brick walls ahead of us. It read: 'ExiSTencE iS fLAWed'. "You'll be going backwards so remember to look back every few steps and make mental notes as you go along."

I nodded and obediently turned my torch towards the two dark tunnels behind us for a better look.

They looked equally creepy—the types of tunnels nightmares contained. Every sound coming from them, however soft, sounded like a threat. I couldn't imagine what going through them all by myself would feel like.

Best to stick close to Paul, I decided. Until I figured out what was really going on, at least. As bizarre as Paul seemed, as confusing as her presence was, the new version of Paul had an odd bravado about her that made me feel as if she could handle anything. Down here, she wasn't the antisocial child-woman who only knew Snakes and Ladders. Here, she was a leader who knew exactly what to do and where to go.

Stick close to Paul and eat more Chinese food.

That was all I knew how to do.

We crawled out of a manhole like rats and ended up in an alleyway full of dumpsters and loose trash. It was night when we emerged. A few homeless people snuggled under the cover of shadows saw us but didn't look particularly surprised.

I think I was more afraid of them than they were of us. I was in unfamiliar territory—their territory. The buildings we stood in the middle of, I did not recognise. The good-quality skyscrapers that looked like they belonged to the Financial District were nowhere in sight.

I heard a soft clang behind me as Paul replaced the cover of the manhole. Her eyes darted around everything afterward and seemed to be rich with thought. "Get rid of the galoshes," she said and did exactly that herself. "I left a couple of crowbars behind that pipe over there, in case you ever need to get the manhole open."

I followed her pointing finger to a silver ventilation pipe plastered against the side of a building and committed it to memory. The silver pipe stood out for it was huge and seemed to go all the way up to the sky.

"Come on, let's move."

I obeyed. I stashed my galoshes behind a dumpster as Paul had done and followed her down the alleyway in the new leather sneakers she had given me to wear with my new clothes.

Paul was fast yet quiet. I could hear my own footsteps but not hers. After going around a few bends, we came to a nondescript back door. Without even looking at me, Paul opened it and went right in.

I hesitated. I didn't want to trespass. I feared doing so would land me in jail, with a criminal record that would make it impossible for me to find work ever again.

"Standing all alone in a dark alleyway in the deep of the night could bring you a fate worse than unemployment, Lane," Paul's voice suddenly said in my head.

I thought she made a good point. There was, after all, free food, clothes and shelter in jail, wasn't there?

So I trespassed. I went right in.

I found myself in a commercial kitchen, surrounded by rows of industrial stoves, steel counters and fridges, underneath blinding white florescent lights.

My new sneakers slid unsteadily as I made my way across the oily ceramic floor in search of Paul. Amidst the heavy scent of dishwashing detergent, I realised I stank. I literally smelled like shit.

I spotted Paul a good distance away, crouched behind a steel counter, listening out the way an animal would.

"Where—"

"Shhh!" Her head darted towards me as her finger shot in front of her lips. She gestured to stay low, so I did.

I found a stack of boxes to crouch behind and followed her eyes to the far corner of the kitchen.

Two chefs, both fat, sat on a bench with their backs against the wall. Both of them had their eyes closed and arms crossed. One of them was even snoring a little. Above their heads was a clock with the hour hand pointed to the number four. Next to them, a pair of swing doors.

"Follow me. Quietly," Paul said in my head. I nodded and did just that with no questions this time.

We made it past multiple fridges and sinks without a sound. Then, my luck ended. As we were going past the counters right in front of the chefs, my new sneakers lost their grip of the oily ceramic floor and my face propelled downwards, directly towards five tall stacks of porcelain plates.

"Shit!" I heard Paul say. Out loud. Next thing I knew, she was right in front of my face, with her hand over my mouth, holding up my body with her own.

How Paul managed to travel fifteen feet across a room full of obstructions in the blink of an eye, I did not know. Had I blocked out part of the event—as Dr Clark always said I had a tendency to do—because it had been unpleasant? I had no idea.

"Be very careful," Paul hissed in my head, her body hot

under mine. Her mouth never once moved. She was so close, I could see how dilated her pupils were and feel her chest moving against mine.

She seemed to be struggling to catch her breath whereas I felt oddly calmer. I felt safer with her right there, protecting me from screwing up. Safer than I felt when all alone.

We stared at each other for a pretty long time, without a word, until Paul eventually decided to let go of my mouth and take me by the hand instead.

She gripped me tightly and brought us towards the swing doors without a sound. The two exhausted chefs never once noticed the two Wonderdrug Psychiatric Centre escapees skulking past their knees.

Beyond the swing doors was a modern industrial eatery with long communal tables flanked by mismatched chairs under dangling Edison bulbs. It was deserted and all the Edison bulbs were switched off so it was pretty dark. Whatever light we could see with came from the brightly lit hotel lobby that was adjacent. The classical music we could hear came from that lobby too.

Paul let go of my hand and crept briskly towards the exposed brick wall which separated the industrial eatery from the lobby. She pressed her back against the brick wall and peeped out. I did the exact same because I didn't know what else I was supposed to be doing in that situation.

The hotel lobby had raw concrete walls, gallery-style fittings and shiny upcycled furnishings. Perfume was thick in the air—the scent of white tea and peony, I think—and there were floor-to-ceiling factory windows that looked out onto a view of Manhattan.

Brooklyn? Was that where we were? I glanced at Paul and asked her that very question with my mind but she never heard me.

Her eyes were on the receptionist at the reception counter—a very nice-looking counter by the way, made of raw brick and glass. The receptionist had his head slanted down to the floor. His shoulders jerked violently from time to time so I figured he was playing a game on his phone or something.

"Are we going to check in?" I whispered. Paul shushed me again and stretched her arm out as if trying to push me against the wall. A strange, vacant expression came upon her face and for a very, very long time, Paul did not move a muscle.

When I say a very long time, I mean like almost a good half hour.

I waited in silence for a whole half hour with her arm across my body and did not dare move one bit. My legs fell asleep and the part of my arm that her hand touched eventually got a little damp.

I found myself wondering if Paul would ever move again and made up my mind to ask to be sent back to the Wonderdrug Psychiatric Centre if we did eventually end up getting caught.

Getting caught and ending up back at Wonderdrug sounded so good, I found myself a little disappointed when Paul suddenly inhaled a deep breath and dropped her arm.

"Are you... okay?" I whispered. I made sure none of my disappointment showed, of course.

Paul never replied that question. Instead, she turned her head up to the ceiling and kept it there as if she were watching something very intently. I followed her line of sight and noticed something most unusual.

There was a white keycard in mid-air, way above the head of the receptionist at the counter. As far as I could see, the keycard was not connected to anything—no strings, no strong wind from below. It was simply... levitating. And then, it was *flying*. Towards us. As if the hotel were haunted and spirits were trying to tell us something.

When the keycard arrived right above our heads, Paul stuck out a hand. The keycard fell right into it. She held the keycard up to me with a huge beam on her face and I could tell she was really proud of everything she had just done.

We went back out via the kitchen then the whole way around the refurbished 1930s building just so we could go back in through the front entrance. 'The Canned Food Factory Hotel' were the words written in bright red lights running down the side of the building.

The receptionist at the reception counter lifted his perfectly-gelled head from the floor the moment we stepped in. He smiled as if the sight of us was the best thing he had seen all day, as if he hadn't just been playing one of the most engaging phone games ever.

"Welcome back, ladies," he said in a manner that was extremely warm and welcoming.

"Hi," Paul replied. She led us right towards the old fashioned cage elevator at the corner as if she knew exactly where it would lead. I gave him a polite smile because I didn't know what else to do.

"I would have liked the suite better, but it's presently occupied," Paul said when we both got into the elevator.

She pressed the button for the tenth floor.

I had no idea what we were doing at that point, so I didn't bother saying anything at all.

Room 103—the room the flying keycard had access to—reminded me of my apartment. It had the same exposed brick walls and tired wooden flooring but was, maybe, eight times larger and had much better furnishings. Its industrial roughness was softened by vintage floral wallpaper on parts of the walls and there were heavy fabric textures all over the room which made it look cosy and luxurious.

A king-sized bed with a steel and leather headboard stood in the middle of the room between two wooden bedside lockers. Heavy floor-to-ceiling felt curtains in grey fell over the large industrial window that was in front of a table made of a plate of glass atop a stack of tin cans. Upcycled vintage closets stood against two walls while Warhol's soup cans and a television screen hung in the middle of the others.

"Thought this place might make you feel at home," Paul said as she closed the door behind us. She flung her backpack onto one of the two leather chairs around the tin can table and grabbed a bathrobe from the closet closest to the bathroom door. "It looks a little like your apartment, doesn't it?" She smiled and went into the bathroom, closing the door behind her.

How in the world would Paul know what my apartment looked like? From reading my mind? Again? I went to the window and looked out.

We had the view of a wall—the windowless side of the building next door.

I decided Paul was wrong. Room 103 did not feel like home. It felt way better than any place I had ever called home. A room that big and posh, with a window that big, I would never have been able to afford under normal circumstances. *Was I actually, really going to get to spend the night in a room as nice as Room 103? Me?*

"What are we doing?" I asked. I simply had to know.

"Starting afresh," Paul replied from the bathroom. "Don't you want to?"

In this fancy ass place? Hell yes. Seriously, why in the hell not? The place was almost as good as Wonderdrug had been, except...

Except I couldn't be sure if it was all really *real*.

Did I really just jump out of a ten-storey window and recover in three days? Had a hotel's keycard really just flown into Paul's hand right in front of my eyes? Could those things even happen in real *life? Or... was there something terrible going on within my brain?*

I chewed my nails and thought hard. According to Paul, I was out for only five days after the falling incident and for three days after my jump from the Wonderdrug Psychiatric Centre stairwell. If I could prove her claims to be true, then I could prove all of this to be real, couldn't I?

I could think of no other way to go about it. I knew I had to see how my body reacted to injuries myself so I searched the room for something to harm myself with. Knives? Fire? Weapons? To my disappointment, I couldn't find any of those things. A t-shaped wine opener with a sharpish tip was the most dangerous object I could get.

I decided it would have to do.

I brought the wine opener out of the drawer it hid in and sat down at the tin can table with it. I turned my palm up towards the ceiling and brought the tip of the wine opener up in the air.

In one quick move, I rammed the wine opener down onto my palm as forcefully as I could manage. Its bluntish tip tore through my flesh so reluctantly, I had to grit my teeth and push down harder on purpose just to get some blood out.

Two strokes, one down towards the left and one down towards the right. One big bloody 'X' and a whole lot of burning pain.

Tears trickled down my cheeks even though I wasn't in the least sad. The pain in my palm felt so real, I decided there and then that everything that was happening in front of my eyes probably was real too.

CHAPTER 12
21 JUNE 2030

We woke around 3pm the next day, mutually ravenous. Paul suggested eating at the eatery next to the lobby—now a coloured, video version of the black and white photo we had been creeping through the night before—and told the hostess who sat us to bill the meal to Room 103.

To my surprise, the hostess—a clean-looking, middle-aged white lady with piercings all over both ears and on one side of her nose—obliged with a big smile and little fuss. The electronic device she wore on a lanyard around her neck verified the existence of legitimate paying guests in Room 103 and had no issue with the said guests running a tab, apparently.

Because there wasn't much of a crowd, we got to have one of the long wooden tables all to ourselves. The table was made of wood from the ceiling of the original factory, a sign pasted on the surface of the table said. The Edison bulbs above our heads emitted a warm orange glow this time, softly illuminating the exposed pipes, wooden floor and red granite wall tiles that seemed to take us back to a time when life was more gritty through and through.

Paul ordered 'Crunchy Fried Chicken Waffles' and a 'Fluffy Vanilla Milkshake' because there were thumbs up symbols next to them on the menu. There was no Chinese for me to choose from so I reluctantly made do with the 'Mac and Cheese Explosion' and an Americano.

I found it hard to believe I was actually still at the Canned Food Factory Hotel. The moment our waiter walked away with our orders, I flipped both palms over to check on the 'X' I had made and...

...found no 'X' on either palm. None that I could see. Both my palms looked absolutely fine. No different from normal, healthy palms. No scars. No wounds. Nothing out of the ordinary. *Why?*

"What do you want to do next?" Paul asked in that moment.

I dropped my palms, thought about her question for a bit but couldn't say for sure. "I guess I could go back to being a masseuse? Or wait tables? I'll just do whatever I can get, I guess. It's gonna be tough getting work without ID though so we'll really just have to take whatever comes."

Paul narrowed her eyes as I spoke and regarded me with an interchanging mix of disbelief and curiosity. "I break you out of Wonderdrug, grant you freedom, and all you want to do is work long hours for very little money?" she said after some time. "Don't you want to try every dish on the planet? Explore every country? Learn everything there is to learn about everything?"

I laughed. "Paul, all those wonderful things require money. Simply staying alive requires money. To get money, we're going to have to get jobs, whether or not you want to. There's no way around it."

She raised one eyebrow in response. "Lane, haven't you seen what I can do? We can do whatever we want. You can do whatever you want. You don't need a stupid job. Not unless you want one for the fun of it, of course."

I stopped laughing at once. I didn't really want a job of

course. None of the jobs I ever held were really all that fun at all. Getting to know Arden Villeneuve at The Gentlemen's Dinner Club had been fun, sure, but the twelve-hour shift and six-day work week that came with it definitely wasn't. So no, I wasn't stupid enough to want a job if I didn't *have to* get one. But me never having to work for money again because Paul, a former patient of the Wonderdrug Psychiatric Centre, daughter of a paranoid schizophrenic, had it all worked out? It sounded impossible. "Can I ask you something?" I decided to say.

Paul looked right back into my eyes and suddenly seemed a little nervous. "Of course."

Hovering all around us were waiters, so I leaned in. "Who are you? How is it you were one thing the day we first met and now, something else altogether?"

Paul heaved abruptly, as if relieved, grinned a little and peeled her eyes from mine. "Well, the person you saw the first time we met was the person I needed Wonderdrug to believe I was. I needed them to have their guard down so I could properly see everything they were really up to."

I frowned. "And what is it they're really up to?"

Paul leaned in with a serious expression all over her face. "Wonderdrug Laboratories has a little known classified department called CRO."

"Crow?"

"Yes, C-R-O, short for Curiosity Research Office. They operate out of the various Wonderdrug Psychiatric Centres around the world. Their mission is to research and utilise women like us. Strange women, as they like to call us."

I frowned again. "How strange?"

Paul watched my face and a twinkle appeared in her eyes. "Isn't it obvious? You fell fifty storeys and didn't die. In fact, by the end of the first day, you were already so much better. That made people talk and that was how CRO came to know of you. They swooped in, found a way to make you look dead, replaced your body with a cadaver and took you in to see how they could profit from your amazing regenerative abilities."

Paul spoke like she meant every word, as incredulous as it all sounded to me. Two words caught my attention. 'Fifty' and 'storeys'. Not 'five' like Dr Clark always insisted. 'Fifty storeys' matched my memory of the falling incident, didn't it? I remembered being on the rooftop right before the falling incident and nowhere else. I closed my open mouth and swallowed hard. "What about you? What do they want from you?"

"I was three, living with my mom at the Manhattan Psychiatric Centre, playing with toys like any three-year-old would, except... with my mind instead of my hands. People, mostly the sane ones, they were horrified. CRO heard the rumours and 'killed' my mom and I like they did you. They wanted to know if my telekinesis had been genetically acquired. My mom gave me the biggest telepathic scolding of my life when we found ourselves trapped in separate wards at the Wonderdrug Psychiatric Centre. After that, I learned never to reveal any more of my abilities. I started pretending to be crazy and mentally slow just as my mom had been doing for years but it was already too late. I was trapped. Until you came along."

Telepathy? Telekinesis? I wasn't sure if I heard her right. "Why didn't your mother come with us?"

"Because she's dead now. Really dead. Which is how you would have ended up had I not gotten you out of there."

A waiter interrupted us by bringing food and drinks to our table. The frying pan he put in front of me was an 'Explosion' indeed. Cheesy, starchy goodness crusted all around the edges of the pan. I felt my mouth water and my stomach squirrel but knew there was just one thing I simply had to know before giving myself thoroughly to it.

"Excuse me—" I said to the waiter, right as he put the last of our drinks—my Americano—between us.

"Lane, no—"

"—what's the date today?"

The waiter—possibly a college student doing the gig part-time—raised his eyebrows at me and smiled. "21 June."

"Of which year?"

"20… 30?" He spoke the digits slowly and turned to Paul with a curious glance when he was done.

She smiled at him in a way that didn't look entirely natural and thanked him to make him go away.

The moment the waiter went out of hearing's reach, Paul's smile dropped.

"Lane, there are things you must never do if you want to remain free," she said with a sternness I'd never thought I'd ever see on her face. "Talking more than is necessary, in a way that will make people talk about you, is a big no. CRO's definitely looking high and low for us right now and they're going to figure out where we are if people start texting their friends about all the strange conversations they've been having with two strange women. Do you understand?"

I nodded but all I could really think about at that point was the waiter's reply. *2030. The year was 2030, not 2033.* Paul had been right about Dr Clark lying, which meant everything she had been telling me about Wonderdrug was possibly also true! It meant I wasn't a crazy person and that I hadn't wasted three years of my life in a coma! It meant I was a woman with a superhuman gift—the 'X' on my palm probably healed overnight—and, more importantly, I was never going to have to get a job ever again! My heart banged hard against my ribs as my mouth curled upwards into a huge grin, even though my brows couldn't stop falling into a frown. "So... what are we supposed to do with ourselves then? Use our powers for good? Save people and stuff?"

Paul snorted. "Of course not. I spent my whole life institutionalised because people want my 'powers' for themselves. They don't deserve to be saved, so, no. We won't be saving anybody."

"Okay. Then... what do we do?"

Paul smiled and a strange look—maybe excitement?—appeared in her eyes. "We enjoy," she said. "Everything the world has to offer, we will enjoy."

I felt joy rush through every pore of my being when I heard those words. Suddenly, being on the run with a patient from the Wonderdrug Psychiatric Centre didn't feel all that bad at all.

We spent what was left of the day trying to explore as much of Brooklyn as we could on foot. I was as much of a tourist as Paul was because, despite having lived in New York all my life, I never once made a stop at Brooklyn, believe it or not. My life had been all about commuting to Manhattan from Queens and back, over and over again. Not being in either Manhattan or Queens for once felt like a breath of fresh air. I felt as if I was away from my place of origin, out in the world on an adventure. I popped in and out of shops with my index fingers flying and my mouth wide open. Paul did too. There was just so much to see and buy. So many things to do and try.

Brooklyn was like an industrial-chic amusement park full of young metropolitan adults out for the purpose of seeing and being seen with people as cool as themselves. Almost everyone out on the streets had shades on and an overpriced drink in hand. Almost every building near The Canned Food Factory Hotel had been repurposed for commerce. Former rundown factories and abandoned office buildings were now inhabited by shops, clubs and cafes of all sorts. Historic buildings and former colleges had been turned into museums, performance venues and fine-dining establishments.

To my relief, Paul hadn't been bullshitting me about the money. She had stacks of notes stashed all around her new backpack and felt comfortable enough with the amount she had to be giving it to cashiers for the most frivolous of items. She bought a $300 block of chocolate carved in the shape of a bear, a digital painting that didn't look digital and would change in accordance to the day's weather, a $2000 watch that did nothing but tell the time, and a heavy brass sculpture of a male hand making the a-ok gesture. Totally unnecessary items but she didn't even care.

She gave me a couple of hundred dollars to spend on whatever caught my fancy too. I bought expensive soaps with the money; flavoured cigarettes, cigarette cases, hand-crafted lighters, nail polish, scented candles, all the sorts of things I never once considered buying back when the money came from my own long hours of hard, laborious work.

I paid extra to get my hair done by a world famous stylist who taught me how to put it up into a big messy updo that was apparently in trend that season. The new look made me look much younger and fresher so I obliged when he insisted I buy a whole basket's worth of hair products to keep my hair up that way.

We picked out more new clothes—plunging little black dresses, insanely high heels, jewellery, little cocktail bags, fake eyelashes—and eventually, when the sky turned dark and the city's lights came on, found ourselves in a magazine-recommended restored 19th century carriage house enjoying octopuses, old-fashioned steaks, red velvet cheesecake and two bottles of wine in candlelight.

By the time we got back into The Canned Food Factory Hotel's cage elevator, drunk as lords, after having stumbled back arm in arm the whole way, I was buzzed from the day of fun and madly grateful.

The moment the elevator's doors closed, I put my lips on Paul's and pressed my body up against hers.

She was startled at first, and a little tense, but when we pulled apart, I saw the way her eyes sparkled and just knew, from experience, that Paul wasn't a worm-throwing child-woman disinterested in romance any longer.

Back in Room 103, Paul backed into one of the wallpapered walls and eyed me with anticipation. I thought she looked a tad afraid so I approached slowly.

When I was close enough to smell her newly applied perfume and warm, sweat-covered skin, I reached out and pushed hair out of her face. "May I?" I whispered, our faces just a couple of inches apart.

She gulped, took in all of my features, then nodded. Her eyes shimmered in the dim light of the room's bedside lamps.

I brought my lips onto hers and grazed them lightly but found her tongue curling against mine shortly afterwards. I responded with slow, gentle kisses but Paul picked up the pace and kissed me back with a fervour that fired up my senses. Her hands travelled down my back, past my hips and pulled all my clothes up above my arms.

"They let you have sex at Wonderdrug?" I asked breathlessly as my bra and dress hit the floor in a crumpled heap. I couldn't believe how good a kisser Paul turned out to be. She was one of the best I ever encountered and I had encountered quite a few before her so that was saying a lot.

"No," she replied and peeled every article of clothing off herself. "But I've read enough minds to know what works."

"Wait, you mean you're—"

I stopped short and gasped for Paul had sunk downwards and was sucking my breast with such finesse, I felt as if I were going to orgasm there and then. When she straightened out and kissed me in the mouth again, I forgot all about what I had been wanting to ask and could think only of how I wanted her to feel.

One of my hands took her breast while the other moved over her clit. I moved my lips over her ear and thrust my tongue in and out in accordance to the frantic beating of my heart. Paul threw her head back against the wall, closed her eyes and moaned. Her body arched against my hands while her hands ran into my hair and panties.

I gasped when she began doing to me exactly what I was doing to her. Every stroke she made brought me sheer pleasure. It was as if Paul knew precisely where I wanted to be touched and how. I repaid her efforts by increasing the speed at which my hand moved against her flesh and began teasing her nipples with my tongue.

"Yes…" she puffed. "Yes.. yes!" Her clit rammed itself against my hand as her hips began to rock. Her free hand dug into my back while the preoccupied one began moving more energetically underneath my panties.

Pleasure engulfed my groin and made my legs go weak. My body began lurching towards Paul's as soft moans escaped my mouth. She was good. Very good. I could feel myself almost going to—

Paul began gasping in pleasure herself. She grabbed my shoulders. She grabbed my hair. Her knees wobbled. Her cheeks turned red.

I moaned and tried to hold myself back. I wanted Paul to experience hers first. I responded to her gasps with persistent, intensifying strokes of the hand until her gasps turned into shrieks and moans then finally, unrestrained exclamations of sheer orgasmic pleasure. A powerful explosion of orgasmic delight engulfed my groin right as her body jerked up against mine. My body began throbbing from head to toe as a delightful orgasm spread across all of my nerves. We crashed against the wallpapered wall, screaming in unison for a good minute until eventually, both of us melted down onto the carpet, winded and moist.

When I looked up again, Paul was looking a little stunned, for some reason. She stared right into my eyes—pupils completely dilated, cheeks thoroughly flushed—and pecked me lightly on the lips. "Let's do it again," she whispered before I could even say a word. "But go deeper."

I grinned and struggled to catch my breath. "Can't we just take a min—"

"No." Her eyes glistened with anticipation as she pulled me over her knees and placed my hand between her legs. "Please."

The look on her face made my groin throb. I put two fingers together and inserted them, very slowly, into her vagina. Paul gasped and clutched at my arm when I did.

"Tell me where to go," I whispered as I explored her depths with both fingers.

She heaved sharply and writhed. "Left…"

I did as she said and came upon a familiar rough patch in the middle of the void of smooth flesh. I rubbed down on it. Hard.

Paul gasped again, louder this time, and arched her back against the wall. She closed her eyes but her mouth remained wide open.

I stroked the rough patch until it ballooned and became terribly swollen. Paul moaned and began taking deep, difficult breaths which resulted in me seeping wetness all over her knee. I found myself rubbing myself against her and moaning along with her when the right amount of pressure hit my groin. When her moans became louder and her breaths became more shallow, I found myself riding her knee more furiously and making the most pornographic of sounds.

I don't know why I suddenly found myself wishing Arden Villeneuve would see us. Perhaps because the beautiful room looked like something out of an arthouse film? Perhaps I wanted Arden Villeneuve to know I was happy without her? I don't know, I really don't, but somehow, I just suddenly wished Arden Villeneuve were there.

I imagined her seated on the carpet right next to us with her fluffy golden hair glowing under light like it always did, watching our faces contort and our bodies squirm. I imagined her long, naked body rocking against her own feet; her face—with those cherubic rounded eyes and impeccably perfect features—losing their composure as she fingered her own full breasts. I imagined her body melting under pleasure, the way it always did every time I made love to her, and saw her mouth let loose desperate gasps as if she was about to die from the delightful sensations building within her. I imagined her reaching orgasm and crying out as she always used to—loud and unrestrained—and I—

—felt the most pleasurable of sensations crest over my groin. I gasped, rocked and lurched backwards when the sensation burst into prominent pulsations of ecstasy that made my whole body shudder and go warm. I felt myself melt into Paul's knee and lose all control of the muscles on my face and eyes right as—

—Paul began crying out helplessly. Her body shook as a thick wetness appeared all over my thrusting fingers and her thighs and knee began to tremble. Together, we made such a racket, I was certain the neighbours would be able to hear but I couldn't stop nor did I want to stop her. We simply screamed and clutched at each other while our bodies went wild until we, at last, both became limp and quiet again.

When I opened my eyes, I found blood on my fingers and Paul staring down at them as if in shock.

Without looking at or saying a single word to me, Paul picked herself up and went to take a shower.

CHAPTER 13
22 JUNE 2030

At 3pm the next afternoon, Paul and I found ourselves back at the same long communal table at the same industrial eatery we had been eating lunch at the day before. This time, however, the energy between us was different.

Paul had on a solemn expression the whole time. She kept her head angled towards her cheese-covered marinara pizza and put bites in her mouth so mechanically, it almost looked as if she were a robot programmed to wipe food off the face of the planet.

In the seat opposite her, I nursed a pounding hangover headache by kneading the side of my forehead between three fingers. The two bottles of wine at dinner the night before had definitely been a bad idea, I realised, when I found myself also hardly able to swallow the hot-smoked salmon bagel in front of me. Finishing food was the least of my problems though.

"Is everything alright?" I decided to ask when the silence between Paul and I became too unbearable. It clearly wasn't—Paul hadn't said a word to me all day—but

I didn't know how else to ease her into talking about it, especially since she wouldn't even look at me.

"Yes," she said to her food.

Damn. "Was... last night... okay?"

"No." Paul looked up for one humourless second and turned her eyes away from mine before I could even register them there. "You're not the type of person I'm looking for."

Okay. My cheeks began to burn as if I got myself too much sun so I stuffed a chunk of bagel into my mouth and tried to look busy until my cheeks calmed down.

"I'm sorry," I mumbled when the dry clump of dough went down my throat at last. I didn't know what else to say. I could tell I had done something horribly wrong and wished my pounding brain would just wake up and tell me exactly what—

Paul slammed a ball of cash and the keycard to Room 103 onto the table. "Look, we should get some time alone and think about where we really want to go from here. I'll see you back at the room tonight." She abruptly got up, made a cringe-inducing screech with her chair as she pushed it out, and walked away.

I panicked. *If Paul never came back, what would I do with myself?* I grabbed the two items on the table and ran after her. "Paul! Wait—"

A passing waitress holding a pot of coffee extended an arm and blocked me. "Would you like the check?" she asked with eyes full of suspicion.

"It's to be billed to Room 103," I said. I tried to move past her arm but she found a way to keep it in front of me anyhow.

"Still requires your signature. I'll get it for you right away if you'll just stay right here, okay?"

"Fine!"

By the time I turned my eyes from the waitress' stern ones, Paul was already halfway across the lobby.

"Paul!" I shouted as loudly as I could. "Can we do

dinner? See you at seven? At the lobby?"

Every single person between me and Paul turned to me and stared in amusement. But Paul did not.

She went right out the main doors of The Canned Food Factory Hotel without turning back even once.

Without Paul by my side, downtown Brooklyn wasn't in the least fun at all.

I got some aspirin for my heavy head but didn't dare spend the rest of the money, lest I never saw Paul again. With shopping, cafe-hopping and practically everything else we had been doing the day before no longer an option, the three hours and fifteen minutes I had before seven in the evening began to feel more like a burden than a blessing. I found myself dragging my feet amidst excited tourists and purposeful locals, feeling very much left out of things again, as I had been for most of my life. I found myself thinking a lot about Paul, or, more specifically, Paul's sudden change of attitude.

Was I a drunken mistake she regretted? Was she simply heterosexual, upset because she knew she had too carelessly given up her virginity to a woman? Maybe what she really wanted was many men and babies and was just afraid I might come in the way of that? Maybe all I needed to do was let her know I didn't expect a relationship with her? After all, I really didn't. I did like her and enjoyed the sex immensely, true, but if all Paul wanted was a platonic relationship, I would be perfectly fine with that too! All I needed from her was, to be very blunt, the infinite cash only she would give me—the cash which allowed me to do whatever I wanted without having to worry, go back to Wonderdrug or, worse, work.

That was the real reason I was so afraid of losing her, I realised. The real reason I wanted to have dinner with her so badly. I wanted to find out what she really wanted of me. *Whatever Paul needed me to be, I would be, no problem. I just needed to make sure she was aware of that.*

In the meantime, the free public library was the only place I dared to—could afford to—be.

The Brooklyn Public Library, a four-storey brick structure, was well lit and airy on the inside. It would have been a really pleasant place to spend an afternoon had there not been children and teens capering about the first two floors, destroying the quiet with their high-pitched murmurs and thumping footsteps.

I didn't know where to go to find a chair to sit in. I hadn't been to a library since middle school. The consensus was that only major nerds and those who couldn't afford to buy their own books ever visited libraries so, because I didn't want to be seen as poor or uncool, I actually refused to step into any library to get the books I couldn't get digitally, even when the consequence was flunking out. Unfortunately, on that particular afternoon in Brooklyn, I no longer had that much of a choice.

I found myself staring at a sign hanging from the ceiling for a good few minutes trying to figure out where to go. 'Non-fiction - L4. Fiction - L3. Young Adult - L2. Children's Library - L1. Information Commons - B1.' Next to the words 'Information Commons' was the icon of a computer and an arrow pointing down at the flight of stairs right under the sign.

I didn't actually want to read anything—I thought paper books smelled dirty, like mould, and preferred not to have to touch any—so I ended up taking the stairs to the basement. On the way down, I thought of a way to make my three hours fly by.

There were only six computers at the Information Commons which was really a small, barely decorated space with a few instructional posters pasted on the walls. Four of the computers were taken by teens working on school papers (I think), one was taken by an elderly woman writing a resume of some sort (again, I presume) but there was one computer that wasn't taken, so I took that.

I opened a web browser, brought up a search engine's homepage and stared at it while tapping my fingernail repeatedly against the keyboard's trackpad.

Should I search for news about the falling incident? Or shouldn't I? Should I? Or shouldn't I? Should I or shouldn't I?

What if the truth about the falling incident was that I had fallen from five storeys and not fifty? What if I found out I wasn't actually dead? What if I really had been admitted to the Wonderdrug Psychiatric Centre because I was simply mentally ill? Then what? Would all the freedom I now possessed vanish in an instant? Was knowing the truth really worth losing freedom for?

Tap, tap, tap, tap, tap. *Should I or shouldn't I? Should I or shouldn't I? Should I or shouldn't I?* Tap, tap, tap, tap, tap—

"Are you gonna use it or not?" a gruff male voice said.

I turned and found a middle-aged man standing next to me with five books stacked in his hands. A translucent file containing a thick stack of papers sat atop the stack. He was balding, smelled like a stale deli, and stared at me in a manner that couldn't be considered friendly.

"Make way if you aren't," he added. Firmly.

I looked around and saw the five other individuals at the Information Commons typing furiously on the computers in front of them with thoughtful expressions on their faces.

I was the only one who had been staring at a screen without typing a single letter. I guess the balding man thought he deserved the computer more than me because he was going to type more on it than I ever would. As if only productive people deserved to get to use free things.

"I *am* using it," I said through gritted teeth. The balding man looked terribly hostile so I decided to be hostile as well. "I need some information and I lost my phone."

Just to prove a point, I typed 'lane thompson death'

into the computer's search field with loud, dramatic clicks of the keyboard. I smashed the enter button so hard when I was done, everyone looked over in my direction.

The search engine delivered results in the blink of an eye. Six news articles in total.

I turned to the balding man and stared till he felt uncomfortable enough to move away. Then, I turned back to the screen as if I really wanted to know what the search results said, even though I didn't really. Not entirely.

Five of the six articles in the search engine's results I had read before. They were about my parents' and uncle's deaths. There was only one new one, titled 'Shanty Apartment Death Ruled A Suicide'.

A suicide? Not a murder? Did that mean Dr Clark hadn't been lying? Tap, tap, tap, tap... *Should I? Shouldn't I? Should I? Shouldn't I?*

The balding man standing at the corner with his stack of books sighed loudly enough for me to hear and watched me with some sort of snarl on his face.

Fucking hell, I thought. I clicked on the article and prayed it would be enough to make the darned balding man take his darned eyes off me.

'Shanty Apartment Death Ruled A Suicide by blah blah blah.

30-year-old Lane Thompson stunned residents of Far Rockaway early last Sunday when she fell from the roof of her rented home—a 50-storey tenement already plagued by a sordid history of murder and forced burglary. The freelance masseuse crashed onto the tarmac below where she lay in a pool of her own blood until paramedics arrived.

Against the odds, Thompson survived the fall but failed to thrive and died the very next day at St John's Hospital where she was being treated in intensive care.

Foul play and gang violence were initially thought to have contributed to her death but cameras around the building revealed Thompson alone on the roof right up to the moment of the fall. Further investigation revealed an unmarried individual with poor academic credentials, zero assets and no history of stable employment. Colleagues at her last known place of freelance engagement, The

Gentlemen's Dinner Club, speculate that her troubled relationships or lack thereof might have taken their toll on her.

Thompson's body was not claimed and has since been taken care of by the state.

The New York Police Department recommends everyone look out for those with symptoms of depression and lead them to doctors for treatment before it becomes too late. Those who recognise symptoms in themselves should also get help as soon as they can.

Depression can cause difficulty with concentration, detail recall and decision-making. Sufferers may also experience decreased energy, feelings of guilt, worthlessness, hopelessness or pessimism, persistent sad, anxious or 'empty' feelings and persistent thoughts of suicide.

Early use of prescription medication and psychotherapy could help prevent depression from worsening further. Talk to your doctor for more information.'

My heart felt as if it were chugging along as fast as a moving train by the time I was done reading. *Suicide? Death? And depression?* I was dead from an ailment I hadn't realised I had? From an action I hadn't realised I had taken? And yet I wasn't really dead at all? *What the fuck was really going on?* I threw myself back into the chair, buried my nose and lips under the front of my t-shirt and tried my very best to remain calm.

The article was dated '12 May 2030'. Seven days, exactly one week, after the falling incident. The date that day? '22 June 2030', the computer said. Just a month and a half after the falling incident, not three years.

I heaved a sigh of relief, thankful that the year the computer said it was matched the year Paul said it was. If the years matched up, everything else she had ever said—amazing regenerative abilities, CRO, not having to ever work for money—would also be true, wouldn't it?

There was only one problem. *Why in the world did I think I got pushed by a blond person with red lipstick when there hadn't been anyone else with me on the roof? And why did the police and my colleagues think I was depressed when I hadn't realised I was?* The smell of a stale deli entered my nostrils.

"You look done," a familiar gruff voice said.

Dammit. Without Paul, I was once again the type of person who needed to fight for everything at every moment in time. The type of person who got thrown into an unmarked mass grave in death. The type of person who didn't even get to use a public computer in peace. I pushed back the chair as rudely as I could, stood, and gave the stinking, balding man the coldest of stares. "Have. It." *Asshole.*

I walked away, back up the stairs to the first floor, but heard the balding man make a sexist comment about me anyway. *Fucker.* Good thing I had better things to think of.

Like... *Why in the world couldn't I remember wanting to jump, or even the actual jump itself?* It wasn't like I had no memories of that night, like it was with the nights my parents and uncle died. I *did* have a memory of the night of the falling incident; I remembered calmly dealing with being dumped by Arden Villeneuve and getting pushed. That was always the memory my mind gave me. *Why?*

Some kid shorter than my armpits rammed right into my legs and nearly knocked me off the stairs. She dashed off without a word of apology just as her friend, equally short, stepped on my new sneakers as he ran by me as well. I wished them both the worst of lives, grabbed the handrail next to me for added support and stopped in the middle of the staircase to properly think.

I had to find out what I was really like right before the falling incident, I realised. I had to know if I was really depressed, or even suicidal. That was the only way I was going to be able to know what really happened on the night of the falling incident. And who would know best? There was only one person who would properly know.

Arden Villeneuve.

At the library's check out counter on the first floor, I asked to borrow a phone. I said I lost mine and needed to call my husband to arrange where we were going to meet later on.

The two ladies behind the check out counter were elderly with greying hair but had thoroughly powdered faces and lipstick that was thicker than mine. They nodded sympathetically and put the desk phone that had been sitting between them onto the counter for me.

Would they have been that obliging if I told them I needed to call my now-married lady sex partner? Probably not, I figured. I smiled as appreciatively as I could make my face do and punched the digits I knew by heart as fast as my fingers could go.

Arden Villeneuve's mobile phone rang for a nerve-wrecking few minutes. During that time, the less-absurd story I had concocted to explain my return from death began to sound ridiculous in my head and I contemplated aborting the call multiple times. I had run my finger over the hang up button and was just about to push down when *she* picked up and said hello in that unmistakably sexy voice of hers.

"Hi, it's... Blaine," I said. I decided, in the spur of the moment, to leave out Arden Villeneuve's famous name, lest the library ladies in front of me got suspicious. "Is this a good time?"

It certainly didn't sound like it was. There were explosions on the other end of the line. People screaming. Children crying. "Lane?" Arden Villeneuve said. She sounded a little shocked.

One of the library ladies looked up from her laptop and smiled at me. I gave her the sort of smile women in detergent commercials always wore and turned away. "No, Blaine. But yes, I do want to talk to you about Lane and her... incident. Unfortunately, I've misplaced my phone so why don't you tell me where and when to meet and I'll see you there. I'm free... anytime."

Something massive and heavy collapsed on the other side of the line. A few men began screaming at each other to run. The library lady who had been smiling at me turned her head back to her laptop at last. The elderly lady who had been at the Information Commons with me before went out the front doors with a stack of papers in hand. A few nerdy-looking teenagers came down the stairs from the second floor.

"Hello?"

For a long time after that, I didn't get any reply.

At 7:10pm, back at the Canned Food Factory Hotel, the door to Room 103 banged shut.

Paul stormed in front of me with both fists clenched, her jaw tight, more angry than I had ever seen her before.

"You should never have made that appointment with that woman or used those search terms!" she shouted with a finger in my face. "We have to move, right now, thanks to you!"

I didn't know what to say. I hadn't mentioned a word about the library when Paul came up to me at the hotel lobby at 7pm but she took one look at my face and just seemed to *know*.

And after that, she went barking mad. She darted to the closet and pulled out all our new clothes like there was not a second to lose. She shoved those clothes into our two backpacks without bothering to remove the hangers.

"What's wrong with wanting to know the truth?" I tried to ask but I was drowned out by the riot of wooden hangers crashing against each other on the bed. Paul pried the hangers from the tops of the backpacks and tossed them like they were empty peanut shells.

"I was just trying to do something meaningful," I added. "What's wrong with that?"

Paul turned to look at me and there was rage in her eyes. "You are planning to tell that woman you didn't die!" she yelled. "To impress her! That's what's wrong with that!"

Oh. Shit. Paul knew every last one of my thoughts, I realised then.

"Yes, I do," she said right away. "Unfortunately. And I also know CRO will find us faster than you can even say 'oh shit' again if you meet her tomorrow!"

God. "I could tell her not to say anything—"

"You can't trust anyone!"

"Paul, please, she loves me. She won't tell a soul—"

"I'm leaving." Paul zipped up the backpacks, threw one over her back and one over her front.

"No, Paul, please!" I ran in front of her and attempted to block her from the front door with my arms outstretched.

"You can go do whatever you want," she said, right before she pushed past me and went towards the front door.

"Stop, please! I can't be out here without you, Paul! I need you!"

Paul stopped but she didn't turn back.

"As a friend," I added, quickly. I took a deep breath. "Look, I won't touch you again, I promise. And I'm really sorry I'm not what you were looking for in a lover but it doesn't mean we can't continue this crazy adventure together as friends, right? Nobody else is going to understand where you came from the way I do. Likewise for me. I need you as much as you need me."

Paul didn't respond but neither did she leave.

Heartened, I took a few steps towards her. "I won't tell Arden Villeneuve I'm not dead if you don't want me to, okay? And I won't tell her where we live so you don't have to move. But could you please just let me talk to her? Just once. I really need to do this. I really need to know what really happened that night."

I watched Paul take one long deep breath. She raised her head and stared up at the wall but didn't turn back. "One time, and you are never to see her again. Are we clear?"

I nodded at once and couldn't help the smile that curled up the corner of my lips. "We are clear."

Paul turned around after that. Our eyes met and I saw an unusual cautiousness in hers.

I smiled, relieved that our quest for enjoyment could now continue as before. "Shall we get dressed for dinner now?" I said quietly. "It will be a very platonic dinner with none of all the things that happened the last time, I promise."

She blinked hard and rolled her eyes in response but did not decline.

CHAPTER 14
23 JUNE 2030

Thanks to Arden Villeneuve, I got to have afternoon tea at Madame Pokerface—a Manhattan high tea room famed for its famous clientele, multiple design awards and insane prices—the next afternoon. And boy, was it a treat for the senses.

What was essentially a black box splattered with messy splotches of pop-coloured paint was also full of rubber furniture—in the same pop-colours of red, blue and yellow—designed like royal furnishings from ages past. It looked as far removed from reality as any place could get and was more like a music video or piece of art designed to make you stop and stare and wonder… why?

The host—obviously gay, dressed in a tailcoat tuxedo with a tall black hat which made him look like a magician—led me to the private corner behind four black walls where Arden Villeneuve sat on a jarringly-red Baroque chair in front of a jarringly-yellow Baroque table. Her mouth fell open when she saw me approach and her eyes became wide.

I felt exactly the same way when I saw her—the body-hugging cream-coloured dress she wore amplified her curves beautifully; her curled hair seemed to be made of the perfect amount of buoyancy and her face was just flawless, as always—but I tried my best not to let my feelings show. I took the jarringly-blue chair the host offered and smiled like being at Madame Pokerface, seeing Arden Villeneuve in the flesh, was not much of a big deal to me at all.

"Thank you, Marco," Arden Villeneuve said with her eyes on me. She peeled them away with effort just so she could smile at him. "We'll have the Fantastic Day, please."

"Excellent choice, ma'am. That set won Best High Tea Taste at the Gourmand Awards in 2028."

"Precisely why I'm choosing it." She gave our host the most charming of grins which instantly lifted him up onto cloud nine. He gushed zealously about how the set was absolutely going to make our day simply perfect, wonderful and magical, then eventually left to get it for us with a bounce in his step.

When we were all alone, Arden Villeneuve turned her eyes back on me.

I couldn't help but stare back. The scent coming from her—that mix of roses, vanilla and champagne—made my heart beat like a drum again. It always did, I don't know why.

"Do you mind taking your sunglasses off?" she asked, without taking her eyes off me.

I had completely forgotten about my sunglasses. I obliged right away and put them on the table, folded.

When I turned back to Arden Villeneuve, I noticed her eyes were bigger than before. Her throat moved upwards then down. Her dress now looked purely white, not cream-coloured at all.

I was as lost for words as she was. *What do you say to a woman you love when you can no longer say you love her?*

"Are you Lane's twin?" she said at last.

There was no easier way to explain the similar face, was there? I said yes. *Just Lane's twin. Not a person who could survive a fifty-storey fall. Not the person who made you come more times than you can remember.*

Arden Villeneuve nodded. Expressionlessly. "It must be really hard losing someone so close. I'm so sorry."

Don't be. I lost nobody. Except, maybe, you. I missed you, even though I won't ever say it. "It's okay."

"Do you smoke?" She reached for the diamond-studded cigarette case on her side of the table and the move drew my attention to the diamond-studded ring on her fourth finger.

"Yes. I do." *We used to smoke after sex all the time, before you went off and married that religious guy, remember?* I reached into the pocket of my jeans and dug out my brand new expensive cigarette case and lighter—a matching set, metal, with the logo of a haute couture brand patterned all over its sides like polka dots, much heavier than those dime-store plastic ones I used to carry. I lit myself a Super Menthol and set both down on the table next to me.

Arden Villeneuve observed my cigarette case and lighter with mild surprise as she lit a Super Menthol herself. When she exhaled, a thoughtful look formed on her face. "I'm sorry, I didn't quite catch your name over the phone. You are…?"

"Blaine. Blaine Thompson."

"Blaine and Lane?"

"Our parents thought it cute."

She nodded and grinned at last. "So, Blaine, what is it you want to talk about?"

"Well, it's about—"

"Sorry to interrupt, ladies, but here is your Fantastic Day set!" Marco, suddenly next to the table again, placed a black clay sculpture with crevices full of tiny finger foods between the both of us. He then set down a glass pot full of golden-coloured tea and a glass bowl full of shrunken miniature oranges in a thick yellowish syrup next to the sculpture.

"This tea, we call 'The Harmless Champagne'." He picked up the glass pot and poured the golden-coloured tea into the black clay teacups that had been in front of us all along. "Looks like champagne but is really only a blend of chamomile, honey, cinnamon and fresh oranges. Those, over there, are wild kumquats in syrup. They blend perfectly, beautifully well with your Harmless Champagne and are very, very, very sweet, so please add them carefully."

He set the glass pot down and pointed a well-manicured finger at the sculpture of finger food that seemed to vanish from the periphery of my vision each time I looked away from it because it was the exact same black as the walls. "Here, we have black truffle sandwiches, caviar pinwheels, homemade clotted cream scones, lemon meringues and hand-rolled truffles covered in edible 24-karat gold dust. Every taste, every smell on this piece of art has been carefully selected to relax you, refresh you and enhance your afternoon thoroughly."

"Thank you, Marco, it's beautiful," Arden Villeneuve said.

"I know. You won't be disappointed, ladies." He wished us a lovely experience and, finally, left us alone again.

We snuffed out our cigarettes and tasted the tea. I thought the ingredients sounded better suited for old people but the blend of raw fruit and natural sweetness turned out to be extremely invigorating. I felt refreshed after a few sips indeed. A pleasant surprise.

Arden Villeneuve smiled and suggested I try a black truffle sandwich. I obliged. I lifted one from the sculpture with two fingers and put the bite-sized sandwich into my mouth. The moment I bit down, an aroma I had never encountered before hit me in the nose. It smelled like earth and tree bark but wasn't entirely bad.

"There's something I need to ask you, Blaine."

I rinsed the overwhelming flavour from my mouth with a large gulp of hot tea and nodded. "Go ahead." Warmth moved from my throat down into my stomach and left me feeling very relaxed indeed.

"How did you get hold of my personal number?"

My heart jumped when I heard her question and the warmth I had been feeling just seconds ago now seemed to burn.

"Lane didn't have my number, as far as I know."

Right. Shit. I had forgotten all about that.

One night, months before the falling incident, a careless reservations executive at the Gentlemen's Dinner Club left the computer containing member details unlocked and unguarded. I thought Arden Villeneuve's number might come in handy some day so I memorised it. Without anyone noticing.

But how was I going to tell that to her face without sounding like a creep? "I found it written in Lane's diary," I said instead, after some thought. "Thought you must have been close friends."

"Close…? Oh, no, I barely knew her. I didn't even know she was a twin."

I found myself blurting out a laugh because her reply sounded like a joke, even though it was barely even funny. "Are you serious? Not even a little bit close?"

"Yes. We were definitely not close. I mean she was my favourite masseuse because her technique was well, the best, but that was it. We didn't talk much, in fact. Nothing more than the basic hello and goodbye, you know?"

Her face was serious as she spoke. She looked like she meant every word. "Really?" I said as a strange coldness began to surround my chest. I felt my smile waning.

Arden Villeneuve frowned and inhaled sharply as if a little irritated. "Did Lane say how she got the number? Staff at the Gentlemen's Dinner Club aren't supposed to know those things, you know. That's why we pay so much to go there."

The strange coldness around my chest spread all the way over to my fingertips. I found myself absent-mindedly caressing my upper canine with my tongue. "I have no idea. She didn't say."

Arden Villeneuve sighed heavily and shook her head as if annoyed. She reached for another cigarette and put smoke between us. "Well, I'm glad you told me anyway. At least now I know I shouldn't renew my membership." She chuckled a little and looked as if she expected me to smile back but I found myself unable to.

Instead, I took a gold-covered truffle and busied myself with chewing it. I thought it tasted awful; I felt like I was eating damp soil.

"So," she said after watching me for some time. "What is it you want to talk about?"

I forced out a smile, hoping it would help dissipate the bewilderment vibrating through my bones, but that didn't work. "I... just wanted to know if you saw Lane the night she fell? If you noticed anything unusual about her behaviour? Because I don't get why she did it. She didn't seem like… the sort who would want to kill herself, you know?"

Arden Villeneuve nodded. "I see. Well, I hate to have to say this, Blaine but..." She shrugged. "I didn't see her the night she fell. I did get a bunch of roses delivered to her apartment that night but the guy who brought it there didn't mention anything out of the ordinary so I'm as clueless as you are. Sorry."

"Why would you send her roses if you weren't... close?"

"Oh, I sent roses to everyone who ever worked for me that day. My way of letting them know I was getting married. Ask Marco if you don't believe me. He got roses from me too."

I stared and didn't know what to say. *Had there been a delivery guy at my apartment on the night of the falling incident?* I didn't remember seeing one, that was for sure. But then again, the Arden Villeneuve in front of me wasn't exactly like the Arden Villeneuve I remembered either. That electrified chemistry we used to always have between us was now... non-existent. She wouldn't hold her eyes in mine the way she used to. She didn't stare at my lips or cheeks. She never even glanced at my chest. It was as if we had been teleported all the way back to the first day we met, back to when we were nothing but service provider and patron with no history together, no different from perfect strangers.

She frowned at me again. "Is everything all right?"

I looked away at once. *No. Everything was not all right.* An awful sinking feeling had begun gnawing at my gut. Thoughts I never thought I'd ever have were tossing themselves about in my mind. *What if... just what if... my brain wasn't entirely in tune with reality? What would my world look like if that happened?* A chill bolted down my spine and made my hands tremble. The teacup I picked up for support rattled against the dish it was on.

Arden Villeneuve shifted in her seat and tapped her fingers against her own teacup impatiently.

I thought that very odd.

Arden Villeneuve had never been impatient with me before. It used to be just… sparks. Two confident women patiently pursuing a sensuous adventure together. *Where was that energising current now?*

Non-existent. In its place, an air of unfamiliarity and awkwardness so impenetrable, I began to think it would be best for me to get away from her. Fast.

Her phone rang, to my relief, and, I think, hers too.

She excused herself, picked up her clutch bag and sashayed away from the table like a larger-than-life goddess of elegance.

The moment she was out of sight, I dropped the teacup in my hands and sank back into the smooth, spongy rubber armchair I was on. *What the fuck?* I saw her face. She hadn't looked like she was lying. So, what? Did it mean our affair—the one thing in my life I had been truly proud of—had been nothing but a figment of my imagination? Did it mean I was so crazy, I didn't even realise I was? What if… everything I saw in front of me wasn't quite the way it really was? What if Paul was just a figment of my imagination too? That would explain her mind-reading, the flying keycard and her super speed, wouldn't it? Or… maybe Paul was just crazy too? After all, I got to know her at a psychiatric centre; a psychiatric centre she claimed was a Curiosity Research Office. To be honest, that did sound absurd, didn't it? I flipped up both palms and looked.

There was no trace of any 'X' on either palm. Nor did my arms look like they had ever been broken.

What if all that I had seen before had never even happened? I was so sure I had seen Arden Villeneuve orgasming so many times before yet, apparently, I never had? *Something was very wrong with me. My memories and reality were not in sync.*

Arden Villeneuve returned in a fluster and told me she had to go. She mumbled something about her manager having messed up the dates of an important interview or something. I didn't care. I was more than delighted to see her go, even though I was polite enough not to let it show.

"It was nice meeting you, anyhow," she said before she left. She was charming and gorgeous, as always, but oddly distant. "Feel free to stay and order whatever you like. Marco will put it on my tab."

I realised she hadn't even touched the food on the sculpture between us. Probably because she wasn't in the least interested in sharing bodily fluids with me. *Unlike what I thought.* "No, thanks. I need to go too," I said and remained seated because I saw the trace of alarm in her eyes right after I said those words. "It was very nice meeting you too though."

She smiled when she saw me not getting up, wished me a nice day then turned and walked away. Out of my life forever, I figured.

I counted to fifty very slowly after she had gone. When

I hit fifty, I took one last glance at the sculpture before me, picked up my belongings and walked away without bothering to taste the rest of those very expensive award-winning sensations.

On the way out, while standing amidst headache-inducing shocks of pop colour, I stopped by Marco to ask if he had received roses from Arden Villeneuve earlier in the year, in May.

He said he had. He found them leaning against the door of his apartment when he got home at night.

I asked him for the date today.

He said it was '23 June'.

When I asked for the year, he told me '2030' and gave me a smile that wasn't exactly as warm or genuine as the ones he had been giving me before.

I walked right out of Madame Pokerface without even pretending to smile in return.

CHAPTER 15
23 JUNE 2033?

Paul ordered room service for dinner that night—dry-aged beef burgers with a side of truffle fries for the both of us because I simply shrugged when she asked me what I wanted. We ate by the tin can table next to Room 103's big industrial window in complete silence. My plate remained untouched even when hers got all cleared out.

"You're missing out," she said when she leaned back into her leather chair to watch me while wiping her mouth on a napkin.

I pushed my plate over to her side with the hand not holding a cigarette, without looking at her. "Have more."

She sighed like an elderly survivor of multiple wars. "How can I help?"

I kept my eyes down and dragged at my cigarette. "Could you tell me what really happened between me and Arden Villeneuve? If you can see her in my thoughts, that would mean our year-long affair really happened, right?"

Paul sighed again. "Unfortunately... wrong. I can't tell the difference between a person's thoughts and a person's memories. I did see her in your mind, yes... in all sorts of compromising positions... but I can't tell if it's something you imagined or if, you know, it all really happened."

Arden Villeneuve looking right into my eyes while half-naked on a massage table... imagined? Arden Villeneuve's toes curling each time I ran my hands along the insides of her thighs... imagined?

But it all looked so real in my head! I sighed. "So you're saying I could be crazy?"

"A lot of people are. Nothing to be ashamed of."

"Why don't I just go see a doctor tomorrow? Maybe what I need is medication. Real medication."

"You can't, Lane. They'll expect some form of ID and you're legally dead, remember?"

"Right. Legally dead. Wow."

"Maybe the best thing to do now is to just... let it go? You haven't imagined anything crazy the whole time I've been out with you so maybe it was just a passing phase? Why don't we go do things again tomorrow? Go back to enjoying ourselves? I found out about a secret apartment at the library you were at. On the fourth floor. We could go check that out? It's funny how I got to know about it. One of the interns found it but didn't dare tell anyone because it was behind a door with a 'no entry' sign and she was afraid they'd punish her for disobeying the rules. I mean how stupid is that? She found a piece of history yet all she cared about was—"

"Paul, stop. I can't enjoy anything if I can't even be sure the things I enjoyed before were real. I need to know what really happened. I can't just let this go. What if Arden Villeneuve was just lying? Maybe she just didn't trust Blaine with the truth? She never wanted anyone to know about us anyway. Maybe she was just..." My heart fell. "Ashamed of what she did with me? Regardless, I need to know for sure. I need to know if... I'm really crazy."

Paul frowned then sighed for the umpteenth time that evening. "Well, I do know of someone who would be able to help, but…"

"But what?"

"She's locked up at Wonderdrug. We'll need to break her out if you want her to read your past."

My heart fell a second time. *Read my past? For real? And what, were we going to jump out of that tenth floor window again? This time with two women in my arms? God.* I thought Paul sounded crazy and yet... she was all I had. I bit my lip and stared right at her. "Why don't you do it? You have amazing powers too, right? You could meet Arden, read her mind, find out what's really going on." I thought it was worth the gamble. *Why not?*

Paul's frown deepened at once. "Meet Arden again? You promised you'd see her only once!"

I reached over and took her by the hands. "Just one last time. Please?"

Paul stared at my hands on hers for a good few seconds then wrenched her hands out of my grasp. "No. It's too risky. Why don't you just take it that she was ashamed of you and we'll just wait and see? I'll watch you. If you develop new hallucinations then we'll find a way to get you to a doctor, how 'bout that?"

I considered it for a second but my heart eventually got the better of me. "No. I need to know what's going on. Now."

"But I don't want to do it!"

"Hey, I helped you get out of Wonderdrug so you owe me."

"Hey! I helped YOU get out of Wonderdrug too so we're even."

"No, I never wanted to get out, remember? I was happy there. I had a good opinion of myself there. And now I've discovered I'm either batshit crazy or a loser my former lover doesn't want to associate with and it's all thanks to you, so you still owe me."

"What's that supposed to mean?"

"It means if you don't come with me to meet Arden Villeneuve, I'm going to confront her outright, tell her who I am and find the truth out for myself."

Paul snorted. "Sure, go ahead. See if she believes you. Make a din and get yourself noticed by CRO. See if I care."

"Fine. It wasn't like I had to deal with any of this shit when I was at Wonderdrug anyway! I don't mind going back!" I kicked back my leather chair, stormed towards the front door and put my hand on the handle.

Paul appeared between me and the front door even before I could begin to push down the handle. She slammed her palm across the door and stared at me with her pupils wide open, her brows furrowed and her breath quick and short. It looked as if she was reading me, trying to see into my soul, trying to see if there was anything I wasn't telling her.

I wasn't not telling her anything. My mind was made up. I simply had to find out what was really going on, no matter what. And I made sure she saw that in my unwavering return stare.

She did, I think. The fierce look she had on her face faltered and she sighed. Again. "Fine," she said in a low voice. "I'll help you. Once. After that, we're never doing anything like it ever again, do you hear?"

I nodded quickly. "Okay."

"If she declines your invitation to meet, which is likely, given her reaction to you earlier, we'll stick with my plan. Wait and see and never contact her again. Are we clear?"

I didn't like her plan but I nodded anyway.

It was, after all, better than doing nothing at all, right?

CHAPTER 16
24 JUNE 2033?

Arden Villeneuve did agree to meet again, to my relief. She didn't sound entirely enthusiastic at first but did say yes once I told her I was leaving the country for good the day after and never coming back. Paul wasn't thrilled—she stormed out of the convenience store we borrowed the phone from—but she did perk up when I told her all about the restaurant Arden Villeneuve wanted to meet us at.

Top's was the sort of restaurant Paul and I would never have been able to get a table at, not even if we had all the cash in the world. You needed a reputation to be able to place a reservation, which was why we got stared at a lot while waiting in line to go in. Everyone—famous YouTubers, CEOs, F1 racers, passersby on the street—seemed to be trying to figure out who we were. They gave us curious smiles with sparkling, friendly eyes, and shamelessly checked us out from head to toe.

Paul and I smiled back like proud members of the nouveau riche, confident in our new clothes and heavy makeup. We strutted to the front like we truly belonged, even when the hostess—a young black lady with a face and body like a movie star's—eyed us with caution.

"Do you have a table, ladies?"

"Yes," I said, fully confident. "Guests of Arden Villeneuve. Blaine Thompson and friend."

The hostess' face changed when she heard the words 'Arden Villeneuve' and the most pretty grin that hadn't been there before appeared on it right away. "Ah, yes. We have you. Miss Thompson and friend, welcome to Top's. Head on into the elevator please, it'll take you right up to Miss Villeneuve." She smiled as if she had known us forever now.

"Thank you," I said.

"Have a lovely evening!"

The four ginormous bouncers with wrestler-sized biceps parted to the side to allow us entry into the plain metal elevator they had been standing in front of. They even smiled at us as we entered and made us both feel very much welcome.

There were no buttons within the elevator but the doors closed the moment we were both in and the elevator started moving up as if it just *knew* where we were supposed to go. Pressure built up in my ears and I just *knew* the world was falling behind even though there was no sound or indicator that confirmed that it was. I looked at Paul as I swallowed hard to rid my ears of the uncomfortable pressure in them and she smiled at me in response. She was enjoying the whole shebang too, I could tell.

We found ourselves face to face with a pleasant-looking male waiter the moment the elevator doors opened. He called me 'Miss Thompson' like the lady below had and instructed us to follow him. It wasn't hard to guess where we were going to go. There was only one set of metallic double doors in the short purple-tinged corridor we crossed as far as I could see. Both metallic doors swung open the moment we got close. The waiter invited us inside—

—and we found ourselves *outside*, on a large platform that protruded out of the building towards a panoramic view of the city at night. It looked as if we were a hundred storeys above ground. There was no railing to save us from rolling over the edge even though huge gusts of wind ran into our hair at great speeds. I was, instinctively, a little nervous about safety but forgot all about it the moment I caught sight of Arden Villeneuve.

Goes without saying, she looked ravishing. She sat right in the middle of the platform, at a round table illuminated in the colour purple, with her hair—purplish in the light—pulled back in a neat twist-wrapped bun and her body covered in a red dinner dress from the chest down. She stood as we approached and gave us one of her charming smiles. "Nice to see you again, Blaine, and nice to meet you...?"

"Paula. My girlfriend," I said on a whim. That familiar scent of champagne, vanilla and roses emanating from Arden Villeneuve's neck made me awfully nervous all over again and since Paul looked great, all dressed up in that brand-new little black dinner dress of hers, I found myself hoping that an intimate association with her might improve Arden Villeneuve's opinion of my social value.

Paul glanced at me with raised eyebrows before turning to Arden Villeneuve and smiling like the hostess below did before. "Hi, very nice to meet you." She extended a hand to Arden Villeneuve like a decent member of society would and I was relieved to see that nothing in her behaviour suggested she ever lived in a mental institution.

My sense of relief turned into alarm when Arden Villeneuve met Paul's eyes with interest and shook her hand for longer than perfect strangers should. Thankfully, the waiter invited us all to sit and their dangerous lingering handshake ended for good.

"May I serve your wine, ma'am?"

"Yes, thank you, Donovan," Arden Villeneuve said.

She seemed a great deal calmer than she had been at Madame Pokerface and no longer stared at me at all. "I got us a 2000 DRC. For us to remember Lane with."

Because I was born in the year 2000. She knew? Donovan the waiter picked up the bottle in the bucket stand by the side of the table and poured white wine into the glasses in front of us.

"To Lane," Arden Villeneuve said when her glass was half-full. She held her glass up and those dazzling sparkles on her fourth finger blinded my eyes all over again.

"To Lane," Paul and I followed. We clinked our glasses and took our first sips, during which I thought I saw Arden Villeneuve peeping at me from behind her glass.

I can't say if it really happened though because she looked away the moment she saw me looking back.

"Thank you," I said when we all set our glasses down. "This means a lot to me." *Way more than you'll ever know.*

"It's only right. Lane did a great deal for me when she was alive."

Really? I looked into Arden Villeneuve's now purple eyes and, for a brief second, felt that familiar, overpowering sense of connection send a jolt of electricity down my spine. Arden Villeneuve removed her eyes the moment that happened so I really can't say if it made her feel the same.

"Lane's massages were simply the best," she added. "She had a gift."

Oh. That sort of gift? Not the other sort? My skin curdled after she said those words so I made the decision to keep my eyes away from hers from that point on.

"Anyway," I heard her say. "What have you girls been doing in New York? Did you collect Lane's remains? I heard they were unclaimed a while back."

I kept my mouth shut because I couldn't think of anything logical to say. Fact was, 'my remains'—whatever the hell those were—were, if they did actually exist, probably still unclaimed, lying in a ditch somewhere, rotting and forgotten, and I was not in the least proud of it.

"Yes, we have," Paul said on my behalf. "But I think tonight should be about happier things. Like your wedding. To that multi-billionaire? Gosh, what does that feel like?"

I heard Arden Villeneuve giggle like a school girl right away. "Oh, it's been wonderful. Like a dream I never expected could come true." She sounded cheery; all that prior solemness in the wake of Lane's death was totally gone.

I couldn't resist the urge to look up to check if she meant what she was saying.

She looked like she did indeed. Her face was all crinkled with smiles. My heart fell and I turned my eyes to my wine right away.

"You look like you're madly in love," Paul said.

"I am. Yes. I just feel so lucky."

"You're not crazy," I heard Paul suddenly say.

I looked up at her in horror but relaxed when I saw she had her mouth over her glass and seemed to be drinking wine.

"You did have a year-long affair with her," Paul's voice continued, in my head, even though her mouth never moved and her eyes never looked my way. "She just doesn't want to admit it because it wasn't love for her. Just... lust, I guess."

I felt my heart plunge. "Lust?" I asked with my mind while pretending to be fully preoccupied with adjusting the napkin on my lap.

"Yes. She's not the type of woman who would ever want to be with a person like you, Lane. Give it up."

Paul put down her glass and smiled at Donovan the waiter who had reappeared by the side of our table with three large plates balanced along his arm. Meanwhile, a part of me just died inside.

"First course: Caviar tartare with filet mignon,"

Donovan said as he set the plates down in front of us. All three plates contained a tiny round mass of compressed black and white dots in the middle. "Very fresh."

I forced myself to smile back at him like a normal, happy person probably would, even though the sight of the dots together made my senses pickle and my stomach heat up with rage.

"This menu's my favourite," Arden Villeneuve told us. "It starts raw—raw fish and raw caviar—then you get a half-cooked pan-seared sea scallop and eventually a completely cooked baked lobster. It's quite the experience, if you like unusual experiences, that is." She grinned and Paul grinned back politely.

I didn't. I kept my eyes on the plate in front of me and put fishy-smelling clumps of dots into my mouth without a word.

The waves soundtrack crashing gently in the background suddenly became especially loud. I glanced at the night sky ahead of us and noticed, at last, the almost invisible plate of glass between us and the deadly hundred-storey drop.

"Is it good?" I heard Arden Villeneuve say. She sounded as if she was looking in my direction.

"Not really," I replied, even though the taste of whatever was in my mouth barely registered in my mind.

"But she will eat it all anyway," Paul added with a huge smile. She looked at me and seemed to be trying to hint me to watch myself with the subtle twitches of her face.

I ignored them both and shoved everything on the plate into my mouth in three quick bites. A sour taste formed in my mouth as I swallowed and never went away, not even when I tried to wash it out with wine.

"Stop it," I heard Paul say in my head. "You can't logically know she lied so you have to act normal. Please."

"What time are you girls leaving tomorrow?" Arden Villeneuve interrupted. She had her eyes firmly on me this time and she looked downright worried.

I couldn't bring myself to meet her gaze, much less answer her. I turned my attention to my glass of wine and poured it all down my throat in one swift move.

"In the afternoon," Paul said quickly. "We're going back to Canada. Where we're from."

"I see. You said over the phone you're never coming back?"

"That's right," I said abruptly and met her staring eyes at last. "You'll never have to see us again."

I saw Arden Villeneuve inhale sharply as she searched my eyes with her large, purple ones. "So this really is goodbye, huh?" She smiled weakly.

I looked away and did not bother with a reply.

I didn't speak again at dinner. Paul filled the awkward silence by chatting aimlessly about the touristy sights of New York and the glamour of Arden Villeneuve's stupid multi-million dollar wedding. I learned Arden Villeneuve's wedding involved elephants, a privately owned mountain and a thousand guests—Lane not included. I found out her new marital home had a white lion enclosure in one of its living rooms and that the bed she shared with her new husband had both massage functions and temperature control. I heard all the details concerning the stone tub full of imported hot spring water from Japan in her new bathroom and the pool that could be converted into an ice-rink at the click of a button.

By the time dessert was done, I was all ready to leave Arden Villeneuve far, far behind. Unfortunately, she insisted on sending us back to our hotel in her diamond-studded limousine and Paul couldn't resist the urge to check the limousine out.

The three of us ended up at the back of the spacious limousine under an artificial night sky made of LED lights, on seats made of calfskin. Paul and I sat next to each other with Arden Villeneuve in the seat right opposite me and I refused to look Arden Villeneuve's way at all. I kept my face at a ninety-degree angle, turned toward the window, the whole way and focused mostly on the club-like music in the background instead of their pointless chatter.

I was done with Arden Villeneuve at that point. I knew I had to be. I knew Paul was right. Arden Villeneuve was definitely not the type of woman who would ever want a woman like me. That made sense. I knew I wouldn't want to be with a woman like me either, if I were her. That was just the way life worked.

The limousine stopped outside the entrance of our hotel eventually, right under the ginormous old-fashioned red lights shouting the hotel's name.

Paul thanked Arden Villeneuve enthusiastically for having paid heftily for dinner but I didn't even bother. When Paul scooted out of the limousine, all smiles, I followed her without even glancing back once.

"Blaine," I heard Arden Villeneuve say, right as her large, soft hand curled around my wrist and pulled me back.

The scent of champagne, vanilla and roses filled my nostrils all over again but I no longer found it pleasant. I sighed and watched Paul disappear through the hotel's glass doors. "What?"

"I am really sorry about your sister."

I turned, with a heart full of hate, and found Arden Villeneuve staring at me with eyes that were uncharacteristically wide. She made no attempt to look away this time; no attempt to change the topic. She simply stared into my eyes, at my lips, at my cheeks, at my ears, as if trying to take in as much of my face as she possibly could. As if... she missed me.

I wriggled my wrist out of her grasp. "Why? Did you have something to do with it?" My voice came out cold.

Her eyes took on a look of shock and she shook her

head right away. "Of course not. Why would you say that?"

"Because I know what went on between the both of you. I know you saw her on the night she fell, I know you dumped her, and I hate that you won't even admit it happened."

Horror crossed her face. "Admit what? I didn't see Lane that night and there was nothing going on between us, I swear. Did she write something in her diary that said otherwise?"

I snorted, shook my head and climbed out of the limousine without another word.

"I'm serious, Blaine, nothing happened between your sister and I!" Arden Villeneuve shouted from behind me.

I went right through the hotel's glass doors without turning back.

CHAPTER 17
25 JUNE 2030?

Paul's side of the bed was empty when I woke in Room 103 the next afternoon. The sight of it made me sit up and wonder, sleepily, if Paul had even been there at all.

Sure, the sheet looked slept in and the quilt looked like it had been pushed aside, but I could have easily done that myself, couldn't I? *I might have slept on two sides of the bed in one night without knowing, right?* I reached over and touched the white sheet on the other side. It was cold. Either Paul had been gone a long time or I had shifted to the side of the bed I was now on very early in the night.

It wouldn't be bad if she did turn out to be a figment of my imagination, I found myself thinking as I yawned and stretched my body across the king-sized bed. My bones creaked as I extended them and afterwards I felt as if my body had entered a deep relaxation. *Being crazy was better than being the sort of person a former lover didn't want to admit knowing, right?* The latter sucked more. Way more. I dragged myself out of bed to get a bottle of water and caught sight of a note on the tin can table, written on The Canned Food Factory Hotel's fancy notepaper.

'Gone to get lunch. Didn't want to wake you cos you were sleeping like a baby. Stay here and don't talk to strangers! I'll be back soon. Love, Paul.'

I picked up the pen lying next to the note and wrote my name under the message.

'Lane Thompson'. My handwriting turned out to be blocky, exactly as I remembered it, nothing like the cursive, artistic-looking writing above it.

I exhaled in disappointment. *Paul was likely another person altogether.* Which meant I was definitely the loser Arden Villeneuve wanted nothing to do with.

Knowing that made me feel very much depressed. Was that how I felt right after Arden Villeneuve dumped me at the cemetery? I wondered.

No. I didn't remember feeling all that depressed on the night of the falling incident. But then again, that didn't mean I hadn't felt depressed, did it?

I left Room 103 to see if the nearest pharmacy had any antidepressants on its shelves. 'Prevention is always better than having to cure,' those antidepressant ads always said. I feared they might be right. Just because I hadn't been trying to kill myself on the night of the falling incident didn't mean I would never try to kill myself ever, right? It was still best to take precautions, wasn't it?

I didn't get far. I had only made it out of the elevator when a familiar figure at the lobby—with shades and a scarf over her blonde hair—made me stop and forget all about what it was I had set out to do.

The woman, tall and slender, in a classic black suit and black heels, had been at the reception counter arguing with the receptionist. She stopped and froze the moment she caught sight of me and her mouth fell open.

"Blaine!" she said and marched over to me while turning back to glare at the receptionist in annoyance. "This is the woman I was talking about! Blaine Thompson.

I told you she lives here!"

The receptionist—some guy I had never seen before—looked terribly apologetic. "Maybe we have her under another name? An alias, maybe?"

I gestured at him to leave the matter alone. Calmly, even though my knees were beginning to shake. Paul would be furious if she knew this was happening, I knew. This was as far from not talking to strangers as I could possibly get. "I did use another name. Don't worry, I'll handle it."

The receptionist nodded at me and grinned sheepishly but didn't stop staring at us—or actually, mainly, at the woman who marched right up to me.

"What name did you use? There's no record of any Paula either."

Of course there wasn't. But I knew it wasn't a good time to get into explanations, not while that receptionist's eagle-like eyes remained on us. "It's complicated," I said quickly. "What are you doing here, anyway?"

"Oh, I... I was hoping to see you before you left. And I'm glad I made it. What time's your flight or ride?"

My flight or ride? Okay... "We... pushed it back. To next week. Decided we wanted to have more time here. There's so much to see and do." I crossed my arms, nodded politely, and refused to smile even though my heart began to pound in that strange way it only ever did in the presence of women I fancied.

"That's wonderful. Do you want to have lunch? Now?"

Lunch? With her? "No." Hours ago, when she was still the woman of my dreams, definitely yes. Now that I knew what sort of person she was? Definitely no. "I have some place I need to be." *Some place far, far away from you.*

"Please, Blaine. I really need to explain some things. About your sister."

My eyebrows shot upwards before I could stop them.

"How about room service? It would definitely be best if we could just go somewhere private. Fast." Her eyes darted sideways as if trying to hint at something.

I followed her line of sight and saw perfect strangers pointing phones and cameras at us, grinning like the receptionist still was. *Shit. Paul would be so pissed if she knew all this was happening.*

"Fine," I said after a sigh. "Come with me."

The space of time between the moment I opened the door to Room 103 and the moment I closed it behind us felt like a whole eternity in itself. Arden Villeneuve, lovely as hell, stepped into my private quarters all alone, bringing that scent of vanilla, roses and champagne with her. *Who would have ever thought a thing like that would ever be happening to someone like me?*

I didn't want her to know I was still in awe of her, of course. Not anymore. I crossed my arms, kept my distance and stared at her as coldly as I possibly could. "So, talk. What about my sister?"

"Could we order lunch first?" she said, looking impeccably neat with her well-pressed clothes and professionally styled hair. The mess of used clothes, towels and unpacked shopping bags all over the hotel room behind her started to look, to me, a lot like pigeon droppings. "I'm starving. Please? Where's Paula, by the way?"

"Out." I gave her a look of obvious annoyance, handed her the room service menu like a waiter would and went to sit on the leather chair by the tin can table, as far from her as I could get.

"I see." Arden Villeneuve plucked off her shades and scarf and studied the menu with her bouncy blonde curls cascading beautifully down the side of her face.

The room became perfectly quiet and I couldn't help but think Arden Villeneuve would never be considering food right now had we been the us I remembered. The second the door shut, I would have tiptoed and put my mouth on hers. We would have been in various extents of undress by now, taking care of a completely different sort of hunger. But, unfortunately, this was the new us now. The us who were strangers, all because she refused to admit the us we were before existed. I did think of putting my arms around her again, in spite of everything, but I made sure those thoughts got forced out of my mind every time they appeared.

When Arden Villeneuve looked up and told me she wanted a Classic Cobb Salad and a bottle of Riesling to share, I went to the rotary dial phone on one of the bedside lockers without saying a word.

I spoke to the room service attendant on the other line in a manner that suggested I was having one of the most boring afternoons ever and kept my back to Arden Villeneuve the whole time. What I didn't let on was that my limbs were tingling with buzzing currents all over again and that my heart was dancing quicker than my lungs could take in air. The recent slap of reality hadn't changed my body's desire for Arden Villeneuve one bit, I realised. It was as if I was biologically predisposed to lose control of all my nerves in her presence; to always want that face, that body close to mine. Arden Villeneuve was like a drug I couldn't get off, an addiction I couldn't shake. Not even when I already knew wanting her was a terrible idea.

I found her seated at the tin can table, opposite the leather chair I had been sitting on earlier, when I hung up the phone and turned back around. Her sunglasses and scarf had been put away and her expensive handbag had been tucked neatly by the side of the leather chair she sat on. She held up her cigarette case and asked me if she could smoke.

I said yes. I picked up my own new cigarette case and went back to the seat opposite her but didn't offer to light her cigarette even though the old me would have most certainly done so. She didn't offer to light my cigarette—like the old her would have done—either. We were both in a completely different world now. A world in which we were polite and distant, where huge plumes of smoke always separated us.

"Will you talk now," I asked. I really would have preferred to go back into the world where we did mostly everything else but talk but I no longer had any idea how to get there. "Lunch is already on its way."

Arden Villeneuve sucked hard at her cigarette and a very solemn expression appeared on her face. "Nothing happened between me and your sister, Blaine. I don't know what she wrote in her diary, but you must know, nothing happened between us at all."

My heart jumped when I heard her words and my ridiculous thoughts jumped out of me along with it. I could see Arden Villeneuve meant every word and it, oddly, made me feel that little bit less depressed again. *After all, being crazy is still better than being the sort of person a former lover doesn't want to admit to knowing, right?* "Prove it," I said. Firmly.

"I can't. I don't know how, but I swear, I'm not lying to you. Why don't you show me what she wrote? There's got to be some other explanation. Just because Lane wrote so doesn't mean it actually happened, right?"

My heart jumped again and this time wouldn't stop jumping. I didn't know what to say. I had no diary to show her. "The diary's not here," was the best I could think of.

Arden Villeneuve's gorgeous eyes turned large again. "Why not? Where else could it be?"

In the land of non-existent make-believe objects, maybe? "I don't know. Maybe her landlord took it?"

"Her land—" she chuckled. Uncomfortably. "Why would Lane's landlord take her diary? Why would *any* landlord take his dead tenant's diary?" She stared at me, her gaze serious and unwavering.

I began to realise inviting Arden Villeneuve up for lunch wasn't the best of ideas at all. "I don't know but I don't have it."

She rolled her eyes. "Stop lying, Blaine."

"I'm not."

"It's all over your face! Just tell me the truth! Why do you keep thinking I had a thing with your sister?"

"Because you did!" *I was there with you, living every moment for an entire year! That is all I remember!* Only I didn't know how to explain it all without sounding perfectly insane!

"I didn't!" Arden Villeneuve insisted.

I struggled to breathe properly. *What, was I really going to have to tell her I was a 'curiosity' who survived a fifty storey fall and then escaped by jumping out of a tenth storey window? Was I really going to tell her Paul was a fellow 'curiosity' who could read minds, move objects with her mind and travel at super speeds?* It sounded perfectly absurd when put within the confines of language.

"Please say something, Blaine."

Goodness. Come on, Lane, think. Think!! I took a deep breath and did my best to breathe normally again. "Tell you what, Arden, I'll tell you where Lane's diary is *if* you tell me how she was behaving the night she fell. And don't tell me you didn't see her because I know all about the cemetery and all the little happy goodbyes you said. I know how many times you orgasmed that night for God's sake!"

Arden Villeneuve stared hard at me and seemed to turn into stone. "I didn't... see her," she said. Weakly. "I swear."

"Alright. In that case, we have nothing else to talk about. Please just leave." I dragged my cigarette hard and turned away from her.

There was a long silence but Arden Villeneuve didn't leave. She simply stayed in the leather chair with her cigarette between her lips and her eyes on the floor. I could hear the tobacco within her cigarette cackling every time she took a puff. From the corner of my eye, I could see her shoulders rising and falling more rapidly than they usually did.

"She behaved normally," Arden Villeneuve suddenly said. Her voice sounded thick, like she was going to cry. "She wasn't suicidal or depressed at all. She seemed perfectly fine when we said goodbye. Better than I was, in fact."

I turned back to her and found her staring into space with bloodshot eyes and a ruddy nose. Her face was blank. She didn't look happy nor did she look sad.

When she turned to me, she simply looked tired. "Will you please just hand me the diary now?"

I took a deep breath then said it. "The diary doesn't exist, Arden. The diary is just something I made up."

"What?"

The doorbell rang in that moment and made us both jump.

"Room service," Arden Villeneuve said. She patted away the tears that had been threatening to come out of her eyes and straightened out her already perfectly straight clothes. "Will you get it, please? I'm not in the mood for… fans."

I nodded and watched her dart into the bathroom as if she had something to hide. It was unusual for room service to arrive that quickly, I knew, but I went to open the door without thinking too much about it all the same.

The door came open and I saw, not room service, but Paul, with one hand full of Chinese takeout and one large bouquet of red roses in the other. She grinned at me, shoved the bouquet of roses into my hands and went right in. "To cheer you up," she said. "And I heard how much you wanted to get the whole eat-more-Chinese-food thing started, so I got you these." She went to place the six boxes of takeout on the tin can table but froze when she caught sight of Arden Villeneuve's bag on the floor next to one of the leather chairs.

I shut the door behind me and turned to Paul. "Paul—"

Before I could even get anywhere, Paul marched to the bathroom door and swung it wide open. The door met the wall behind it with a startling loud bang.

Arden Villeneuve screamed like she had been caught

with her pants down even though she had only been standing in the middle of the bathroom, impeccably dressed. She regarded Paul and me with wary eyes then said, "Hi. Paula."

'Paula' stared at her without blinking for a few seconds, after which her face suddenly morphed into one of fury. "Get out. Now!"

"Okay! Okay…" Arden Villeneuve frowned at me and the roses in my arms as she went towards the door. She looked… scared. "I'll wait outside, okay?"

Paul slammed the door right in her face without giving her a reply. Then, Paul bolted the door's two locks and dashed over to the vintage closets like her life depended on it. "We have to go, Lane!" She dragged our two backpacks out of the closets and began stuffing all our clothes into them the way she had done once before.

"Why?" I managed to say when the meaning of her actions finally registered within my brain.

"Arden texted CRO while you were ordering lunch! They're coming for us right now!"

"CRO? Arden doesn't know about CRO—"

"She thinks they're part of Wonderdrug! She thinks they're doctors and they told her we're mentally insane so no prizes for guessing whose side she's on now!"

"Wait, I didn't see her talking to anybody when I was—"

"CRO's fast as hell, Lane, so I suggest you move!" Paul pushed past me and darted into the bathroom. "Grab that sculpture I bought! The one with the a-ok sign. Smash it over her head! We can't have her following us!"

What? "No, wait! Paul, she admitted to knowing me and she looked… pretty darned upset when she was telling me about it."

"Not now, Lane! Just knock her out!"

"No! I'm not hurting Arden! I love—"

Paul emerged from the bathroom with her hands full of toiletries and hand towels and there was rage all over her face. "Stop it, Lane! That woman'll never love you the way... you want her to." She marched over to the backpacks and stuffed the toiletries into various empty pockets.

"How do you know? I've seen the way she looks at me, or at least, *peeps* at me! I'm pretty sure she doesn't feel nothing towards me!"

"She doesn't love you!"

"But I love *her*! Can't you understand that?"

Paul zipped up the last of the backpacks' pockets and stared at me with the most unusual expression on her face—like she was furious and confused yet amused and not convinced all at once. The expression vanished when Paul took in a deep breath and licked her lips. "Lane, that woman likes money, power, fame, and you're right smack at the bottom of the consumerist food chain. She likes that you know how to push every last one of her buttons but you're not good enough for anything else but sex! Not good enough for her to marry, not good enough for her to associate with! Can't *you* understand that!"

The sound of Paul's voice seemed to morph into claws once it hit my insides. It clawed at my heart so tightly, my heart hurt, and the blood that travelled out of it subsequently began to feel sour. I did understand Paul's words. Oh, all too well, because they were simply, matter-of-factly, true. I knew I had nothing to offer Arden Villeneuve. I had no lion enclosure, I had no ice-rink swimming pool, I didn't even own a beat up car or a cheap home. That was the reason I never dared tell Arden Villeneuve I loved her. I knew she would reject me outright. I was a nobody. I was, frankly, ashamed of myself and everybody, even Paul, knew I should be. I felt a lump appear in my throat and felt it grow with every subsequent breath of mine. I blinked hard to make sure the lump stayed away from my eyes. "Fuck you," I said.

I went right up to Paul and glared with all the fight I had left in me. "You spent your whole life in an institution, behaving like a retard. You've achieved even less than I have which makes you more of a loser than I ever will be! Nobody's ever really loved you, nobody's ever considered spending their life with you, so you don't get to tell me what I can or can not do! What the hell do you know about love or life or anything anyway? You've done shit with yourself so stay the hell out of my affairs!"

Tough-looking Paul stared at my lips and froze. She became completely speechless. Her eyes widened. For a brief second, I thought I saw hurt flicker through her eyes but the hurt quickly vanished and the look in her eyes became colder than ever. She straightened up and looked me right in the eye like an opponent ready to take on the fight. "Are you coming, or not?" she asked. Her voice was low. Dangerous.

I held my ground. "I need to finish my conversation with Arden."

Paul sniggered and took her eyes off me. "Sure. Who am I to say no?" She swung one backpack onto her back, one onto her front, grabbed the six boxes of Chinese takeout she had left on the tin can table and marched to the door.

"Paul, can't you just wait—"

She didn't. The door to Room 103 slammed shut a second later.

Just like that, Paul was gone. All I had left of her was the bouquet of roses she had shoved into my arms and the bags of unpacked shopping she hadn't bothered taking with her. The roses were smaller than the huge ones Arden Villeneuve once bought for me but they were just as red and fresh. Looking at them didn't cheer me up at all though. Not one bit.

Less than ten seconds after Paul left, the doorbell rang again.

I opened it right away, hoping Paul had forgotten

something so we could, perhaps, discuss everything that had come out of our mouths more rationally this time.

But it wasn't Paul I saw. It was Arden Villeneuve.

I let her in of course. Why wouldn't I? I could never say no to Arden Villeneuve. I realised that about myself then.

"Is uh… is everything okay?" She stared at the bouquet I was still clutching in my arms and checked out the room in a way that suggested there might be a great deal of danger right around the corner.

"Yes."

"Where did Paula go?"

I shrugged and kept my eyes down so she wouldn't see the sudden surge of loss I felt. *Where did Paul go?* That I wanted to know too. *What was I going to do out here without Paul? How would I survive?*

"Should we go after her? I could go with you if you want."

I shook my head and put the bouquet down on the tin can table. One thing at a time, I decided. *Right now, there was something else I really needed to do.* I went to the industrial window and dragged the floor-to-ceiling windows on both sides of it together. Room 103 became grey and dull, devoid of colour.

"What are you doing?"

What I had been wanting to do for too long. I peeled off my white singlet and bra and went to kiss Arden Villeneuve on the lips.

I wanted my kiss to be a kiss she would never forget—a kiss she could use to define all other kisses—but Arden Villeneuve stiffened and didn't open her mouth for me. Instead, she kept her eyes wide open and stared at me as if in shock.

"I'm married," she said when I pulled my lips away and opened my eyes again.

I watched her eyes glance subtly at my naked chest and smiled with my intentions all over my face. "Does it matter? Really?"

She swallowed hard, dropped her eyes down to my chest again, then shook her head ever so slightly.

My small smile turned into a full on grin. *I knew it.* I had known it the night of the falling incident, while smoking on my apartment's rooftop. That was exactly why I hadn't been suicidal or depressed at all. I just knew with enough time, with enough persistence, I would reunite with Arden Villeneuve's body again. What I had to offer her body was as addictive as a drug. I was a bad habit she would never be able to fully shake. Not because I was the hottest woman around or the most successful, no, it was simply because I understood who she was. Arden Villeneuve had a weakness for unusual, unexpected experiences. She needed it for her work as an actress, which she thought of as art. She needed unusual experiences to feel like her life had been lived to the max, to feel like she had explored all possibilities. And I *just knew* how to give her what she needed. For example, how commonplace was it for a woman to get sexually propositioned by her dead lover's identical twin?

I reached over, unbuttoned Arden Villeneuve's jacket, peeled off her black inner blouse, pushed my breasts against her stomach and surrounded her nipple with my lips. She didn't protest at all. In fact, her eyes grew shiny and her mouth fell open. I sucked her in rhythm with her beating heart. *Thud, suck. Thud, suck. Thud, suck.* She reached for my shoulders then clutched at my back. Her heart began to beat more furiously under my ear. When she gasped at last, I *just knew* we were the old us all over again. *I did it! I found a way back!*

I pushed her down onto the bed and went in between her endless out-stretched legs. Her black lace panties came off and my lips reunited with her clit. She was already moist down there and only got more moist as I sucked and licked and sucked and licked while she watched me on propped up elbows. She gasped again, grabbed at the bed sheet with tight fists and threw her head backwards. "Fuck, how do you know how to do that…" she whispered.

She didn't care for a reply. Arden Villeneuve rammed her clit towards my mouth and began to moan. I sucked her with increasing speed and added a finger into her vagina. Her moans grew louder and more desperate. I could tell she was having a remarkable time because she was saying… "Yes… Yes! Yes!!! Yes!!!!! Yes!"

Blood rushed to my groin. I felt myself become wet too. When she began screaming in helpless pleasure and trembling violently against my face, I just knew I wanted everything she was having. I could hold back no longer. I wanted to feel her the way she felt me.

I ripped off my pants when she collapsed back down onto the bed, limp and flushed, and climbed up to join her on the bed. I put one leg on the floor, one leg over her and slowly lowered myself.

She eyed me with hunger and closed her eyes the moment our clits touched. Her mouth fell open again and her face contorted into one of pleasure.

This time, I moaned along with her. She was swollen and hard so rubbing against her felt absolutely heavenly. Straightforward pleasure engulfed my private regions. It was delightful enough to get me out of my mind, out of my thoughts, out of my disappointment and misery, rage and bitterness, and that was just all I really needed there and then.

I rubbed harder. Her cries of pleasure filled the room right as a thick wetness gushed against my groin. The pleasure in my groin intensified with every subsequent thrust of my hips and I knew right away I was going to come—

I screamed and dropped my head as an intense orgasm shot across every muscle of my body and made me go weak. I vocalised the sensations that overpowered me and let them take over the muscles on my face. My arms trembled and lost strength. My thighs began to throb. I felt nothing but good and happy; happy with myself and also the world. I moaned with contentment. Warm relaxation surrounded my bones. I heaved a deep sigh and wanted to lie down but—

"Don't stop, Lane!" Arden Villeneuve pleaded. Her eyes met mine, large and shiny. She began to rock her hips up towards me with fervour.

I resumed thrusting my drenched clit against hers and next thing I knew, Arden Villeneuve was screaming like she was dying of pleasure all over again.

And so was I.

We lay side-by-side, face-to-face, in silence, afterwards. Her hand fell on my cheek and her thumb caressed it gently, as if trying to get a feel of my flesh. There was sadness, tenderness and... I think... love in her eyes, to my surprise.

"You love me?" I couldn't help but ask.

She bit her lip, observed every part of my face intently and her face turned crimson. Tears appeared in her eyes and rained down on the bed, culminating in a large damp patch on the bed sheet. Arden Villeneuve began to sob and seemed unable to speak.

"You love me," I realised. It was all over her face. *Paul lied. Or she had been wrong.* Arden Villeneuve did love me. I could see it, right before my eyes.

"I didn't think she would try to kill herself," she whispered, her voice choked. Her hand vibrated violently against my cheek as if she couldn't quite stop it from shaking. "I thought she was cool with just having fun. I never would have... if I knew she would be hurt or... sad or…" She burst into furious sobs and all I could think of to do was get closer. I put my head against hers and hugged her shaking body. Tightly.

"It's okay. It's okay," I whispered, silently delighted

about having her back in my arms again. "You didn't kill me. I didn't even jump. I was pushed. Somebody pushed me, I think."

Arden Villeneuve pulled back and stared at me in shock. She sniffled hard and looked both confused and relieved at once. "How do you know? Did Lane write all that in her diary?"

"There is no diary, Arden. I just know because…" I took a deep breath and braced myself. "I am Lane. And I missed you. A lot."

I expected shock, some terror, and maybe also delight and love, but Arden Villeneuve gave me none of those things. She simply blinked hard and removed her hand from my cheek so quickly, it felt as if she had only suddenly realised her hand had been lying there. When she looked away, it looked as if there was disappointment in her red, swollen eyes.

Her reaction made me very uncomfortable. *Was it normal to react that way when faced with a revelation like that? Wasn't it more normal to be horrified? Or... relieved?*

Arden Villeneuve clearly wasn't afraid. Or even surprised. Not in the least. She just looked simply… awkward and… crestfallen.

Why?

The doorbell suddenly rang again and made us both jump up. We both turned to the door.

"Must really be room service this time," Arden Villeneuve whispered with a sad, sad polite smile. She wiped her tears off her face and stood up to pull down her shirt, jacket and skirt very quickly.

I didn't understand her smile at all. It wasn't the sort of smile she normally gave me after sex. It was the sort of smile she'd usually save for strangers she barely knew.

The doorbell rang again.

"Could you get it? I'll wait in the bathroom."

Before I could reply, Arden Villeneuve was already halfway there. I went in search of my own clothes; not an easy task with the curtains closed—everything looked the same shade of grey. I found my bra and top next to the tin can table and my jeans and panties on the floor by the bed. The doorbell rang for a third time.

"Just a second," I shouted and struggled to put on everything as quickly as I could. It was difficult because my legs were still weak from the orgasms I just had and my head was a little dizzy.

The doorbell rang again. And again. And again. Three times consecutively.

Fucking bad service, I thought as I shoved my final piece of clothing—a crumpled white singlet top—over my head. "I said just a second!"

"Room service!" the person on the outside hollered.

"Will you just—" I stopped in that instant because something caught my attention.

That voice outside? *It was one I knew.*
But where from?

"Room service, ma'am," the voice said again.

"Blaine, get the door," Arden Villeneuve shouted from the bathroom.

"Room service!" the voice shouted from the outside.

That was when it hit me. The voice outside became as familiar as my dead relatives' faces and just as terrifying once I remembered where I knew it from. Blood from my head rushed to my feet. I was left cold and outright giddy with fear.

That person on the outside? *He* was not room service, that I knew for sure.

CHAPTER 18
25 JUNE 2033?

Into the closet? Under the bed? In the bathroom? There weren't that many hiding options in Room 103. I took a deep breath and dashed towards the place I figured was best, right before the bathroom door opened and Arden Villeneuve emerged. "Blaine?"

Blaine? Didn't she believe me? I held my breath and kept as still as I could, thankful I already had my clothes on. I couldn't see the rest of the room from where I was but decided it might be better that way.

The doorbell rang again. Footsteps moved away from me and I heard the door to Room 103 open.

Please let it be room service, I prayed with my eyes tightly shut. *Please let me be wrong. Please let it be overpriced salad and wine. Please.*

"I don't know where she went," I heard Arden Villeneuve say.

"What do you mean?" *that* voice replied. Footsteps, many more footsteps, entered the room. "I just heard her voice in here."

Fuck. Shit. Could it really be? The footsteps got closer. I bit my lip and tried to breathe without moving my body—an impossible feat, I realised. The body is not something you can control, not when your heart is pounding in overdrive.

Creaks sounded as wooden doors and drawers got thrown open. A thud on the carpet. Multiple individuals looking into closets and under the bed?

"She was right here. She said she would open the door."

"What about the other one?"

"She left with bags. I could only stay with one of them."

Somebody shoved the shower curtain aside violently. Another slammed the bathroom door against the wall. My muscles began to quiver. I could see them vibrate.

"The toilet is clear," an unfamiliar gruff male voice said.

Silence. So quiet, I could almost hear people breathing near me. I was doing my best to breathe without making a sound when, all of a sudden, a familiar scent entered my nostrils.

The scent of headache-inducing cologne. It was so close, so thick in the air. *What was it? Cedar and mint? Leather?* I pursed both lips and backed up as far as I could go.

Somebody dragged the floor-to-ceiling felt curtains open and let sunlight back into Room 103. That was when I saw *him*—his hair neatly-gelled, his face, freshly-scrubbed as always. He was in a business suit this time; no longer in a white coat. Three other men in similar business suits stood behind him but *he* was the one with the hand on the curtain and face pressed against the floor-to-ceiling industrial window right in front of me.

I sucked in my stomach, extended my neck and tried to make my body way thinner than it really was, even though it was close to impossible. My breath sounded deafening to me. I prayed it was not as loud for them as it was for me.

Dr Clark slammed a palm against the glass of the industrial window and banged hard a few times as if trying to make sure the industrial window couldn't be opened. *It couldn't. I already tried.* There was a new expression on his face—one I had never seen before. *Displeasure.* Calm and always patient Dr Clark was actually displeased, right in front of my eyes.

I squeezed my eyes shut. There was nowhere else for me to go, nowhere else to hide. *CRO is fast as hell, Paul had said. Paul had been right. She was probably right about everything else too.* Doctor Clark didn't look like a doctor anymore. He looked like an agent on a hunt. I began to wish Paul were here. *Paul would know what to do. Paul always had a plan. I really should have just listened to her!*

"How the hell does a person just vanish into thin air?" Dr Clark asked.

"You tell me," Arden Villeneuve replied. She sounded more frustrated than he did. "Are you sure that's Blaine Thompson? Because she moves, walks and talks exactly like Lane Thompson. And I mean *exactly*."

Because I am Lane, Arden!

"Like I said, Miss Villeneuve, Blaine has internalised her sister thoroughly. What the mind believes, the body enacts. If you think you're hungry, you will feel hungry. If you truly believe you're somebody else, you will be somebody else."

Arden Villeneuve didn't say anything in response to that.

"That aside," Dr Clark continued. "Did you manage to get the diary?"

"No. She wouldn't tell me where it was."

"Did you even try?"

"Yes! Look, Mr…"

"Doctor. Dr Clark."

"…Clark. I'm very tired. I spent all morning trying to find your girls and as far as I'm concerned, one of them was right here waiting for you. My part is done. I want to see you delete the footage now."

A pause. I suspected they were sizing each other up.

"I can't. We haven't found our patients—"

"That's not my problem! I've done what I can, what more do you want? Are you blackmailing me or something?"

"Of course not. But neither can we delete anything before we find our patients. I've already explained—"

"Oh for God's sake! Fuck you! You don't get to steal data from my computer, knock on my door in the middle of the night and tell me what to do! Get out!"

"Miss Villeneuve, please—"

"I said Get Out!"

I had never heard Arden Villeneuve that angry in real life before. It sounded more like a movie from where I was standing. Very unreal.

"Alright, please stay calm. We will go." Footsteps moved towards the door. "But, if you do see Blaine or Paul Rafferty again, please just call us, okay? They're dangerous and need to be put away. Do you understand that? *Do not* try to hide them. You'll only be putting yourself in danger."

"I did *not* hide them!"

"Okay. Okay. I got it." Dr Clark's voice sounded much further away now. "You have my number and... also, just so you know, I really enjoyed your last movie."

I heard the door to Room 103 slam shut right afterwards.

Silence after that. Nothing moved. Nobody made a sound.

Then, out of nowhere, a loud crash. Glass breaking and a heavy thud. I opened my eyes.

Heavy grey felt was all I saw. I edged forward and peeped past the felt, out at the rest of the room.

The glass plate atop the tin can table that had been in front of the floor-to-ceiling industrial window was gone. Only the table's stem of tin cans, piled one on top of the other, remained on the floor, on its side. Around it were pieces of shattered glass, Paul's bouquet of roses, and a lamp that used to sit on the wooden locker next to the bed. At the other end of the room, by the bed, Arden Villeneuve stood with both hands in her hair. She kicked the mattress and swore.

A mix of emotions swirled in my stomach; fear was not quite it anymore. Fear was there of course—how could it not be there—but there was some other, more powerful emotion riding on it. A very energetic emotion. I clenched my teeth and realised what it was.

Confusion.

I stepped out from behind the floor-to-ceiling curtains, also thankful that all those years of shitty laborious jobs had left me so thin. Had Dr Clark been more persistent, had he pushed the curtains aside that little bit more, I would have been spotted. Easily.

Arden Villeneuve sensed my presence and turned right away. Her hand flew to her mouth. She stared at me like I were a ghost.

"Blaine," she said.

There. I saw her say it. Blaine with pursed lips to make the 'B' sound. "I'm not Blaine, Arden," I said. "There is no Blaine. I made that up."

"Okay, sure. Regardless, you need your meds, okay?" Arden Villeneuve dropped her eyes down to the leather chair next to me, where her very expensive top-of-the-line handbag lay next to the chair's leg. "Let me call your doctor for you."

"You don't believe me?"

"No, I do. I really do. Just let me get my bag…" She edged forward.

I put myself between the bag and her. "I mean it, Arden. I *am* Lane. I didn't die. Don't you recognise me?"

"Yes. I do. You *are* Lane and the year *is* 2033. Okay?"
What?

"Lane, your doctor cares about you, very much so, so

let's call him to take a look, how about that?"

I didn't know. Was that okay? Was that not okay? In my experience, Wonderdrug hadn't been all that bad, but Paul seemed to think it was hell. What she definitely had been right about was how difficult it was to get out once you were in and I couldn't be sure I wanted to leave everything I now had access to just yet.

Arden Villeneuve jumped forward and grabbed her bag before I could make a decision. She fished out her phone and tried to dial so I lunged forward to take it out of her hand.

"Blaine, no!" She dodged and held it up to the ceiling to keep it out of my reach since she was almost a full head taller.

"You called me Lane during sex!"

"I did, yes, but... I didn't actually mean it!"

What?! She tried to move away from me so I jumped and knocked the phone out of her hand like a basketball player would do. It fell onto the floor. She crouched to pick it up so I kicked it away and grabbed her by the arms.

"You told him I moved exactly like Lane! What if I really *am* Lane? Let's talk about this!"

Arden Villeneuve didn't reply but spent all of her energy struggling to get out of my grasp. Because she was taller, and thus larger overall, I had to use all of my core's strength just to keep her from moving closer to the phone.

"Look, I can tell you everything you did with Lane! How you kissed, how you touched, everything you said! Just stop and listen to me!"

"You read it in her diary!" Arden Villeneuve yelled. She squirmed harder and turned all red in the face.

"There is no diary!"

"Yes there is! Lane left it for you before she jumped so you could experience life on the outside! You read it so many times you began to think you were her! But you're not, Blaine! Lane's dead and gone and you are certainly not her!"

What? Wasn't the diary and Blaine both things I made up in the spur of the moment? Me, Lane?

Arden Villeneuve shoved me hard onto the ground and made an abrupt run for her phone. She picked it up before I could get up and put it to her mouth.

"Wait! How do you know Lane's really dead? You didn't see her body, right? I could still be her, couldn't I?"

Arden Villeneuve's face crinkled and tears sprung out of her eyes again. "People don't survive falling from buildings nor do they come back from the dead, Blaine. Plus there is another reason I know you are definitely not her." She took a deep breath and looked me right in the eyes, solemn this time.

My skin grew cold. "What's that?"

"You said you missed me. Lane would never do that. That's why I enjoyed her fucking company so much!"

What the—?

Arden Villeneuve lifted her phone to her mouth and said, "Call Wonderdrug Doctor."

"Calling Wonderdrug Doctor," her phone said in response.

Fuck. Paul was right again. You can't trust anyone indeed.

The line connected right away. "Is she still there?" Dr Clark said on the other side of the line.

"Yes. Hurry!"

Arden Villeneuve ran to block the door with her body and gave me a look that said she wouldn't be moving away from it, no matter what.

There was no chance to think properly. Either Arden Villeneuve was right or Paul was. I was either mentally unstable Blaine or Lane the curiosity. *Who did I want to be more?* The choice was a no-brainer.

I went to the pile of unpacked shopping bags in the corner and dug out the brass sculpture Paul had suggested before she left. A male hand in an a-ok gesture—way heavier than I thought it would be. It had the weight of a full sack of potatoes in one handy hand-sized structure and was heavy enough to make my muscles ache. I clutched the sculpture's wrist with all my strength to keep it from slipping down onto the floor and marched towards Arden Villeneuve.

Her eyes became big with terror when she saw me with it. "Blaine, don't!" She pressed herself against the door as if that would get her any further away from me.

"Will you let me go? Before Dr Clark comes back?"

She gulped. "I can't. I'm sorry. They have my footage. Please understand."

"What footage?"

"From my cemetery. Me and Lane. They said they'll make it public if I didn't help them get you."

"So what? Let the public see it. You've done nude scenes and sex scenes before. What's the big deal? Let me go."

"No! I can't! It'll ruin my marriage. And my reputation. Nobody else must ever know."

Oh? Her words went right into the depths of my heart like a thick dagger with perforated edges. I narrowed my eyes and stared right into hers. "So... you're just going to spend the rest of your life denying you ever knew Lane Thompson?"

Arden Villeneuve swallowed hard and looked away. She didn't answer.

I smiled when I realised Paul had been right yet again. Arden Villeneuve didn't love me. Not as a whole person. That was the truth. I wasn't good enough for anything other than exciting, unexpected physical pleasure indeed.

"Please don't do anything you'll regret, Blaine," Arden Villeneuve whispered.

"You're right," I said and smashed the sculpture against her head with all my might. "That's precisely why I need to do this."

Arden Villeneuve lost her hold of her phone and sank to the ground like a puppet that had lost its strings. A large red bump appeared where the sculpture met her skin. I shoved her motionless body out of the way, whispered an apology I knew she couldn't hear and ran out of Room 103 like a sprinter determined to break a world record.

As I ran, I realised Dr Clark and Aunt Mary had both seen this coming. I *was* dangerous, just like they said. Arden Villeneuve would have been fine and dandy had I been put away and locked up like they said I needed to be.

Perhaps they really did know me better than I knew myself after all.

CHAPTER 19
25 JUNE 2030?

I went out the nondescript door at the back of The Canned Food Factory Hotel—past the hotel's industrial kitchen, out into the back alley—because I knew that was what Paul would have chosen to do. When I left Room 103, I made up my mind to make only choices Paul would make because with Paul, I had always been safe. No CRO agent or doctor ever got close to us when we did things her way. Paul knew how to stay safe so everything Paul ever said was now word.

Don't talk to strangers. Keep a low profile. Find your way back to the nuclear bunker if we ever lose each other.

Got it, Paul.

I darted from one dumpster to another, using the bulk for cover. I made sure I checked around corners before proceeding ahead and kept my eyes peeled for men in business suits.

There were no men in business suits as far as I could see. I saw only shoppers, tourists, beggars and locals holding over-priced drinks on the streets. I noticed everybody else was out in the open whereas I was the only person in the back alley amongst cats.

The cats glared at me and turned their heads away snobbishly each time I glared back at them. I got the feeling the cats hated my presence and I found myself hating theirs too. I narrowed my eyes and snarled at them with teeth bared as I forced myself to think. *How did we end up at The Canned Food Factory Hotel? Which manhole did we come up from?*

I recalled Paul and I, quiet as thieves in the dark of night, running through a similar-looking alleyway as air-conditioning boxes on the sides of buildings poured heat down upon us. Above us, the starless sky had been shaped like an 'L'.

I looked up and squinted against the glare of the midday sun. The patch of sky above me was shaped like a '7'. *'7' was 'L' upside down, wasn't it? The manhole was likely right up ahead!*

I kept going until I spotted a familiar-looking manhole at one end. A manhole with the words 'MADE IN CHINA' inscribed on its cover.

Yes. That was the manhole we came out of alright. That was what my gut told me.

"Lane!"

A female voice. Unfamiliar. She called me Lane, not Blaine. Did that mean I was Lane for sure? Or had I heard her wrong? I turned like a deer in headlights and saw—

—a silhouette standing at the other end of the alleyway, the end which led out to the street. The blinding sunlight behind her meant I couldn't see her face or the colour of her skin or hair. What I could see was how slender her frame was and how tall she seemed. She seemed to be in boots with a hooded jacket pulled up over her head. Her hands looked thick and unnaturally shaped, like she was wearing leather gloves.

Why would a person wear leather gloves in the middle of summer? Was her hair blonde? Did she have red lips? Was she the person who pushed me? Or was she just another CRO agent or... the police?

The silhouette moved towards me with hasty steps.

Instinct told me not to wait to find out who she was. The silhouette was not Paul, that was all I needed to know. Anybody else could mean danger or entrapment. *I was better off alone.* That, I had learned in my early twenties. *Always better to be alone than with someone who might hurt you.* I scanned the area quickly for a way to open the manhole's iron cover.

"Listen, you're in danger," the silhouette said from the distance. She spoke as if trying to calm me down, with both hands slightly raised, the way hostage negotiators in movies often had theirs raised. "You need to come with me. She'll lead you to them again if you stay out here."

I didn't get what the silhouette meant. *Who was 'she'? Who was 'them'? What danger?* So many questions, so little time. *Think, Lane, think. What would Paul do?*

She would look for the crowbars she hid behind the huge silver ventilation pipe. The one which snaked all the way up to the sky. *There!*

Genius, Paul, I thought when I dug behind the silver ventilation pipe and found a solid metal bar within my grip. *God, how I missed her.*

"We need to go now," the silhouette said, just a few feet from me now. "The Office will be here any minute."

The Office? As in the Curiosity Research Office? Unfortunately, I was in no mood for conversation at that point. I shoved the crowbar into the side of the manhole cover and pried it open. It was not as easy as I thought it would be. The darned cover was insanely heavy; I had to kick with every last push of energy I could muster to make the cover crash to the side with an explosive clang. *Manhole open!*

The silhouette jumped into a run. I tried to get myself down the hole but she was pretty fast; not as fast as Paul but not a lousy runner either. Before I could get away, she was already right behind me, larger than life. "Lane, stop," she said. I spotted her tongue sticking out as she made the 'L' sound. She pulled me up from the manhole in one big huff—a rather incredible feat for a woman as slim as she was—and swivelled me around so that I faced her.

Once face to face with her, my knees went weak and my heart nearly stopped from shock. I couldn't understand what I was looking at.

The silhouette—definitely a woman—had skin that was not white or black or brown but... a pale greyish, greenish blue. Her lips were a dark shade of grey and her features looked both Asian and Western all at the same time. Now that she was close, I could see she had dark brown hair and eyes, but even so, she didn't look entirely like a normal human being because of the colour of her skin.

Instinct kicked in again. I grabbed the crowbar from the ground and tried to smash her on the head with it but she stuck an arm out and held the heavy bar up before it even had any chance to get anywhere near her. "I'm not the enemy—"

"Hey!"

We both turned and saw a man in a business suit running towards us. He had a gun! *One of those men in Room 103!*

He fired and got me right in the arm. The impact pushed me backwards and made me yelp. My arm began to burn like it was on fire and I saw blood coming out of the new hole in my jacket. *Fuck!* The odd-coloured woman ripped out a gun from under her jacket and fired back.

She got the man right in the middle of the forehead with just one shot. He tumbled to the ground but seven more men in business suits appeared right behind him in that moment and started shooting at her and me.

Fuck! Fuck! Fuck! Why didn't any of those people think murder or wounding other people was bad? Another bullet hit me in the same arm and that burning sensation I had been feeling intensified. Adrenaline propelled through my muscles and I just knew I had to get away. From *all of them!*

Fast! I flung myself into the manhole and grabbed the sides of its slimy moss-covered ladder just in the nick of time. I slid down like a fireman would.

"Lane, wait!" the odd-coloured woman shouted. Shooting continued from above.

You can't trust anyone, Paul said. *Right, Paul. Right again.* I landed knee deep in stinky sludge and dashed right into the protective blanket of darkness.

Once my eyes adjusted to the lack of light, I realised the sewers weren't as dark as I remembered them to be. The hour of day had something to do with it. Long beams of cold, white sunlight streamed down from above through grills, showcasing the slime on the walls in gory detail. It was still spooky of course but somehow now felt safer than the world above where guns and other people ran rampant.

I looked out for the specific pieces of graffiti Paul once pointed out. 'Opportunities are everywhere' was one of them. I chose the tunnel on the left when I saw it and prayed it would lead me to 'Not your damn robot!', 'Guys Like Us Got Nothing To Look Forward To' and 'ExiSTencE iS fLAWed' eventually.

Good thing Paul made me focus then. The underground was like a maze, I realised, with a zillion possible turns. I could tell it would be hard for the odd-coloured woman or any of those suited men, if still alive, to figure out which turns I had taken. One wrong turn and they would be somewhere else, far, far away. All the same, I moved as quietly as I could. Better to be safe, Paul would say.

I waded like an alligator would towards its prey, with my hand over the two burning, damp holes in my jacket. The liquid around my calves smelled like a mix of shit and detergent but I didn't mind the stench this time. It no longer bothered me.

Overhead, the city rumbled on, unconcerned. I thought it sounded like a whole different universe now. A universe I no longer belonged to.

A man in a ratty singlet, with a beard that went all the way down to his chest, shoved a kitchen knife in front of my face the moment I popped my head through Paul's fallout bunker's open circular door.

"Get the fuck away from me!" he shouted as if I were the one brandishing a knife at his face. His teeth were mostly black and there was a prominent patch of dirt in the middle of his sweat-covered forehead.

I put both hands up at once, partly to show how harmless I was and partly to shield myself in case he tried anything violent. "I'm just looking for a friend," I said. "She told me to meet her here. I'm not looking for trouble."

The man noticed the holes and blood on my sleeve and gave me a look that was both suspicious and disgusted, as if I were the one with black teeth and a body that hadn't been washed in weeks. "Nobody's meeting nobody here!" he shouted. "This is my place now. Step in and I will kill you!"

I nodded and backed away quickly. After what I had seen on the way over, I didn't doubt the authenticity of his words one bit. "Could you at least tell me if she came by?"

"Yes. She didn't!"

With great effort, and with a riot of creaks and whines coming from the door, the bearded man shut the circular door in my face. The sewers became ten times darker after that.

I put my arms down and sighed. *Now what? Where would Paul go if not here? Canada? Some place enjoyable? Some place nobody else knew about?*

I got the feeling Paul did once talk about a place nobody else knew about but, for the life of me, couldn't remember where that place was or when she talked about it.

Fuck, fuck, fuck, I thought, when my arm began to feel thoroughly numb. *I really should have paid more attention to Paul before. And maybe I should also have taken that fortune cookie's message more seriously.* Had I been serious about eating more Chinese food, had I followed those boxes of takeout when they left with Paul, had I refused to meet Arden Villeneuve at any of those non-Chinese eating places, I never would have ended up as depressed and injured and confused as I was now, right? I would have been healthy. That fortune cookie had been stating the truth, I decided.

Question was, had Arden Villeneuve?

CHAPTER 20
DATE UNKNOWN

The answer came to me in a dream many hours later. I dreamt of Paul and I back in Room 103, seated at the tin can table—whole again, with its plate of glass intact—by the floor-to-ceiling industrial window. We each had a plate of burger and fries in front of us. I was smoking and she was leaning over and saying...

"I found out about a secret apartment at the library you were at. On the fourth floor. Behind a door with a 'no entry' sign. A piece of history yet all she cared about was."

In my dream, I told her I wasn't interested. Not in that. I was more interested in knowing the truth about my uncle's and parents' deaths.

"Oh, that's easy," she said. She waved her hand like a magician trying to entertain children and Room 103 morphed into Uncle Tim and Aunt Mary's kitchen the instant her arm came down. Paul evaporated and vanished from sight.

I felt dread at once. Not surprising because I always felt dread in that house, even before there had been a dead body on the kitchen floor, but in my dream, my sense of dread was more intense. Likely because there *was* a dead body on the kitchen floor.

It was Uncle Tim or at least it used to be. He had become a dead burly redneck soaking in a pool of his own blood and looked a little like a piece of rotten meat swimming in gravy. His face, with a huge bloody gash on his forehead, was contorted in horror. Aunt Mary was right behind him, staring down and screaming as if she had encountered a very large and menacing rat. Her lung capacity was unreal; she never once paused to take a breath. She eventually turned to me while still screaming and pointed a fat, dirty index finger right at me. Rage and hate were rich in her eyes. She began to look as if she were trying to kill me with her high-pitched scream.

I turned and ran out the kitchen as fast as my legs could go but stopped running when I noticed the living room around me.

It wasn't Aunt Mary's living room I was in. It was my parents'. And there they were on the couch, dead and stiff, with their mouths wide open. The small flat screen TV in front of them was on. The enthusiastic morning news presenter on it wouldn't stop smiling and talking about nothing important at all.

"Paul!" I found myself shouting, almost as loudly as Aunt Mary had been screaming. "Paul!!! Help me!!!!!"

Paul materialised in front of me with a bucket-sized box of Chinese takeout in her hands. It looked very heavy but she smiled as she effortlessly threw its contents—brown, mucky shit water—right at my face.

I woke up with shit water really on my face, with shit water up to my armpits. I found myself being pushed around by the force of shit water rushing past my body and could feel myself rubbing slime off the sewer walls with my back.

What the fuck? I didn't remember setting myself down in

the middle of shit water. I remembered having picked the highest and driest platform to sit down on. It had been safe before. So safe I even found myself drifting into sleep; the safest place to sleep in the sewers, I thought.

Clearly, more often than not, I thought wrong.

Many more hours later, I climbed out of the very same manhole I jumped into hours earlier. It wasn't ideal—I knew there was the risk of aggressive, gun-toting individuals jumping me the moment I emerged—but I didn't have a choice. I didn't know any other way out of the sewers and I could feel myself dying of hunger and thirst. Thankfully, the manhole remained uncovered and there seemed to be nobody around when I emerged.

A very good thing because I was almost as blind as a mole after all those hours in darkness. My eyes took longer than usual to adjust so my face stayed scrunched in a perpetual squint as I stumbled through the now familiar alleyway while holding on to the sides of buildings for support.

When I finally could see properly again, I noticed no sign of a crime scene. *Where had all the shot bodies gone? The man with the bullet hole in his forehead? He looked very much dead the last time I saw him. Where did he go?*

I couldn't think of a single answer and honestly didn't care enough at that point. I was too desperately hungry and thirsty. I knew I had to find a way to get food and water into my body so I searched a dumpster.

A box of discarded cupcakes, some cans of unopened Coke, a few boxes of Chinese takeout with scraps at the bottom and a recently expired box of cereal saved me.

They all tasted way better than Madame Pokerface's exorbitantly priced Fantastic Day tea set ever did, in my opinion.

I made it through the doors of The Brooklyn Public Library just ten minutes before it closed for the day. The first thing that got my attention, as I walked into the refreshing, air-conditioned compound, was the way everyone walking out looked at me. They all brought their hands over their noses and turned their faces into scowls. They eyed me from head to toe and edged as far away from me as they could possibly get.

For the first time since getting out of the sewers, I noticed the stench coming from my body. I realised I smelled like excrement gone sour and soon noticed I looked quite like it as well. My previously white singlet was now coloured with a mix of brown and yellowish stains. My jacket had holes and my jeans were clearly damp and muddy. My skin, where exposed, was also crusted with mud, or should I say, what I think was probably mud.

Unfortunately, there was nothing else I could do but keep my head high. I ignored the eyes on me, climbed the stairs to the fourth floor—the non-fiction section—and went in search of a door with a 'no entry' sign on its front.

"Excuse me," a male voice said the moment I stepped onto the landing of the fourth floor. "You can't be here."

I turned and saw a big-sized, youngish-looking security guard—possibly just out of college—looking right at me. He had both his hands on his hips, a mammoth of a belly and a stern face with patchy-red cheeks over the dollop of fat where his neck should have been. There were many objects on the belt around his hips but the one he seemed to be thrusting forward most—possibly on purpose, for me to see—was the holster which held a revolver.

Great. Not again. I smiled at him with the calm of a seasoned criminal. "Can't I?" I asked, in the most docile manner I could muster. "Isn't the library... public? Free for all?"

"Well, it is," he said, somewhat breathlessly, as if he had some chronic issues with his lungs—asthma or something. "But you're not... dressed appropriately."

"Oh! Okay. I see. I guess I'll just have to get a move on then." I pointed my thumb back towards the stairs but darted forward at top speed instead.

"Hey! Stop!"

Goes without saying, I didn't. The bookshelves on the fourth floor were scattered in a non-linear, over-lapping, maze-like fashion—for reasons likely more aesthetic than functional—so I figured I could zigzag across the entire floor without being seen or caught. Most of the time, at least. I jumped behind the first row of bookshelves I came upon and scanned my surroundings for doors with 'no entry' signs on them.

There were no such doors. Only doors for staff, gents, ladies, storage. The usual stuff. No 'no entry' on any of them.

"Ma'am, you need to leave," the guard shouted. I could hear him breaking into a jog and panting in the quiet of the library. All the other patrons were already either at the check out counters on the first floor or out the doors so it was really just me and him up on the fourth.

I shot around the maze of bookshelves as quickly as my tired legs could move and looked around like a soldier on the offence.

There! Nondescript white door with a 'No Entry' sign. Three o'clock. Only fifty feet away.

"We're closed, ma'am! Everyone needs to leave!" the guard shouted again. I could hear him panting as if he had been running for his life for hours. Clearly, he wasn't physically fit enough for the job and it occurred to me then that he might have been hired simply because he looked menacing and not because he could harm anyone or guard anything.

I realised I could dodge him much faster than he could get to me and be much quieter while at it too. All without that much effort on my part. I thought it ridiculous that I was actually able to do so so easily.

"Why don't you just come back tomorrow morning?"

he yelled eventually. He stopped between some bookshelves and began heaving really dramatically as he looked all around. "On somebody else's shift, for God's sake." he added, in a much lower voice.

He hadn't realised I was right behind him, simply waiting for the perfect chance to dart over to the nondescript white door on his right.

The moment he turned and walked down the aisle on the left, I made a dash for the door, thankful for the soft carpet that cushioned away the sound of my feet.

The silver ball of a handle on the door wasn't locked and turned easily, to my relief.

I slipped in and shut the nondescript white door behind me so quietly, I didn't even hear a peep myself.

I found no secret apartment behind the door, only a rust-covered black spiral staircase nestled tightly within four severely-peeling cream walls. Just the sort of staircase a person would climb if they wanted a look into the world of the dead and sinister.

I gulped but put my feet on the staircase's rusty rungs anyway. I knew I needed to find Paul—that was most important. There were people more terrifying than the supernatural out there in the world. Only with Paul would I ever be safe. *Only with Paul had I ever been safe.*

The rusty staircase groaned and made a ton of noise each time I put my weight down, as if reminding me I was most definitely uninvited, but I persisted in making my way up.

I really, really needed to find Paul. Really, really needed to.

"Paul?" I whispered when I got to the very top and saw a secret apartment around me at last. "Are you here?"

Nobody replied. The secret apartment was smaller than I imagined it would be and looked way more haunted than I ever imagined possible. There was no furniture anywhere; the wooden floorboards under my shoes looked like they were rotting and every last one of its windows had been boarded up. The apartment's wallpaper—once colourful, I think—was now brownish with water stains in some parts and bloated like water-filled seaweed in others. The ceiling was peeling like the walls around the staircase had been, except it was also falling all over the floor like giant pieces of dandruff. Fixtures of a kitchenette remained—an island counter, built-in cabinets and a kitchen sink—but all were too cracked, too rusted, and too dirt-covered to ever be used again. There were two closed doors at the far end of the secret apartment. The sort of doors that likely had demons hidden behind them.

I didn't dare go any further. "Paul?" I whispered. "It's me, Lane."

I got no answer but below me, something swung open.

"Ma'am, you can't be in here! This is private property! I'm going to have to call the police if you won't leave!"

Fuck, how did he know? Saw me in security cameras or something? I looked around for a place to hide and quickly realised there was none. The secret apartment was too bare; I would be seen no matter where I ducked. The demon-hiding doors at the far end were my only hope.

The staircase below groaned again, way louder than it did when I was on it.

I jumped on my toes and ran towards the demon-hiding doors as quickly as I could.

The door on the right opened into a small bathroom with stained tiles, mouldy dated toilet fixtures and a really foul smell. I could see no place to hide in there so I quickly went for the door on the left. I swung it open, stepped right in and I saw—

—Paul, seated on a picnic mat in the middle of a bare space that might have once been a bedroom. The window behind her was wide open—wooden boards similar to the ones over the windows outside lay carelessly tossed on the floor some distance away—so there was air, light and sounds of life from the outside in the room. She had the two backpacks I recognised, empty Chinese takeout boxes, snacks, mineral water bottles, cigarette butts, cigarettes and papers all around her, and a pen in her hand. She stared at me, then behind me and began looking quite horrified.

Two heavy thuds landed outside, on the wooden floorboards I had been standing on just seconds earlier. I turned towards the sound and felt the floorboards under my shoes vibrate as well.

"The hell? Ma'am? Where are you?"

I turned back to Paul and was surprised to see her and everything that had been on the floor around her just seconds ago gone. Instead, she was right behind me with her back flat against the wall separating the empty room from the rest of the secret apartment, with the two familiar backpacks hanging on her shoulders. She glared at me and looked incredibly pissed.

I put my back against the same wall right away. "Sorry," I whispered. *For not believing when you said Arden Villeneuve didn't love me, for all the things I said about you and for this.*

"Shut up," she hissed and peeped out.

The guard's footsteps got closer, as did his voice. "This place is not safe for sleeping in, ma'am. There's a shelter just a few blocks down. You can still make it there before it fills up today if you run now."

"What are we going to do?" I whispered to her.

"We?" she whispered, just as softly. "I'm going to go and leave you here for him because this is your problem, not mine." The determined look in her eyes told me she meant every word.

I grabbed her arm and squeezed it. Hard. "Don't, please. There are people trying to kill me and I don't have any money. I won't survive a week out there without you."

The guard's heavy footsteps got even closer. The dusty floorboards in the room we were in began to visibly shake.

I looked at Paul and pleaded with my eyes. Please help

me, I mouthed.

She looked right back at me, her pupils huge abysses of black, then rolled her eyes and sighed. She wrenched her hand out of mine.

The guard stepped into the room.

I'm not entirely sure how but next thing I knew, I was in a squat behind the island counter in the secret apartment's kitchenette, out of the room we had been in just a second earlier. Paul had an arm around me and a hand over my mouth. She gestured at me to be quiet and let go of me to go peep around the corner. I followed suit.

I saw the guard standing alone in the now empty room, muttering something unkind about homeless people. He rammed the open window shut and walked out shortly after with disbelief all over his face.

Paul darted back behind the counter when he emerged and pulled me along with her. She turned to me and put her arms around me once again.

Next thing I knew, I was back in the previously empty room, behind the wall again, safe in Paul's embrace. She stared at my face and I stared at hers. I stared at her lips and she followed suit with mine. Something about the way she looked at me made my heart jump. A rush of chemicals moved underneath my skin. I realised, while looking at her face, that she really was the smartest and bravest woman I had ever known.

Outside, the rusty spiral staircase groaned dramatically, as if it was on the verge of collapsing.

Inside, Paul and I remained inches apart, close enough to feel each other's warmth. I found myself wanting to kiss her, so I did.

Paul let go of me and backed away the moment my lips touched hers. She frowned and regarded me with disgust. "You just slept with Arden Villeneuve," she said.

I did, yes, but I didn't understand what Paul was trying to say.

She rolled her eyes and moved a good distance away

from me. "I'm not like everybody else. Just because everybody thinks it's normal to love a million different people at the same time doesn't make it right for me."

Oh. Okay. And I was not 'the type of person' she was looking for. How did I forget? I sucked in my lower lip and tried my best to look apologetic, even though I wasn't. Not really. I had enjoyed the sensation of her lips on mine again, even though the moment had been brief. "Sorry. I thought since you bought me roses—"

"Only to cheer you up." Paul sighed, reached into her pocket and dug out a wad of cash. She held it out in front of me. "Here. Make it last or use it to get a job, I don't care. You're on your own."

I stared at the cash in her hands and felt like a horrible person. "Paul, I'm not here for the money. I missed being with you."

Paul rolled her eyes again and set down the backpacks on her shoulders onto the floor. She removed the picnic mat from one of them, spread it out in the middle of the room the way it had been before and put the cash she had been holding on one of the edges of the mat. She then took more items out of her backpacks—a stack of papers, that pen, a pack of cigarettes and a lighter—and set them all around her. She sat down, lit a cigarette and refused to look at me.

"You smoke now?"

Paul ignored my question and released a large cloud of smoke into the air between us. She picked up the pen and began drawing boxes on her stack of papers like an artist in a fit of inspiration. She then added words in the middle of the boxes she had just drawn. I couldn't read what the words said because they were upside down, cursive and too far away to see properly.

I went to the part of the mat where the wad of cash wasn't and knelt down in front of her. "I am incredibly sorry, Paul. For everything. Especially what I said about you growing up in an institution. That isn't your fault or even a bad thing. I really shouldn't have said it like it was."

Paul said nothing in reply. She looked like she didn't even hear me.

"Truth is, I was furious because you were right. I'm good enough for nobody. I've known so for the longest time, I just didn't want you to know it too."

I saw her hear me. For a brief moment, her eyes glanced up and her throat moved but right afterwards, Paul continued pretending like she hadn't heard a thing. She dragged on her cigarette like a seasoned smoker and continued drawing on her stack of papers without a word.

"Thing is, in high school, I was really popular, even though I had no money and just about the lousiest grades in the world. I was really popular on Instagram, for some reason, so the cool kids thought of me as their own. I got to date the prettiest girls, the most handsome jocks, the richest kids, practically anybody I wanted. I never thought the fun would end but of course it did, in time. The kids who used to worship me started getting degrees and good jobs then nice homes and partners with big paychecks. We stopped hanging out because my face alone was no longer enough to keep me in their league. They started following new people, made new friends, found new lovers, while I eventually got used to being single and, well, mostly alone. Nobody wanted to build a life with me because I had nothing to offer in real life. I had no money, no assets, no promise of a bright future... All I had was... Arden Villeneuve. And even then, I didn't. Not really." I sighed. "Now, all I have is you. So wherever it is you want to go, whatever it is you want to do, I'm all ready to do it with you."

Paul frowned, to my relief, and properly looked up at me at last. "I don't think you're ready for what I want to do next."

"I am. Just give me a chance. Please."

"No. I've known you long enough to know you. You can't handle it. We're better off going our separate ways now because you're only just going to get in the way and ruin everything. Again."

"I won't. I promise. I've learnt my lesson. I'll do everything you say from now on, I swear."

"Well, the last two times you swore, you broke your promises so—"

"I won't again. Not anymore. Paul, you need a friend as much as I do. It's not going to be fun going about life alone. Trust me, I've been there."

She narrowed her eyes as she observed me. "I could always just give you more money now, if that's what you're afraid of."

"I don't want your money. I want... to be with you."

Her eyebrows went up and I saw her inhale sharply. "Are you sure?"

"Positive."

On hindsight, I really should have asked what she was planning on doing first.

CHAPTER 21
DATE UNKNOWN

Paul and I left the library with our backpacks the next morning, the moment the doors opened and the first hoard of patrons entered. She said I had taken the word 'secret' right out of the phrase 'secret apartment' so we couldn't stay at the secret apartment a minute longer. The guard from the day before was planning on gaining fame and possibly a promotion from the 'historical treasure' he discovered and he had been bent on telling everyone and their mother about it the evening before, she said. But, it didn't really matter, Paul said. The secret apartment was unliveable and she needed to move over to Manhattan to get things done anyway.

Things unrelated to enjoyment, I discovered, when she rejected the four-hour spa treatment I suggested we do next.

"I don't want people thinking I'm just a loser who's achieved nothing," she told me with the raised eyebrows of sarcasm as she marched us to the subway station closest to the library. "I've since decided to do as you suggested. Use my 'powers' for good, save people and stuff. Prove myself worthy in the eyes of the world."

The hardness of her face as she said those words made my cheeks burn with shame. "I'll help you," I said right away. "Who do you want to save?"

She didn't have time to go into that, she said. Not when on the move. It was too complicated and she didn't want to risk other people listening in.

We stopped in the middle of the subway station's foyer, near the gates, with the peak hour rush flowing all around us. I was clean again—thanks to the soap, water and hand towels Paul stole from Room 103—and had on a new set of clothes, but commuters glared at us with disgust on their faces all the same. They hated us because we blocked their paths and added additional seconds and hassle to the daily journey they already detested to the core. I understood that because I too had been a miserable commuter once before but Paul didn't.

She—the one who had chosen to stop where we were—didn't move away. She didn't even notice the glares. Her eyes were on her shoes and there was that strange vacant expression on her face again, the one she had on the day we got to The Canned Food Factory Hotel. She looked as if she were lost in deep thought or stuck in a trance of sorts. Frankly, she looked thoroughly weird.

Someone rammed against me as he or she passed and made me stumble backwards. My hands jumped into my pockets and checked frantically for my wallet the moment that happened and stopped checking only when I remembered I no longer owned a wallet. *Right.* I depended on Paul. She had stacks of cash. Stacks I feared she would lose if we stood where we were a minute longer.

"We should go," I told her. "The city's full of crooks who deserve to be shot."

"Shh, I'm trying to concentrate." Paul closed her eyes right smack in the middle of the subway station's migratory rush and became completely motionless.

Another commuter knocked against me as he passed

and yet another knocked against her. They both gave me ugly stares so I felt compelled to show them gestures of apology even though deep down inside, I wished them both the shortest, most treacherous lives known to man.

"Paul, why don't we do this somewhere else," I said when the two angry commuters finally moved out of sight.

Her eyes shot open as I said those words but they didn't turn to me. They fell instead on a man in the distance—an olive-skinned workman dressed in a dark blue jumpsuit that was completely covered in paint of all colours.

He was all-alone, leaning against a wall and playing with his phone, possibly waiting for somebody.

"Wait here," she said and very abruptly marched towards him.

"Why?" I asked but she had already gone.

Adrenaline shot through my veins as I watched her for I couldn't tell what she was planning on doing to him. *Saving him? Just talking to him?* I decided to look around for the nearest exit in the meantime, in case I would need it at short notice. When I turned back to check on Paul, I found her already right in front of the workman.

She looked as if she were merely walking by him, with no ill intentions whatsoever, until I noticed—

—the bunch of keys flying out of his pocket, into the hand Paul held open next to her thigh.

I panicked because the scene was as clear as day, yet nobody but me seemed to notice.

Paul brought the keys to her front and, without even looking down, wrenched one of the keys away from the keychain that held them all together. She shoved the key she had removed into her pocket and stopped in her tracks as if she had suddenly remembered something she had forgotten. Commuters behind her glared and said unkind words to her face but she didn't seem to care. She turned around and marched back towards the workman like a woman in a hurry.

As she passed him, the bunch of keys in her hand flew back into his pocket as magically as they had emerged. The workman didn't even look up from his phone once. Nobody else noticed the keys at all.

I couldn't help but smile when it was all over. Paul was incredible, I was aware of that then. I knew I would kiss her again in a heartbeat, if she would only just let me.

Paul didn't walk back to me right away. She went round the edges of the station, in a circle, with her head angled upwards as if she were trying to find a signboard or something.

Why? I followed her eyes and saw nothing out of the ordinary—just ads and travel information and the like. I only got what she was doing when I looked away from her eyes and down at her hands.

At thigh level, wallets were flying, all by themselves, out of pockets, into the open front pocket of the backpack on Paul's back. Some were pretty visible, even from where I was, so I didn't get why nobody else noticed them flying. Everybody else seemed to be simply preoccupied with their own rush, their own thoughts or their own music, and nobody actually saw what was happening right under their eyes. Literally!

By the time Paul returned to my side, the front pocket of her backpack was stuffed to the max with wallets of all shapes, sizes and colours. She brought the backpack to her front, zipped up the front pocket like there was nothing unusual in it and smiled at me with twinkles in her eyes.

"How 'bout we do Chinese followed by a four-hour spa thing next?"

I changed my mind about what crooks deserved and said yes right away.

When darkness fell, when the day of fun—we did two movies and more Chinese after our trip to the spa—was done, Paul tipped us into a driverless taxi and typed an address I didn't recognise into its control panel.

"Is that our new hotel?" I asked.

She put her finger to her lips, pointed to the little holes at the sides of the car's doors and didn't reply. Built-in microphones, I realised. *Risky.*

I nodded, smiled and ran an imaginary zip over my mouth. The hours of fun and relaxation had done wonders for my spirit. The tight knots in my neck had been rubbed away, my hunger had been satiated, my tired legs had been rested... I was happy again and in the mood for adventure. I thought of the taxi ride as another fun experience and wasn't in the least worried about where we would end up.

We ended up in front of a row of pre-war elevator buildings somewhere in Manhattan. Instead of going into the buildings though, Paul led us across the road and made us stand in the shadows of an alley opposite them.

"Where are we?" I asked after I followed her lead and pressed my back against the alley's grimy brick wall. I thought she looked more beautiful than ever in the dimness of the alley and couldn't stop staring at her.

Paul lifted her expensive $2000 watch and said, "You'll find out in exactly one minute." She turned her head towards the road and held her gaze there so I did the same.

Exactly one minute later, a taxi screeched to a stop at the exact spot ours had stopped at moments before. A man dressed in a shirt and tie stepped out with a briefcase in hand. His brown hair was so neatly gelled, it shone like plastic under the orange glow of the street's lamps. His face looked familiar too. Too familiar.

My heart jumped then sank with dread when I realised why. All the happy sensations I had been feeling for most of the day vanished in a flash. The hairs on my arms stood on ends. "Dr Clark?"

Paul never replied. Her eyes watched Dr Clark the way they had watched so many other men before him but I got the feeling she was uncharacteristically a little nervous this time.

Like the other men before him, Dr Clark had no idea Paul was even close. He walked up to the main door of one of the buildings, tapped a card on the security panel at the side of the main door and went right in.

"What if he calls the rest of CRO?" I whispered. "They have guns and they use them! I saw them do so myself!"

Paul shushed me. Her eyes fell on the pavement across the road.

A discarded flyer on the pavement suddenly rose, as if it had suddenly gotten caught in a gust of wind. It fluttered towards the door Dr Clark had gone through and ended up between that door and the wall, right where the door's catch was, right before the door closed shut.

"Now."

Now what? Before I could even ask, Paul was already halfway across the road. I dashed after her with legs that were unsteady as I watched her push open the door that hadn't locked properly because a flyer had been in the way of its catch. She tossed the flyer and held the door open for me as she beckoned me to join her inside.

The door locked behind us the moment she let go of it. I found us in the lobby of a rather nice apartment building—one with a floor of black and white squares, with vintage-looking letter boxes in the corner—but Paul spent no time at all admiring our surroundings. She pressed a button that opened an elevator and said, "Come."

I obeyed, as always. Only this time, I didn't feel all that safe as I did so.

On the fifth floor, seven well-polished apartment doors lay along a stretch of orange carpet in between freshly painted grey walls. It was yet another building I wouldn't have been able to afford to live in yet Paul glided through the perfumed corridor as if she had been living there for decades. I followed her and stopped when she stopped outside a well-polished door with the words '5D' in gold letters on it.

The door opened—all by itself and ever so quietly. I saw a living room behind it. A small but cosy space with mostly grey walls and a single blood-orange wall on one side. There were no windows... or maybe there were, just none that we could see, perhaps hidden behind the two sets of thick cream curtains at one end.

Paul tiptoed in and gestured at me to follow.

I did, of course. Where else was I to go?

To the left of the entrance was a small open kitchen complete with ovens, a dishwasher and laundry equipment. A bar counter with two black leather barstools on chrome legs separated the kitchen from the living space on the right in which Dr Clark lay slumped on a white sofa. He had his briefcase on the sofa next to him, his legs propped up on the stone coffee table in front of him, his tie loosened, shirt unbuttoned, eyes closed and he held his glasses in one hand. The other hand pinched at the flesh in between his nose and he looked thoroughly beat. He had not the slightest inkling he was being watched and didn't notice when Paul shut the door behind us.

His briefcase opened itself, as if the apartment was haunted, and a gun—a real, solid, metallic black handgun—flew out of it. The gun floated up towards the ceiling as a hotel's keycard had once done and ended up right in the middle of Paul's open palm.

A gun? I began to feel afraid again. For us or for him, I wasn't sure. From experience, the wrath of Dr Clark's gun-toting men in suits was worse than the wrath of Paul indeed, but the idea of a gun in *her* hands—the hands of a woman who had spent many years in a mental institution—didn't sit all that well with me either.

More so after she lifted it and aimed its barrel right at Dr Clark's tired head.

"Hello, Mr Anderson," she said with an unexpected calmness that sent shivers down my spine. *Mr what?*

Dr Clark shoved his glasses over his nose and opened his eyes immediately. Shock was on his face as he took in the sight of us. He blinked hard a good number of times. "Paula! And... Blaine?"

Blaine, he said. Not Lane. *Blaine* with both the upper and lower lips sucked in. And... Paula?

"How did you get in?" he asked. He had that look of genuine concern, the same kind of look he often gave me in therapy, but his hand was in an unusual position this time. It was sneaking into the pocket of his pants.

"Paul," I whispered but didn't actually have to. Her eyes were already on his hand and her mouth was starting to curl upwards as if there was something hilarious about his hand being where it was.

Dr Clark screamed in pain. His hand, which had a phone in it, emerged from his pocket contorted in the most unnatural position, as if controlled by some supernatural force he could not overcome. The phone yanked itself out of his grasp, levitated towards the goldfish bowl on the console below a big ass wide-screen TV, and plopped into the water with a giant splash.

Both the goldfish in the bowl and I jumped in shock.

"No calling the Office, Christopher," Paul said with smiling eyes. "I want it to be just you and us tonight."

"Paula, no," he said and sounded as if he were trying to discipline a child or a pet. "Be a good girl. You were always a good girl, weren't you? Why are you behaving like this today?"

He glanced at me and frowned more. "Did... Blaine put you up to this? Why are you calling me Christopher?"

What? Who? Me? No! And why was Paul Paula now?

Paul's eyes hardened in a way I had never seen them do before. She began to look almost pathologically cold, the way school shooters usually did right before they carried out their deadly deeds. "No, she did not. But I have to say, I did learn a thing or two from her."

What??? When? How? What did you learn?

Paul didn't explain further but Dr Clark's face and body—stripped of colour and shaking uncontrollably—did. Whatever Paul had learned from me was terrifying. That much was clear.

Paul requested I tie his hands and legs up with the nylon rope and duct tape she had in her backpack so I did, even though it felt incredibly weird doing so.

I did ask her—in my head, so Dr Clark wouldn't hear—what exactly it was we were trying to do, but she never heard me. She was too busy, at that point, checking out the selection of paperbacks on his bookshelf while keeping the gun pointed towards his head.

"How did you get my address?" he asked me with a frown when I rolled the fourth and final round of duct tape over his wrists. He was on the carpet next to the stone coffee table—a white and fluffy carpet that looked very expensive—with eyes larger than ever and limbs fully tied up, thanks to me. He eyed me cautiously, like I wasn't someone he could fully trust, and I wasn't in the least surprised.

"It was me. I read your mind," Paul said before I could reply. She sat herself down on the stool—a solid white plastic box—right next to him and grinned as she admired my handiwork. "Then I used telekinesis to open your door. Piece of cake."

Dr Clark stared at her for a good few seconds then chuckled, albeit nervously. "Teleki—? There's no such thing, Paula," he said and sounded like he meant it.

Paul grinned more, not in the least fazed. "Nice try, Mr Anderson, but I already know all about CRO. All about us. And, all your dirty little secrets and habits. Hashtag asphyxiation, granny, three way... MILF."

He frowned again, this time with concern all over his face. "All I ever tried to do was help you get better, Paula. You're very sick and you need medication right now. You too, Blaine."

Blaine? Was I really—

"Let's just speak truthfully, for once, shall we?" Paul scooted closer to Dr Clark and rammed the gun right into the middle of his chest. "We're not sick. You know we're not. In fact, I would even say that you and the whole damn organisation you work for are the sick ones. What you guys do *is* sick."

"That's just your delusion talking, Paula! You've been off meds for way too long. You have schizophrenia and you need help. I can help you!"

"Oh, please, you're not even a real doctor! All you have is an irrelevant degree in statistics, am I right, Mr Anderson?"

Dr Clark was rendered speechless but I thought he made a good point. *Paul dumb and harmless one day then smart and ruthless the next?* It did sound like a personality disorder of sorts to me.

"Blaine," he suddenly said. "Stop this!"

I turned to him, met his eyes and saw, for the first time ever, something I never thought I'd ever see in them.

Fear. "I don't deserve this," he said in a voice that quivered. "All I ever did was try to help."

I froze. *Another good point.* Dr Clark hadn't actually done anything awful to me, had he? Not in Wonderdrug nor out in the world. I was only afraid of him because... Paul said I should be.

"Lane, don't listen to him," Paul said. "He lies."

"She's not Lane, Paula. And I'm not lying. She's Blaine! Lane Thompson is already dead!"

"Oh, just shut up!"

I looked from one to the other and couldn't decide which one of them to believe. *What had Dr Clark called me when I lived at Wonderdrug? Lane? Or Blaine?* Lane, I think. But I couldn't say for sure.

"I have medicine right here," he said with a sudden burst of enthusiasm. "I could give you both some now. It will calm you down a great deal and help you see things as they really are. Why don't we try that, huh?"

Paul rammed the gun hard against his head. "Stop the doctor act now!"

"Okay! Okay! Okay… What is it you want then? Huh?" Dr Clark swallowed hard and suddenly looked like he was on the verge of crying. "Just tell me. I'll give it to you. You don't have to shoot me."

A big grin appeared on Paul's face and her eyes sparkled in amusement. "Unfortunately, I do."

"Why?"

"Because I want to save people. From you. I just wanted to see what you'd say once I told you that."

I gaped at him, then at her, and felt my heart sink to the carpet when I remembered why Paul—or Paula—was so bent on saving people.

CHAPTER 22
DATE UNKNOWN

"Paul, let's talk about this first," I decided to say. I didn't want Dr Clark to die or become disabled for life because of me!

"There's nothing to talk about."

"You can't just shoot him for no reason!"

"Oh, I have many reasons. One: He killed my mom. Two: We need his—"

"Your mom's not even dead, Paula!" Dr Clark shouted. His face turned from white to cherry red and the whites of his eyes did likewise. His lips began trembling. "She's been discharged, that's all! You're not understanding things right!"

What? Not dead? My mouth fell open and I turned to him in surprise but Paul simply scoffed.

"How many alternative truths do you guys have up your sleeves, Mr Anderson?"

"I know you're upset because she hasn't visited in a while but that's no reason to—"

"Christ! Shut up! Enough with the stories!"

"They're not stories, Paula, I'm telling the truth! You

have schizophrenia. You're not seeing things right!"

"Stop!"

"Blaine!" He turned to me so suddenly, I backed away a little in shock. "Help me stop her! She needs medication. Take the gun from her, please!"

"He's lying to you, Lane," Paul said. "There is no Blaine!"

"Yes there is! Blaine, you're Lane's twin! You read her diary when she died and got confused. You were ill to begin with, that's why you were living at the Wonderdrug Psychiatric Centre! You have an identity disorder and schizophrenia, just like Paula! That's why you were on the same floor!"

What?! Wait, wasn't that what Arden Villeneuve said too?

"Jesus! Maybe it wasn't such a good idea letting you talk, huh?" Paul turned the gun towards his mouth and searched the room for the roll of duct tape I held behind my back.

"Paula's denying you treatment, Blaine!" Tears fell out of Dr Clark's eyes at last and he began to weep like a little boy tormented by bullies. "You did something terrible to Arden Villeneuve. You need help! You need to take the gun and fight for your right to be treated! Please!"

"You don't need treatment because you're not sick and he's not a doctor! He's lying about Arden Villeneuve! She's fine! She's not dead! It's a trap!"

"Paula's dangerous! She'll hurt you if you don't take the gun from her!"

"Says the man who ripped flesh out of your thigh!"

"We didn't do that! You ripped flesh out of your own thigh, Blaine! That's why you need our help!"

"God, will you just stop with the stories!"

I struggled to catch my breath as my mind spun. *They both seemed to be telling the truth, which meant either of them could be wrong or lying. How was I to tell?*

"Paul, let's pause a moment and discuss this," I decided to say. Her reckless swinging of the gun made my stomach queasy, as did the genuine fear in Dr Clark's drenched eyes.

Paul stared at me in exasperation and tightened her grip of the gun. "There's nothing to discuss, Lane. He's trying to make you think you're crazy so you'll willingly let him lock you up and do all sorts of tests on your body. And mine too!"

"Paul, don't. Please," I whispered. I set aside the roll of duct tape in my hands, walked towards her, slowly, and reached for the gun.

Three shots rang out like deafening claps before I even got to touch it.

When I turned back to Dr Clark, there were two deep red circles in the middle of his forehead. Two holes—a little like the two that had only recently been in my arm—from which thick dark red liquids flowed. There was shock in his blue eyes as they stopped blinking. He tipped sideways and fell to the ground like a sack of potatoes.

No more words came out of his mouth after that. His eyes never got the chance to close.

"You killed him," I said as red liquid spread across the fluffy white carpet and made its way towards my sneakers. *Or had I killed him? Brought on his death by planting thoughts into Paul's head?* I edged away from the red on the carpet and her. "Why?"

Paul stood, heaved a sigh and stretched her neck. The look on her face wasn't one of guilt or even horror—it was relief. "We need his eyeball, Lane. And stop acting like this is such a big deal. You've killed more people than I have so you don't get to judge."

I became stiff at once. "I... never... Why do you say that?"

"Read it in your file." She stuffed the gun into the back of her pants and began rummaging through Dr Clark's briefcase as if it were the perfect time to multi-task. "You're 'a genius who's gotten away with murder three times', according to CRO. Three people dead with you in the vicinity? That doesn't happen to other people. Frankly, they're quite afraid of you. And... I like that about you."

I did not like *that* about me one bit. My skin tingled and began feeling as if something was heating it up from the inside. "I don't even... I don't remember killing anybody."

Paul fished out Dr Clark's employee pass from the briefcase and shrugged. "Maybe that's just the way you get things done? Maybe you won't remember all this either."

How was that even humanly possible?

I could see Dr Clark's death everywhere. His corpse, the room full of blood, they were now perpetually at the periphery of my visual field, no matter where else I tried to look. I couldn't stop seeing the shock on his face in my mind. I couldn't stop remembering the silence that came upon the living room the moment all life left him. Through the holes in his skull, I could see collapsed flesh, bone and brain! And his eyes! They wouldn't stop staring at me! They were full of horror. *He had been so afraid before he died. He hadn't even had the chance to calm down before he died!*

"Can you get us a knife?" Paul said with a frown. She stuffed Dr Clark's employee pass into her backpack as she watched me with a twinge of concern.

A shot of fear ran down my spine. "Why?"

"We need to get his eye out, remember? That's what we killed him for."

My knees buckled when I heard those words and I found myself in a squat, holding onto the floor for support, shaking from head to toe.

As if killing the man and digging his eyeball out wasn't bad enough, Paul insisted we spend the next twenty-four hours *resting* at his apartment. I didn't want to but I couldn't make myself go anywhere else because I was a total wreck by that time, curled up with my chin on my knees in the corner of the living room, with a face drenched by hot, incessant tears.

THE WOMAN WHO MADE ME FEEL STRANGE

I wanted very much to ask where we would be going next, if Paul had more death planned in the future, but I simply... couldn't. I couldn't stand, I couldn't speak, I couldn't... anything. Not with the dead body—now turning purplish—staring at me.

"You must try his shower," Paul said at some point. She peeled off all of her clothes and became completely naked while standing right in front of me. "It has a ten-minute water jet massage function that's really just about the most relaxing experience ever invented. I think it'll make you feel a lot better."

I moved my eyes away from her naked body and kept them away. There was nothing sexy about a murderer, I realised. Nothing sexy at all. I didn't look up when she set her clothes to wash in Dr Clark's washing machine, nor when she invited me to take a shower with her. I looked up only when she moved away from me and I heard the shower in Dr Clark's ensuite bathroom run.

Ten minutes. That was how long I had alone with my thoughts, I knew. I had to get my thinking done before Paul came out of the shower. I tossed my head back, closed my eyes and thought as quickly as I could.

I was in an apartment with a dead body. The gun that made the dead body was still in the possession of the woman who pressed its trigger. The dead body thought I needed meds. The woman who killed the body thought I didn't, but then, she was also perfectly fine with me being a serial killer which meant her opinion wasn't something I really should be taking into consideration. Dead body said woman was really a mentally ill patient. Woman said dead body was not even a real doctor. Doctor or mentally ill patient? Which one of them to believe?

Doctor, I decided. After all, he was the one who hadn't killed anyone yet. He was the safer bet. *He said I needed meds so I would have to go find some and eat some. Fast. Before the mentally ill patient got out of the shower. And I had to stop thinking at once because I had been thinking for way too long already. The mentally ill patient would be done with her jet water massage any minute now and I didn't want to be caught looking for meds.*

I jumped up, opened my eyes and found myself face to face with Paul. Her hair was dripping wet and her face was damp like a ghost's would be if it had only just crawled out of a well. All she had on was a towel wrapped around her body. I gasped and jumped back before I could stop myself but quickly regained my composure.

"Are you okay?" she asked.

Of course not. We just killed a man, his dead body was still on the floor and I might just get shot anytime. By you. I nodded and said I was.

Paul reached for my arm and looked right into my eyes, as if reading me. Her touch was unnervingly gentle. Her eyes were solemn and full of concern. "You don't need to lie. I'm not going to hurt you."

I couldn't hold my gaze in hers. I found her eyes no longer beautiful. In fact, the sight of her now made my skin crawl. I nodded, with my eyes back down on the carpet, and tried to pull my arm away from her grasp while keeping my face as blank as was possible.

"Lane…" She grabbed me by the wrist before I could pull away completely.

I couldn't look at her. I couldn't bear the sight of her face a minute longer and the weight of her gaze on me made my knees wobble all over again.

"Lane! I wouldn't ever hurt you!"

I forced myself to look up, lest my life depended on it, and was horrified to find her face right in front of mine, her lips close enough to touch. As if that wasn't bad enough, they were also getting closer.

I took three steps back and yanked my arm out of her grasp because I never wanted to have to touch those lips again. Not ever. But instinct made me smile and say, "I know."

A new expression flickered in her eyes but she blinked it away before I could read what it meant. Her hand curled into mine and she said, "Come." She pulled me along with her.

Not again, I thought.

Paul stopped so abruptly, I nearly crashed into her. She turned and stared at me with a face of worry so I put on that instinctive smile again. Think nothing, I told myself quickly, lest my thoughts made my face reveal secrets without my knowledge. *Maybe that was how Paul had been reading my mind all this time? She had been reading my face? But think nothing, show nothing and I should be fine, right? Blank brain, blank brain, blank brain...* Keeping my brain blank took a whole lot more effort than I anticipated—it required constant effort—but I think it worked.

Paul didn't seem to suspect anything, although she did heave deeply as if a tad irritated and let go of my hand. She went ahead to Dr Clark's briefcase without me, pulled out a laptop and brought it over to his body on the floor. As if he were just an object and not a dead human being, she picked up his pale, purple-tinged thumb and pressed it down against the laptop's trackpad.

Nothing happened. *His finger was too dead, maybe?*

She covered his thumb with her hand, rubbed it vigorously like she were giving it a hand job then tried again. This time, the laptop whirred to a start. A pleasant musical tone sounded as its screen lit up. Paul typed a long line of text on the keyboard and pressed the 'Enter' button.

A white document appeared on the big ass TV screen next to her. "Look," she said to me.

I saw a table with columns labelled 'Room Number', 'Name', 'Illness', 'Delusion(s)' and 'Status' on the TV screen.

'P. Rafferty' was the first on the list. 'Room 1'. Illness: 'Schizophrenia with Occasional Catatonia, Mental Retardation'. Delusion(s): 'Telekinesis'. Status: 'Escaped'.

'B. Thompson' was right at the bottom. 'Room 20'. Illness: 'Self-Mutilation, Depression, Suicidal Ideation, Identity Disorder'. Delusion(s): 'Superhuman Regenerative

Abilities'. Status: 'Escaped'.

Between the two names on the list were more female ones, most with schizophrenia listed as their primary illness and all with status listed as: 'In Treatment'.

The document didn't say I had schizophrenia—Dr Clark had been wrong about that—but neither did it say my name was 'L. Thompson'. *What did that mean? Were Dr Clark's last words to be trusted, or not?*

"Room 16. Cola Lam," Paul said. "She's the one who can read your past. She can give you the answers you seek."

'C. Lam', the document read. Illness: 'Schizophrenia'. Delusion(s): 'Muscle Memory Reading'. Status: 'In Treatment'.

Paul dug out a stack of papers from her backpack and spread them out on the carpet for me to see.

They were the same papers she had been drawing on the day before at the secret apartment. Now that she had them pointing towards me the right way up, I could see they weren't random doodles of art at all. They were detailed blueprints. Of the 'Wonderdrug Psychiatric Centre, New York, USA'. Rooms were either labelled by number or by function. All exits, entrances, elevators, stairwells and security camera locations were clearly marked out. In one sheet, the one labelled 'Level 16' at the top of the page, I recognised the shape of the long corridor on it and the location of the nearest stairwell. It was the very corridor Paul and I had run along the day we escaped Wonderdrug. Paul put a dirt-filled fingernail over one of the boxes on that sheet—a box with the words 'Room 16' written within it.

"That's where she is. We'll get her out first, then you open the doors towards the left while I get the doors on the right. After that, bring everyone to the middle of the corridor. We'll take the lifts back down."

I stared at the pair of double lines with 'X's on both sides, labelled 'Elevator A' and 'Elevator B', and I found it much harder to breathe. "So... that's who you're intending to save? The patients at Wonderdrug?"

"The curiosities trapped by CRO—yes. We need the numbers to survive. I realised that only after I lost you. Two of us alone, with only one place to live, that just doesn't give us enough options."

I swallowed the clump of nerves in my throat and took in a long, deep, difficult breath. "It says illness and delusions, Paul. Right there. It says you have schizophrenia. It says I'm B. Thompson."

"They write in code, in case the files get out. 'Delusions' is code for 'advantage'. 'Illness' is what they use to justify keeping you locked up. And they must have changed your name after they spoke with that movie star lover of yours. To keep the story consistent."

I nodded for a good minute as a whole new perspective of our situation began to sink in.

"No," Paul said abruptly, with a frown. "Look, I'm sorry there's not more evidence but everything I'm telling you is the truth. We're not mentally ill! Look!"

She navigated the laptop back to its desktop and opened a file labelled 'wd-former-patients.cls'—a file format I did not recognise.

The new document also contained a table. It was almost similar to the one in the document before, except in the new table, the first column was labelled 'Number' instead of 'Room Number'. The length of the table was also longer, going all the way to number '67', and the status of every person listed on the new sheet was 'Discharged'.

"'Discharged' is code for deceased while captive," Paul said. "See how many there are? They've been killing people like us for years. My mom's number 55. There. Rose Rafferty."

Number 55: 'R. Rafferty'. Illness: 'Schizophrenia with Occasional Catatonia, Mental Retardation, PTSD'. Delusion(s): 'Unspecified'. Status: 'Discharged'.

Status: Discharged.
Discharged.
Dis-charged.

My heart began to run again, this time at the speed of a moving train. I didn't know what to say. I knew exactly what I would think of the D-word but I didn't dare actually think it lest my thoughts made my face change again. I decided it was best to focus on what Paul just said... *There's my mom, Rose Rafferty. There's my mom, Rose Rafferty. There's my mom, Rose Rafferty. Rose Rafferty, Rose Rafferty, Rose Rafferty, Rose Rafferty...* That was the only way I could keep my own thoughts away from my mind.

"Lane, look at me. Just look at me! Look at me!" Paul put her hands on my cheeks and wrenched my head up towards her eyes when I didn't comply.

I did look at her eventually because I got the feeling she might just kill me if I didn't.

Her eyes were anxious in a way I had never seen them anxious before. "Lane, my mother *is* dead. That is the truth. And all those other women on the list are too. Wonderdrug lies because they believe sacrificing us for the betterment of mankind, for the betterment of their company's coffers, is what's right. But it's not. We deserve proper lives and happiness. You deserve a proper life and you deserve to know the truth."

I nodded again. The goldfish splashed around its bowl; the washing machine kept on grinding; the dead body wouldn't stop looking at me; the red on the carpet looked darker. I thought of nothing but *the truth, the truth, the truth, the truth...*

Paul watched me for the longest time but eventually sighed, lowered her head like a plant that had wilted and let go of my cheeks. "Get two spoons and a chopper," she said and got up to go to Dr Clark's briefcase again.

"Why?"

She pulled a plastic box out of the briefcase and held it up for me to see.

It was Dr Clark's multi-compartment pill box—the one with a different compartment for every different colour of pill; the one which contained the cotton candy pink pills I now wanted desperately to eat.

"We need to grind the pink ones to remove their time-release properties," she said. Matter-of-factly. "And we need Mr Anderson's right wrist."

Okay. I nodded like a good employee would, took the plastic box from Paul and headed towards the kitchen with it.

When my back was completely turned and I was far enough away from her, I shoved four pink pills into my mouth and swallowed.

CHAPTER 23
DATE UNKNOWN

The four pink pills didn't change a thing. I woke up anxious in a self-driving taxi in the dark of night, with Paul next to my side, and remembered everything.

Every microsecond before the gun fired, I remembered. Every twitch of fear in Dr Clark's huge blue eyes, I remembered. Every dead stare. Every difficult breath of mine. The red on the white carpet. The way Dr Clark's wrist split from his body when the chopper *I found* came down on it, I remembered.

But I didn't know what to do next. I saw us already in the heart of the Financial District, right in front of the boxy, good-quality twenty storey building which had the words 'Wonderdrug Psychiatric Centre' plastered above glass doors on its front.

The words were made of a shiny metal, backlit with a bright white light. They seemed to shine like gaps of daylight amidst the darkness of the night around them.

Shit. What did I last remember?

I remembered sinking down into Dr Clark's white sofa—which looked a little like a fluffy white cloud to me at that point—with spoons still in my hands. I remembered feeling heavy and dazed and seeing my eyelids droop like curtains over my eyes.

What day was it? The same day? Or a different day?

Paul didn't say. She fed cash into the self-driving taxi's payment machine and dragged me out without caring whether or not I actually wanted to be out.

Instead of going right in and asking for help like any sane, logical person would, she had us crouch behind the row of bushes in front of the entrance while she observed the situation inside and checked the time on her watch.

The LED signboard on the wall next to the glass doors in front of us had big red letters that said the Wonderdrug Psychiatric Centre was 'CLOSED'. The reception counter beyond the glass doors—a classy white marble centrepiece that matched the white marble floor and white marble walls around it—was empty. There was a lone security guard strolling the lobby aimlessly but he went behind a white marble wall and didn't emerge again after that.

"Now," Paul said and dragged me by the arm again.

I stood my ground and shook her hand off this time. "I don't want to do this," I said. Firmly. I really didn't. My fingers were still trembling from the shock of Dr Clark's *murder* and my thighs remained wobbly. I felt as if I had only just made it out of the most horrifying haunted funhouse by the hair and would vomit if I had to do anything thrill-related again anytime soon.

"I need your help," Paul replied. Equally firmly.

"No you don't. You said I wasn't ready for this and you know what, you were right before. I can't handle this. I'm sorry. You're better off on your own." *And I'll be better off back in the care of the Wonderdrug Psychiatric Centre, never having to see you again.*

Paul frowned at me and curled her hands around my arm like an eagle might do with its talons. "You need to see this," she said in a low, dangerous voice. "You need to know that everything I've been telling you about

Wonderdrug is real."

"No, I don't." What I truly needed was medicine, a doctor and... protection from Paul, or Paula, I thought. *Wonderdrug is real, Wonderdrug is real, Wonderdrug is real, Wonderdrug is real...*

She rolled her eyes, sighed then pushed something hard and cold into my lower back. Dr Clark's gun, I realised soon after. The very gun she killed him with. "Come with me, help me open half the doors on the sixteenth floor, or I will shoot you." She sounded perfectly serious; there was no hesitation or self-doubt in her voice at all.

In that moment, it became painfully clear to me how much I *didn't* want to die. I thought about all the things I hadn't yet tried—the better job, the further education, the better housing, the places I hadn't yet seen, the things I hadn't yet done—and realised Dr Clark had been so wrong when he said I had suicidal tendencies. The news article and my former colleagues had all been wrong. I didn't want to die. Not at all. I wanted to live!

I was not suicidal at all. Not in the least!

"People don't always say or know the truth about things, Lane. The ones who lie lie because they want you to behave in ways that will benefit them. The ones who believe the ones who lie don't know any better. You need to make your own conclusions, Lane. You need to see Wonderdrug for what it really is, with your very own eyes. Come with me and let me show you what's really going on."

She shoved the gun deeper into my lower back after that so I agreed immediately.

The security office of the Wonderdrug Psychiatric Centre was located on the third floor. To get there after hours, you needed an employee pass to open the glass doors at the main entrance, a registered retina to open the ten foot chrome barricades behind the reception counter at the lobby and an approved wrist chip to get the elevator moving. None of those were a problem for Paul who had come well-prepared with Dr Clark's arsenal of belongings, bodily or otherwise.

All I could do was pray we would be caught by the ten or so black-globed cameras on the ceiling of the lobby and stopped by whoever happened to be watching.

"Not going to happen, Lane. The cameras switch off for five minutes during the security reboot that happens at 3am every second Sunday of the month. Guess what day and time it is?"

Wait a minute... Hadn't Paul said a Wonderdrug security reboot was a rare occurrence?

Paul stopped in front of the tall chrome barricades with Dr Clark's eyeball in a Ziploc bag and turned to me. "Fine, I lied. Sorry," she said, without much expression.

She shoved the gun into the back of her pants so that she could dig into the Ziploc bag and take the eyeball— washed, so it was now white with grey streaks, with a blue circle in the middle—between two fingers. She held it up to the retinal-scanning device in front of us and the tall chrome barricades opened immediately.

Paul lied. Paul lies, I realised as I made my way past the barricades. *Sorry, sorry, sorry, sorry...*

The black door labelled 'Security Office' opened all by itself the moment Paul and I stepped close to it. I suspected a chip in the dismembered hand Paul had in her backpack might have activated a sensor of sorts but she, as usual, smiled so proudly when the door opened, it looked almost as if she was trying to tell me the opening of the door had been her doing.

The room we stepped into was almost pitch-black, lit only by the blue specks of light blinking on the towers of humming data processors near the door and the white light coming from the thirty screens above a state-of-the-art control panel at the other end of the room. It was cosy and quiet the way a night out under the stars with cicadas buzzing incessantly in the background might be considered cosy and quiet, and it was unbearably cold. There were two security guards seated at the control panel, with their backs to us, staring at the thirty screens in front of them.

"Reboot done," the security guard on the left—a middle-aged African-American woman with long copper-coloured hair bound in a tight plait—said as all thirty screens abruptly turned black. She pushed a few buttons on the control panel then added, "All systems back to normal."

Black and white footage showing various areas of the Wonderdrug Psychiatric Centre began appearing on all screens. Twenty-four of those screens never changed: they showed a fish-eye, overhead view of the twenty floors above ground and the four underground. The remaining six screens changed every minute or so and showed various stairwells, elevator interiors, storage rooms and toilets.

In one of those six screens, I spotted the guard we had seen at the lobby washing his hands in a toilet. When the screen changed, I saw a roomful of nurses seated at desks, in front of laptops. On the screen next to it, there were a couple of guards, with rifles in hand, strolling about corridors that looked similar to the one we had run along the night we escaped.

"Awesome," the guard seated on the right of the control panel—middle-aged, Hispanic and male, in the early stages of losing his hair—said without much enthusiasm. He leaned back in his chair and stretched.

Neither of them noticed us sneaking closer to the middle of the room. We used the towers of data processors for cover and blended with the dark because of our black and grey outfits. I considered screaming or calling out for help but the gun Paul kept against my waist made me decide otherwise.

When we got behind the row of data processors closest to the control panel, a small Ziploc packet of pink powder—four pink pills ground into dust by me—levitated from Paul's upturned palm and started flying towards the seated guards' backs.

The packet went towards the mug on the table next to the female guard—a white mug with the picture of a comic book's male superhero on it—and tipped all of its contents in, right before she picked up the mug and put it to her lips.

Un-noticed and now empty, the packet flew back to us and hovered right in front of my face.

"Keep it in your pocket," I heard Paul say in my head. Her lips did not move.

I obeyed because her gun remained against my waist.

Another packet of pink powder came out of Paul's pocket and flew towards the guards in the same way the previous one had done. This one went towards the mug on the table next to the male guard instead—a black mug with the words 'Well Done, Dad! I'm Awesome!' down its front. Before it could get its contents in though, the male guard reached for the mug and removed it from the table.

Yes! I thought when I heard a loud sucking sound emanating from the male guard's lips. The mug was empty.

He set the mug back down but the packet of pink powder hovering in mid-air behind him didn't continue towards it. Instead, it sank down under the control panel and hid in the shadows as if it were a helpless creature that feared being seen.

"Want another?" the male guard asked the female guard. "I need more."

The female guard shook her head and yawned, her mouth wide like a zoo animal's would be after a full meal. "No, but could you get me a Hyperpro? I feel like I just did Zoleplax or something."

"That's why I've been saying, you need to take a Hyperpro at the start of every shift. The only way to power through the day, remember?"

Yeah. Who could forget? The catchy Hyperpro jingle that had once been everywhere came back in my head on loop.

"*Hyperpro, Hyperpro! The only way to power through the day! Hyperpro, Hyperpro! Makes sleepy, sluggish, lazy you go away!*"

"Mm hmm," was all the female guard said to that. She inhaled deeply, the way people sometimes did when their muscles were thick with sleep. "I think it's all the carbs I had for dinner." She crossed her forearms on the table in front of her, buried her face in them and stopped moving.

The male guard glanced at her, chuckled and shook his head in a manner that suggested sympathy. "I need the locker room key to get it for you, Yolanda. You didn't put it back."

The female guard did not reply. She didn't even budge.

"Yolanda?" The male guard reached over and shook her gently but she didn't move.

He pushed her head up to the ceiling and shook her more violently while calling her name repeatedly but she never did open her eyes.

"Shit!" The male guard reached for the walkie talkie next to his mug and—

—Paul, together with the gun on my waist, vanished from my side.

A loud thud sounded up front. When I turned back, I saw the male guard flat on his back on the ground with Paul standing above him. She rammed the black mug she had in her hands—his mug!—down against his head.

The mug shattered when it hit his forehead and left a reddish bump and a large gash from which blood spewed. The male guard yelped and went limp. His eyes rolled to the back of his head and closed.

Paul grabbed the female guard's white mug from the table and readied herself for another high-powered smash.

"Paul, no!" I jumped out from our hiding place and dashed towards her as quickly as I could—

—but the white mug hit him before I could get there.

It broke apart and drew more blood. The male guard jerked violently then became perfectly still.

I pushed Paul aside and put my finger under the male guard's fleshy nostrils. A weak stream of air could be felt. Faint but most certainly present.

"He's dead," I said to Paul right away. *He's dead. He's dead. He's dead,* I thought, over and over. My heart thumped hard in my chest and I felt my knees wobble violently.

"We better drug him, just in case," Paul said. She grabbed the packet of pink powder from under the table and tried to pour its contents into the male guard's mouth but I snatched the packet away from her at once.

"Enough! This man's a Dad. He has a kid waiting at home somewhere—"

"So? He would shoot you to get himself a pay raise! You can't trust people on payroll to do the right thing, Lane!" She tried to snatch the packet of pink powder back from me so I quickly emptied it onto the floor.

"Stop it!" Paul dug her gun out from the back of her pants and pointed it right at my face. "You don't understand what people are really like. You need to trust me!"

Trust a person who's constantly threatening to end my life? I bit my lip and raised both hands in defeat. "I don't want to die, Paul," I said softly. "But fact is, we need help. We're not normal, we're murderers."

She rolled her eyes. "Shut up, we don't have time for that right now. The chopper's in your backpack. Use it to get yourself a right hand. It's the wrist chip that opens the doors so make sure there's at least an inch of wrist above where you make the cut."

I stared at her and shook my head. "I don't—"

"Do it, or you will die."

Guess what I chose?

Paul moved really quickly after we got the male guard's right hand. She brought us up to the sixteenth floor via elevator and we ended up at the very same corridor we once fled.

Everything was as we had left it; the lights on the metal squares above the handles of the doors were all still red, not green; the corridor smelled just the way I remembered it.

With the gun pointed at my head, Paul pushed me towards the door closest to the elevators and shoved a 'remover' into my hands. "This door's Cola's. Remove her tracker, get her out and do the same with the other ten doors to your left. Tell everyone to meet in front of the elevators. Are we clear?"

I nodded because I knew that was what she wanted to see.

Paul blinked a few times, gave me a look I didn't quite understand, then took a nervous breath. "This is how you open the doors," she said as she tapped Dr Clark's dismembered wrist onto the metal square on the door.

The metal square's red light turned green the moment the wrist touched it—a green I recognised from before.

Paul opened the door, shoved the male guard's dismembered hand into mine and pushed me in.

I expected a small room with black painted walls but what I saw was nothing like that.

I found myself in a high-tech laboratory of sorts. There was what looked like a laboratory set up on one side of the room—complete with sink and microscope—and a long desk with computers and eight monitors on the wall on the other side. The room smelled surgical, the way my pillow at Wonderdrug always smelled, and was perfectly silent. There were many boxes of latex gloves stacked to the ceiling right beside a door that was slightly further in.

"She's the one who can read your past. She can give you the answers you seek."

Could she? Really?

I stepped towards the monitors on the wall and took a good look at the four monitors that were switched on. All of them showed black and white images from cameras mounted on ceilings. One showed the very lab in which I stood, with me in it; another showed a small room with black painted walls and two doors—the room I had expected to see; the third showed an empty bathroom that looked exactly like the bathroom I used to use while living at Wonderdrug; and the fourth showed a ward exactly like the one I remembered living in! It had the same bar table, queen-sized bed, bookshelves, white chairs and all. The only object I didn't recognise was the person lying in the bed, fast asleep. She looked really small and thin.

A really short and skinny woman, perhaps?

I went to the black door next to the boxes of latex gloves and tapped the male guard's dismembered hand against its red-lit metal square. The blueness, hardness, coldness and fleshiness of the dismembered hand made my stomach churn so I averted my eyes and pushed the handle down without waiting to see if the red light turned green.

It must have turned green because the door opened without a hitch. I found myself back in the space I recognised—the small room with black painted walls. It even smelled familiar. Like paint.

I went towards the door at the end and unlocked it with the hand. The red light turned green. Easy.

I pushed in but froze at once. The woman on the bed was not what I had been expecting to see.

In the flesh, in colour, it was clear she wasn't even a woman at all. She was just a child. Seven or eight years of age, maybe? No older, definitely. She was in the same blue gown Paul and I used to wear.

What did the document in Dr Clark's laptop say her illness was? Schizophrenia? Was that why we were all on the same floor?

No, I decided. I was not going to deprive a child of medical treatment. I would have to go back out to the laboratory room and look for a way to get help. I turned and was about to open the door when I heard—

"Hi." The voice of a young girl. Right behind me.

I turned back and saw tiny black eyes, now open, staring at me. The child they belonged to sat up and reached for the pair of black-framed glasses resting on the side table next to her bed.

When the child put the glasses on, I saw Cola Lam for who she really was—an intelligent-looking Asian child with a bobbed haircut and lots of curiosity in her eyes. She looked like the sort of kid who could wow crowds at Math Olympiads. I hid the male guard's dismembered hand behind my back, for her sake, and struggled to think of a logical way to explain my presence in her ward.

"Are you trying to set me free?" the child asked before I could think of anything. She glanced at the 'remover' in my other hand with a look that suggested she knew what it was.

I didn't know what to say. *Yes, but no? I was supposed to but no, I don't think so?*

"Come here," she said gently, as if she were the adult and I were the child. "Let me look at you."

She sounded almost like a doctor, which felt very weird because her manner didn't match her tiny frame, high-pitched voice or cute facial proportions at all. Yet I felt compelled to go towards her. There was just something about her calm, unfazed demeanour that suggested she might just really have all the answers after all.

The moment I got to the side of her bed, the child put her hand on mine. Her hand was only about as wide as a tomato but her touch was firm. The dismembered hand I accidentally swung forward didn't appear to bother her at all.

She stared into space and suddenly said, "Ah!" As if she realised something. "Okay, now I get it," she added after some time.

"Get what?" I asked. My voice came out shaky. I

realised I was more afraid of her than she was of me.

The child swivelled around and lifted her blue gown so that her unclothed back faced me. "Just do it," she said. "Don't worry. You're not depriving me of anything. I want to get the hell out of here too."

I blinked hard and blinked again. Then I made myself take a few long, deep breaths—the sort I heard could calm you in times of anxiety.

"Paul isn't crazy, Lane. I really can tell you everything you want to know but first, you need to get my tracker out. Hurry, we don't have much time."

I couldn't believe what I was hearing. Her manner of speech was completely unlike a child's. Because her mouth wasn't visible to me in that moment, I couldn't decide if she had really spoken those words or if... psychosis was making me hear things.

"Just do it, Lane!" she said. Just like Paul would have.

I ran my fingers down her tiny, warm body and did to her what I had once done to Paul. The tiny blood-covered chip came out of her back as easily as Paul's had done before. Seeing it brought on a sense of déjà vu. I couldn't help but remember Paul and I holding similar chips in that stairwell I jumped from.

The child replaced her gown and turned around as if she knew the tracker was out. She hadn't even twitched. "Somebody did push you," she told me. "The woman with blonde hair and red lips? That really happened." The child's lips moved this time. I saw them move myself.

I gulped. "Who is that woman? Why did she push me?"

"I don't know. I don't know the people you do, but I do know you didn't kill Uncle Tim or your parents. You were fast asleep both times."

My heart jumped. "I was?"

"Yes. You were," she said with the conviction of a professor confirming a scientific fact. "A blue woman did it. Both times. She even left you a message and a phone number. Said you are to find a way to call her if you ever end up stuck at Wonderdrug." The child read out the phone number. It was local, a New York number, but not one I recognised.

"When did she say that?" I had no idea what a 'blue woman' meant. *A woman who was sad? Or a woman who was physically blue?* I had no clue.

"She sat on your bed and spoke to you before she gassed your parents and injected you with the serum that wiped your memories. She came to check on you the night she killed Uncle Tim too. I think she cares about you."

What in the hell? Why would someone who cared murder my relatives? "Who is she?"

"I don't know. I could probably tell you if we had more time but we don't."

The door that led to the outside suddenly slammed open. Paul barged in with her hand on the handle. "We have to go! The alarm just went off! Come on!"

Paul propped one of the white armchairs against the door to keep it open then vanished as suddenly as she had come. The child jumped off the bed and ran after Paul as if she knew exactly what was going on. I ran after the child because I didn't know what else to do. I couldn't hear any siren but Paul had definitely been in a panic. *What did that mean?*

Once we got out to the corridor where the elevators were, I heard the alarm Paul had been shouting about at last. It was deafening and incessant, blaring like sirens I only ever heard in war movies during scenes involving air raids. I stopped following the child and stared because the corridor was now full of women in blue gowns. They all looked as bewildered as I felt. There were only two men amongst them—one old, one young.

"Dad?" the younger male was saying to the older one. "You've been here the whole time?"

"Dustin? Oh my goodness, Dustin, you're sick too?"

"Why didn't you just tell us you were in a hospital, Dad? All this time we thought you were just being a jerk!"

"What do you mean? I wrote your mother and you so many emails, none of which either of you replied!"

"You must have gotten the addresses wrong. We never got them!"

"Everybody, listen up!" Paul suddenly shouted. She was right in front of the elevators, holding one of them—'Elevator A', according to her sketches—open. "Get in! We're going to make a run for it!"

She looked... scared. I had never seen Paul scared before so I could tell 'a run' definitely hadn't been part of her plans. Some of the patients dashed past me and went towards her as if they trusted her—the child was one of them—but many others stared at her with that same dazed look I believe I had on as well.

"Lane! Come on!" I heard Paul say. Her eyes were wide and frantic like a mad person's when I caught sight of her; her cool and controlled manner completely gone. She was trying to get the patients within the elevator to move further in but her eyes kept turning towards me. "Come on, Lane, move!"

I didn't move. I didn't want to. The chaos of the moment was all too much for me to take. I didn't know what to expect or what I wanted out of all this. The child's words had shaken my understanding of reality all over again and I didn't like how I was feeling. I had enough of confusing contradictions; enough of not knowing, rethinking and running all the time. All I wanted at that point was stability and inner peace—exactly what I had at Wonderdrug before Paul came into my life and ruined everything! I also wanted to drop the disgusting dismembered hand I was still holding on to but, for some reason, couldn't relax my fingers enough to let go.

A chime sounded from the other elevator—'Elevator B'. The number '16' appeared on its indicator and its chrome doors began to open.

"Lane, hurry! Now!" I heard Paul shout.

I didn't move. It was too late, I knew. I'd just be

running into the arms of the person or persons coming out of the other elevator. I stood where I was, relieved that the choice had been made by somebody other than Paul for a change.

Five armed security guards barged out of 'Elevator B' the moment the doors opened. Four of them had rifles which they immediately used to shoot down the patients running towards 'Elevator A'.

The only one of them without a rifle was also the only one of them without a right hand. He had a blood-soaked jacket wrapped around his stump, blood all over his forehead, pale lips and eyes fixed on the dismembered hand in mine.

When his eyes climbed upwards and met mine, I saw nothing but hate and fury.

"Eleven o'clock, P-eight-seven!" He pointed a finger at me with the hand he had. "Get her!"

The armed security guard closest to him turned his rifle towards me and I felt a sharp, painful sensation in my shoulder immediately after.

My legs lost strength and I felt myself melting into the ground, along with the other patients around me.

My vision became a blur, first of blue, then of black.

I found myself thinking that Paul had been right about the male guard without a hand. Whether she had been right about everything else, I couldn't say, but with regards to the nature of the guard without a hand, she had been so right.

I didn't understand what people were really like indeed.

CHAPTER 24
DATE UNKNOWN

The next time I opened my eyes, I found myself on the back of a man. His stark white t-shirt smelled unwashed and fresh-out-of-the-store but his head—full of thick, light brown curls—smelled like a mix of male sweat and shit.

I recognised the growl overhead and the darkness of our surroundings shortly after. *Of course.* We were back in the stinky underground maze of sewage tunnels. Every vagabond's favourite mode of transportation.

What the hell happened? Hadn't I passed out just feet away from my old ward? Why was I not back at the Wonderdrug Psychiatric Centre yet?

The man I was on grunted and pushed me higher up on his back. He turned his head and strained his neck to look at me. "You awake? Everything okay?"

His finely chiselled profile was familiar—I had seen it at the Wonderdrug Psychiatric Centre during the chaos along the corridor. The man I was on was one of the two men who had been present. The younger one. Just no longer in that blue gown. He wasn't ugly and had I been into men, I probably would have found being on his back quite the treat. "I'm not sure," I said. My voice came out fine.

A woman I didn't know, with bangs and straight

blonde hair just above her shoulders, ran up to walk alongside us. She was in grey jeans and a black long-sleeved shirt—an outfit eighty percent of women in New York would wear—and had on a pair of black galoshes that came to her knees. She was possibly about my age, or just a little younger, and she smiled at me but all I did in return was stare at her with my mouth wide open.

The woman I didn't know looked exactly like my mother. She had the same platinum colour of hair, same rich blue eyes, same large lips, same cleft chin, same high forehead.

"Hey," she said to me.

I frowned. No matter how I looked at her, she wouldn't stop looking like my mother. "Hey," I replied.

The man I was on stopped walking in that moment. I turned back to the front and realised it was because the woman in front of him had stopped walking as well.

It was Paul. Or Paula. Just up ahead. In black galoshes too, wearing an outfit I didn't recognise, with a new backpack on her back, holding a torch. She had her back to us and didn't bother turning fully around. All she did was glance at me briefly from the corner of her eye before she resumed her march forward like a woman in a hurry.

She looked just as capable as she did the first time I saw her move through the sewers, way before I realised she had no qualms killing people, but was a tad tired and glum this time. She moved the way a person who had been through a life full of shit would move. Irritably. There was no gun in her hands. Not anymore.

Both the man I was on and the woman who resembled my mother resumed following her, as if there was an unspoken rule that they should.

"What happened?" I asked. I had to know.

"Paul offered us a chance at freedom and fun," the man I was on said breathlessly. "She dragged you out too. I don't know how."

"It was pretty chaotic," 'my mother' added.

Why get me out when I had screwed up her plans big time? What was this? Entrapment? Was I a prisoner of war now? "Where's your dad and everybody else?" I asked the man I was on.

"He didn't make it. None of the others did." I felt him sigh under me and push me higher up on his back again.

"What day is it? What year?"

The shoulders under my arms shrugged and 'my mother' made the same gesture.

I stared at her and couldn't peel my eyes away.

She really did look like my mother. Just, maybe, a more child-like version of her. What my mother might have looked like before she had me.

"What's your name?" I had to ask. My mother's name had been Leona.

"Dustin," the man I was on said. "Are you ready to walk? I don't know how much more of this I can take."

I laughed, politely, but stayed right where I was. I had touched enough of that greenish-brownish water to know I was better off never touching it again. Not if I had a choice. "Sorry, still a little dizzy," I said, even though I wasn't in the least dizzy at all.

'My mother' laughed along, in a sweet-and-shy-little-girl way. "I'm Gemma," she said and looked away like she was embarrassed by her own name.

Gemma. Not Leona. "Do you have any children?"

My question startled her. "No. Of course not," she replied. "I... I've never even been in love, to be honest. I've been sick my whole life, since I was a baby, so I never actually left the Wonderdrug Psychiatric Centre at all."

I blinked hard and tried to remind myself we were likely not related but no matter how I tried, her face—innocent and fresh like some sweet young thing—remained exactly like a young version of the blonde woman I knew to be my mother.

"Hey, hold up!" the man I was on suddenly shouted.

He jerked me upwards and began to run and I soon realised it was because Paul was no longer in front of us.

She had run off, deep into the darkness—
—and left the three of us to fend for ourselves.

CHAPTER 25
DATE UNKNOWN

Hours later, when light appeared through the holes in the sewers' ventilation grates, I caught up with Paul. At last.

I found her next to a moss-covered ladder, with her back against a damp brick wall and a cigarette between her lips. She had been deep in thought—wearing an expression that spoke volumes of ennui—until she noticed me.

The moment our eyes met, I kicked my heels up in the slush and ran towards her. When I could reach her cigarette, I snatched it out of her mouth and tossed it into the slime that came up to my knees and left my jeans soggy. The half-smoked cigarette bobbed on the surface for two seconds before vanishing from sight, likely never to be seen ever again.

"What the hell do you want of us?" I shouted as I stared right into her eyes. Dustin said Paul's gun—empty of bullets—had gone into a dumpster along with her old backpack and old clothes so I was no longer afraid of her killing me with it. I even dared let the fear, apprehension and uncertainty that had been brewing within me the whole time in the sewers explode in the form of rage. "Why in fuck's name do you keep dragging me away from medical care?! What the fuck do you want of me?"

Paul stared back for a moment but averted her eyes and

crossed her arms shortly after. "Wonderdrug is *not* medical care. I've told you a thousand times, why won't you just get it?"

"Because it sounds ridiculous, Paul! Because your words don't match the Wonderdrug documents you showed me!"

Paul didn't argue. She simply turned her eyes onto the brick walls all around us and exhaled an unnaturally long, tired sigh. "What did you do in Cola's room? Did you talk to her?"

"Is that why you dragged me out? Because I talked to Cola? Because I didn't open the rest of your doors?"

She sniggered but didn't look at me. "No, it's not, believe it or not." She sighed again. "What did Cola say?"

"She told me I'm not a murderer, believe it or not. I'm not like you."

"So CRO got it wrong?" Paul began nodding like one of those noddy table-top dolls. "CRO gets things wrong, I should have known." She laughed to herself, rolled her eyes and shook her head. Then she turned back to me.

"Let me guess, you think I'm a monster?"

I frowned. Yes, I did think of her as a monster, but I didn't get the look she now wore on her face. There was a twinge of sourness all over her downturned mouth and she wouldn't meet my eyes. I had no idea what that look meant.

"I made a mistake, okay? I thought if I actually did something incredible you would just…" She sighed. "I didn't think it would do the exact opposite and make you… just…"

What? "Just spit it, Paul. What is it you want? What are we doing, really?"

She inhaled a deep breath of air and said, "I don't know."

I couldn't stop my mouth from falling open. "You don't—? After all that we did—you did—you don't… *know?*"

"My plan was to get a bunch of curiosities out so we could all collectively share the benefits of our different advantages. I never expected to end up with two *normal* human beings so excuse me if I don't know what to do with them just yet!"

"What the hell does that mean?"

"Those two made it out only because they were low priority! The guards were aiming for the ones with advantages first. You, me, Cola, all the other women. Those two?" She laughed dismissively. "Men don't ever have advantages and that blonde girl…" She raised her palms towards the ceiling, shook her head and sighed like a woman disappointed. "I failed, okay? I failed and I suck and I've since realised I'm just like everyone else in that I've no clue what I'm really doing. At all!"

I didn't get it. "Gemma told me she's been sick her whole life so she can't be all that normal."

"She is normal. Her grandmother, Dustin's grandmother, they were the ones who had advantages. They were the real curiosities! Get it? No, you probably don't get it! I could tell you all the secrets of the universe and you'd still just think I was crazy, wouldn't you? All because a doctor *told you* I was."

I noticed the flicker of pain in Paul's eyes as she spoke with her jaw clenched but didn't know how to reply because she wasn't wrong. I did still think she was crazy. Hell, I believed I was crazy too. I really thought all of us—Dustin and Gemma included—needed medical attention urgently.

"Everything okay?"

Paul looked up and behind me right away. I turned and saw Dustin and Gemma standing in the distance, staring at us.

Neither of them looked like they dared come any closer.

"Yeah," Paul said and took five steps away from me as if we had been doing something we shouldn't have. Her face changed; the hurt on her face turned into that look of confidence and nonchalance she always wore.

"Why did you run?" Dustin added.

"I needed the exercise," Paul said. She shrugged. "Besides, the tunnel was straight the whole way through. I knew you guys would catch up with me. Eventually."

Both Dustin and Gemma nodded but didn't look entirely convinced.

"Anyway, the safe house is just up this ladder," Paul said to them. She then turned to me. "Everyone coming?" Her eyes were hard and she looked like she didn't care either way.

"Yeah," I said, after a bout of quick thinking. I had no idea how else I was going to get out of the sewers and the long walk we had just done had tired me out thoroughly. I would go with Paul and friends to get some rest and food first, I decided, since I didn't have any money on me. Once I felt better, I would walk and find my way back to the Wonderdrug Psychiatric Centre. That was the plan. *My* plan.

I was so done following other people's plans.

Paul's mouth smiled but her eyes didn't. She refused to look at me for a long time after that.

The 'safe house' was right in front of the manhole we emerged from, on an isolated street, behind a large padlocked metal gate with the words, 'No Trespassing', 'Danger!', 'Caution!', 'Safety Equipment Required Beyond This Point' plastered, on metal boards, all over it.

"A construction site?" Dustin said as if disappointed. He gazed up at the possibly thirty-storey cement skeleton behind the gates and frowned. His hand went over his eyes so I couldn't tell if blinding sunlight or displeasure was the real reason he kept on frowning.

Gemma, on the other hand, gaped like she had just entered an amusement park. Her eyes grew large with interest and she looked happiest of us all.

"This would have been a state-of-the-art condominium with one of the best views in New York had its owners not committed fraud," Paul said as she unlocked the padlock of the metal gate with a key she removed from the pocket of her jeans—*the* key she had stolen from a workman at a subway station during rush hour, I realised. "Their bank accounts are frozen so construction can only resume when their trial ends—next year. You won't find another home in Manhattan with as much space and privacy as this one, I'm telling you."

The large metal gate squeaked open without any issues. Dustin kept his mouth shut when Paul invited us all to step in and watched sullenly as Paul closed and locked the gate behind us. We then followed her into the bellows of the skeletal structure that was a mix of brick, cement and steel set upon a vast patch of grassless, muddy sand.

I felt tiny and insignificant in contrast to the structure's massive stature as we went down a flight of cement stairs into the basement and I worried, many times, about the warnings on the gate. We were 'Trespassing'! The place was Dangerous and required 'Caution'! We didn't have 'Safety Equipment' or know the first thing about keeping safe at a construction site! We could easily step on all the wrong surfaces or touch all the wrong pillars and die, I suspected. I didn't feel at all safe whilst at Paul's 'safe house' this time.

There was almost no light down in the basement. Paul was the only one of us with a torch and her torch's light only covered the area right in front of her. I could see the clutter of dust particles it illuminated—and could feel them entering my nostrils, smelling a lot like plaster—but not much else. The spaces next to us and behind us remained impossible to see. The darkness made my skin tingle. I got the feeling it might be hiding ghosts and humans, all with bad intentions.

The deeper we went, the darker the basement became.

Paul was right about the building being private alright. The complex layout of walls was perfect for a long game of hide-and-seek. I lit the plastic lighter I found in the pocket of my jeans but its light didn't make the room any brighter. If anything, my plastic lighter's light made the room more creepy than before. Its flickering orange flame cast moving shadows across the walls and heightened all my worries regarding the presence of malevolent spirits.

"So much for a view," Dustin said, the displeasure on his face apparent, even in the darkness.

I got what he meant. The basement we were at had nothing on the clean and cosy Wonderdrug Psychiatric Centre, that was for sure.

"The view is upstairs. Stunning but deadly," Paul said. "I don't recommend sleeping there but it's really your choice. That's what freedom's all about, isn't it?"

Dustin said nothing in response.

Paul took a piece of white chalk out from the pocket of her backpack and drew a long line down a wall sitting in the middle of nowhere. "We'll sleep behind this wall tonight. Dustin, you're coming with me. We need to get candles, food, water and bedding for tonight. Lane, I need you to comb the whole site with Gemma, make sure no stragglers are with us. We'll meet at this very spot in three hours."

"Whatever," Dustin mumbled.

My stomach growled and felt as if it were dissolving under the acidity of the fluids that churned within it so I didn't say no either.

"What are stragglers?" Gemma asked, shortly after we split from the other two and made our way through the rest of the unfinished basement with Paul's torch in my hand.

"They're like homeless people," I replied as I shined the torch from left to right then back again.

No rooms, no doors, no locks; just raw, incomplete walls and absolute quiet; nothing to protect you from being seen or touched by the unknown. My skin pickled and unease rippled through my muscles. It reminded me of the way I sometimes felt when lying on Aunt Mary's couch back when Uncle Tim was still alive and home.

"Why would anyone be homeless?"

Why? I stopped walking forward and turned the torch onto Gemma instead. She looked calm. Way calmer than me. As if we were simply walking through a sunny, climate-controlled museum and not a filthy, stuffy, hazardous incomplete building.

"How old are you?"

"Thirty."

Just three years younger than me? She didn't look it; she looked way younger. More like a teenager who just hit puberty than anything else. Was it her colouring or the wide-eyed innocent stare she always had on that made her look that way? Or was it the high-pitched angelic tone of her voice or the fact that she was half a head shorter than I was? I couldn't quite put my finger on it. "You're thirty and you don't understand why homelessness happens?"

She shook her head and made her fluffy blonde hair flap around like maize in the wind. The serious look in those babyish eyes of hers convinced me, once again, that she wasn't just putting on a dumb blonde act of sorts.

I regarded her with narrowed eyes. "What did you use to do at Wonderdrug then? If you were there all your life you must have done… something?"

"Oh yeah, of course. I did tests all the time. Different tests. All over my body."

"You mean doctors did tests on you?"

"Yes, well, doctor actually. I only have one. Dr James." She smiled shyly then shrugged. "I have a rare brain disease which makes me mutilate myself in my sleep. There's no cure for it right now so Dr James has been working on coming up with one, just for me. That's why he does all those tests. Just the way things are for me."

Wait a minute... Coincidence? Or family? "Where are your parents?"

"Dead. My father died in a traffic accident and my mother died of the brain disease I inherited. That's why I have to live in a hospital. I would die like her if I didn't get meds regularly."

"So being out here could kill you?"

"Yeah, but I really wanted a taste of life on the outside, you know? All those movies and games made it seem like so much fun. I know I'll end up back in hospital once I start self-mutilating again, but for now, while there're still traces of meds in my body, why not?"

"Wait, so you're saying you mutilate yourself and… your wounds heal?"

"Yeah."

"Very quickly?"

"Uh-huh."

I took a deep breath to calm myself as excitement shot through my whole being. *My mother's face, self-mutilation in sleep and* also *quick healing wounds?* What were the odds of all that happening if we weren't related in any way? *Next to impossible.* I realised Gemma could just be a… sister I had never known of? Or a relative? A relative my other relatives never talked about? "Can I see?" I asked. "The parts of your body that have healed?"

"Sure." Gemma pulled up her sleeve and showed me her arm. "They're everywhere. I spare only my neck and face for some reason."

I frowned when I saw her arm and had to lift it towards my eyes to be sure I was really seeing what I thought I was.

It seemed real alright; the raised brown patches, in all sorts of shapes and sizes all over her arm, never changed or vanished no matter how I blinked and tried to see otherwise. Some patches were shinier than others, some were darker, but none of them looked like anything I had ever seen in my life. From afar, Gemma's arm looked more like that of a spotted animal's than that of a human being's.

"Were you born with these?"

"No, these are the parts that healed. Scars, from wounds I inflicted on myself."

Scars? I shined the torch right at them for a better look and decided I didn't have any scars on my body. Not on my palm where I had once made two large, deep strokes, not where I had ever seen broken bones, torn flesh or bullet holes. "Do you mind showing me the rest of your body?"

"No, I don't mind at all." She unbuttoned the lower buttons of her black shirt and showed me her stomach. "Dr James makes me show him my body all the time. I'm kinda used to it."

It was me who wasn't used to the way her stomach looked. There were strange brown holes and raised bits of flesh everywhere, like Play Doh that had been kneaded carelessly in an uncontrolled manner and hadn't been smoothed out. On top of that, some parts were coarse in texture while others were inhumanly smooth. It all looked very odd, like one big confusing mess of abnormal flesh. I felt myself gulping but kept my face straight out of politeness. "Does it hurt?"

She shook her head. "Not now but it did when the injuries were fresh. The burns were the worst."

"Can I see those too?"

"Up here." She unbuttoned her shirt all the way up to her neck and showed me the raised clump of pinkish flesh clinging on to the inner side of her right breast. It was different from the brown patches on her stomach and not just in colour. It was much thicker and stringier, like a blob of pink goo had grown over her original skin.

I bent down for a closer look and felt myself shudder against my will. There was just something about the whole abnormality of Gemma's flesh that made me awfully uneasy. Nervous too.

"Paul," Gemma suddenly said.

I swivelled around at once and shined the torch in the direction of Gemma's gaze.

I saw Paul standing about ten feet away from us. She had something yellow in her hand and looked downright furious. The shoot-a-doctor-in-the-head extent of furious. "Chalk," she said, as if with restraint. "Mark an 'X' if you get into trouble so Dustin and I will know not to wait around for you."

She tossed the yellow chalk at us like it were an egg she wanted to pelt us with and it landed right at my feet.

"Just so you know, the scaffolding around here is not stable so feel free to step around recklessly if you're feeling suicidal. That's all I came to say." She turned and went round the corner without another word.

Just like that, she was gone. Again.

"Why is she always so angry all the time?" Gemma asked.

I stared at the yellow chalk on the floor then at the breasts Gemma continued to leave exposed and realised I might just have figured out why.

There were no stragglers in the basement nor anywhere else within the construction site. We covered all twenty-five unfinished floors in exactly three hours and went back down to the basement to sit and wait behind the wall with a line of chalk down its middle. Gemma fell asleep on my shoulder shortly after but I couldn't rest, despite being as tired as she. My mind spun with questions and theories while my body created a mess of cigarette butts on the concrete floor around me.

In the two hours or so that followed, I tried hard to think back on everything that occurred after I woke up from the coma caused by the falling incident. I found myself making a few startling conclusions. One: Every single person I had spent a great deal of time around since—Dr Clark, Paul and Arden Villeneuve—lied in some way or another. Two: Their versions of the truth often contradicted each other's so Three: None of anyone's proclamations of the truth could be taken at face value. Four: Fortune cookies couldn't be relied upon either—I had eaten nothing but Chinese food in the hours leading up to Dr Clark's murder and it hadn't done shit for my health or sanity—so Five: Since nobody and nothing could be trusted to give me the truth wholesale, I was on my own in figuring everything out.

I flicked the only lighter I possessed on and off till it ran out of fuel and decided all I really needed to do was choose who I wanted to believe. Paul, Cola, flying objects and vanishing injuries represented one version of reality while Dr Clark, Arden Villeneuve, the dismembered security guard and Gemma represented another. Did I want to be Lane, the lucky and free curiosity or Blaine, the schizophrenic, depressive, self-mutilating patient of the Wonderdrug Psychiatric Centre? I had chosen to be Lane once before and it led to death and injuries mere days after. If I chose to be Blaine this time—chose to accept that Paul simply made up a ton of bizarre theories and was very dangerous—would that eventually lead to a better, safer life overall?

And on the topic of Paul... I didn't get why she was behaving like a jilted lover now when she herself turned me down—twice—when I did—before I got to see her for the sort of person she really was—want a romance with her. *What the hell was up with that?*

Three hours after our supposed meeting time, Paul and Dustin appeared with their backpacks and hands full of all sorts of store-bought survival items and grins on their faces. Paul's grin was huge and genuine-looking. Dustin's not so much. He grinned the way one would only grin in the presence of a boss or a customer—too consistently happy to be humanly possible. I suspected the four hefty cartons of mineral water bottles in his arms might have had something to do with it. Paul dropped her grin the moment she caught sight of Gemma on my shoulder and afterwards refused to look in the direction of my face ever again.

"Did you find anything?" she asked, as if I were her employee and it were my obligation to answer whatever she asked, whenever she asked. Dustin dumped both the four cartons and his swollen backpack onto the floor and came over to join Gemma and I in the exact same position we were sitting in—butt on the ground, knees up, back and head against the wall.

Only when he was close did I notice the sweat trickling down the sides of his face, his pale lips and the difficulty he was having with catching his breath. He looked as if he had been put through a strenuous activity his metrosexual body had been in no way prepared for. "No, nobody's here," I said to Paul. "Why are you so late?"

Gemma lifted her head from my numb shoulder and rubbed sleep out of her eyes. "You're back," she said.

Paul didn't look at her, nor did she answer my question. She began removing cans of hotdogs, sardines and tuna from her backpack and stacked them against the wall opposite us. "Come on, unpack the stuff," she said to Dustin. "What are you waiting for?"

He groaned but got up and did as she said anyway, for reasons I didn't understand. Four bundled sleeping bags came out of the backpack he had thrown onto the floor. He threw them at Gemma and I and barked at us to lay them out in a manner that was not entirely polite.

Gemma did as he said. I, on the other hand, ignored him and went right next to Paul and looked her right in the eyes. "Hey, you got a minute?"

She turned her back to me and walked away with a camping lamp, a can of hotdogs and a packet of hotdog buns in her hands. "Dustin, get the picnic mat," she said. She set her items down on the empty space behind the sleeping bags Gemma was diligently unwrapping then switched the camping lamp on. Warm orange light flooded the area around us and highlighted the unhealthy levels of dust hovering in the air.

With the light, I could see Dustin's eyes better and it became obvious they were dead and tired. He laid out the picnic mat in front of Paul with grunts that made lying out a picnic mat seem like the most strenuous activity in the world, but his face remained stoic, the way hardened individuals kept theirs when faced with adversity.

Dinner was canned hotdogs stuffed in supermarket-bought buns. They tasted like plaster and had the texture of jelly clumps surrounded by dry, rough cloth—a far cry from the freshly-grilled gourmet sausages the Wonderdrug Psychiatric Centre sometimes served with cheese, sour cream and fried chopped garlic along with chips or fries.

I tried to suggest we go out for breakfast the next morning—since dinner felt so profoundly unsatisfying after the long, desperate wait for it—and maybe look into getting a hotel room to bathe in but Paul cut me off immediately.

"We no longer have those options," she told me with hard, cold eyes. "Thanks to your movie star lover's exposé of our former living habits."

She looked away, her body language hostile, and said nothing more after that so I didn't either.

I ate the plaster dogs anyway, with hands that were muddy with sewage and sweat and a face that was as joyless as it was blank.

Nobody spoke nor did anyone pass anybody else any food. There was no happy laughter, no sharing of relief, nothing. All four of us simply shoved pale buns through our mouths like it were a repetitive task we had no choice but to do—and I guess it probably was.

By the time my share of dinner had been consumed and a sharp, persistent pain replaced the gnawing, gaping ache that had been in my stomach all day, I found myself questioning the true value of freedom.

What was the point of freedom if all it did was make your life way harder than it had to be?

I couldn't come up with any good answer to that.

CHAPTER 26
DATE UNKNOWN

I slept like a log, despite the conditions, and woke up right in time for breakfast—a single box of muesli bars on our picnic mat, right in the middle of Dustin and Paul who were already eating theirs in silence.

I never liked muesli bars. I always thought they tasted like perfumed cardboard and would have chosen to go without had I not had the long trek back to Wonderdrug—or even the nearest police station, if I could find one—ahead of me. But since I did, I took two muesli bars for myself. One to eat and one for the road, in case the road turned out to be one helluva long road.

Paul watched me like a hawk as I took the two bars from the four in the box. Neither she nor Dustin said a word to me, nor did they look particularly happy, so I mumbled something about getting fresh air and headed on up to the second floor where there would be wind, sun, a view and reprieve from awkward energy.

Gemma, who had woken up last, came after me with one of the two remaining bars of muesli. I didn't want her to join me—I didn't want to have to answer her weird questions about the most banal matters of life or feel like I was having breakfast with my dead mother—but said okay because I could tell, from the desperation in her smile, she didn't want to be left alone with the sullen-faced two either.

We climbed up a table-sized stack of loose bricks right next to the edge of the second floor and angled ourselves towards the view of ant-sized cars whizzing between skyscrapers in the distance.

"I think Paul and Dustin had sex last night," Gemma said as she ripped open her packet of muesli.

I nearly choked on the muesli I had only just shoved into my mouth and had to wipe away the bits that came flying out when I coughed. "Why do you say that?"

"They were naked and Dustin was doing that rocking thing men do when they have sex in the movies. He was making those sorts of sounds too."

Right next to us while we slept? And I never woke up? I found myself giggling in amusement as an image of them both in the situation Gemma described came to mind.

"Have you ever… tried sex yourself?"

I stopped giggling to stare at Gemma with my mouth open. "Are you kidding? In this city, everyone past puberty would have had sex *at least* twice before the age of sixteen."

Gemma dropped the muesli bar from her mouth and her expression fell. "Oh."

My heart dropped along with her face. "Sorry. I didn't—"

"No, it's okay, you just don't know very well what it was like for me just like how I don't know very well what it was like for you, and probably everybody else. It's normal."

"Right."

She shrugged and gazed out at the horizon as she resumed eating her bar of muesli. "I'm still glad I got the chance to see them do it though," she said in between bites, while grinning shyly. "And all this and the sewers, it's… great. I can't believe I'm actually here." She beamed and looked as happy as a child on vacation, without a care in the world.

No facade, no lies, no hard feelings, no grudges, no

worries, no regrets, that was how Gemma took on the world, I realised. Watching her made me wonder if not knowing might be the true secret to perpetual happiness. After all, if you didn't know how cruel the world really was, you would feel safe and at peace and happy-ish the whole time, wouldn't you? Maybe ignorance was all each and every one of us really needed?

"Hey Gemma, the last muesli in the box is for you."

Paul's voice. I turned and saw her standing behind us.

She had her eyes on Gemma and she was smiling. In a friendly way.

Gemma smiled back in that sweet way she always smiled and looked a little bashful. "No, I'm fine, thank you."

"I want you to have it," Paul said.

"No, it's okay, I'm not—"

"Just go. Take it. Eat it if you want, hold it if you don't, I need to talk to Lane." Paul didn't sound unkind but she did sound firm.

Gemma looked at me then at Paul and hopped off the stack of bricks like a very obedient child.

Once Gemma had gone down the stairs, Paul turned to me. Her eyes met mine and I think I saw her cheeks go red. "May I sit?"

I shrugged then nodded and quickly finished up the last of my muesli while she took Gemma's place on the bricks, just in case I would need to run or fight at short notice. I also made sure my other bar of muesli was snugly tucked into the pocket of my jeans and not in any danger of falling out during dramatic movements.

"Do you like her?" Paul asked once she had gotten comfortable.

"Gemma?" I turned to face Paul and saw that her cheeks were now redder than ever. "Only about as much as I would like an elderly relative. She looks exactly like my dead mom. That makes liking her sort of... weird, don't you think?"

Paul laughed and licked her lips and seemed to be trying to say something but didn't.

"She does remind me of the old you though," I added when the pause between us got too long for comfort. "The you I played Snakes and Ladders with?" *The you who didn't go around killing people.*

Paul laughed again. Nervously. "Gemma and I are total opposites. And neither are you related to her, in case you're wondering."

I frowned a little and eyed her with suspicion. "How would you know?"

"CRO tested your DNA against hers when you first got in because they thought you might have come from the same lineage too. Gemma's grandmother had superhuman regenerative abilities, you see. She was Latina with olive skin, dark hair and dark eyes, just like you, so naturally they thought there might be something there, but, there wasn't. The DNA test was 100% negative. No relation whatsoever. Not even remotely."

I frowned more. "I don't understand what you're saying."

"I'm saying you and Gemma may have been switched at birth. If Gemma looks like your mom, it could be because she *is* your mom's kid and you could very well be that Latina's grand-daughter. That would explain everything, wouldn't it?"

It would, but... only if CRO and the DNA test actually did exist. "How do you switch babies without anyone knowing though? Two babies without the same hair or eye colour on top of that."

"I don't know. But that doesn't mean there aren't people out there who do, right?"

Right, but.. only if CRO and the DNA test actually did exist. Unfortunately, there was no way I was going to be able to know for sure. I decided to remove the frown from my face and change the topic before Paul got enraged again or something. "Is that all you wanted to talk to me about?" I asked.

Paul kept her eyes on the view, took in a deep breath and said, "No." She turned her face to mine and I saw sadness in her eyes, clear as day. "What I wanted to say... is... I love you, Lane. I don't want you to go."

What? My heart skipped a beat and I found myself nervous and struggling to breathe normally. I frowned again. "Why? I'm not the type of person you're looking for, plus, you slept with Dustin. Just last night!"

"I did. And yes you're really not the type I want to love but... I've since learned it's not up to me." She swallowed hard and stared right at me, her eyes large and sad, her pupils completely dilated. She looked... scared; desperate for my approval; as if she really was in love with me.

"Hey, can we go?"

Paul and I pulled our bodies away from each other and swivelled around at once.

It was Dustin, standing by the stairs behind us, with his eyes right on us. He looked irritable and bored—the way some of my former lovers sometimes looked when I talked to them about my struggles regarding work and money. "It's late."

"Give me a minute," Paul said. The vulnerability she had on her face just seconds ago vanished and all that was in its place was a confident lack of emotion.

"I can go on my own, you know. Just give me the money and the key to the gate, or give me the money and let me out."

"No. Just wait downstairs. I'll come when I'm done."

"No. We have to go now." Dustin crossed his arms and refused to budge. "We won't have time to get all the shit you want before the sky turns dark otherwise. I say we're going now." He kept his eyes on her and never once looked away.

"Fucking bad timing always," I heard Paul mumble under her breath. She sighed and turned to me, her eyes wild and shiny but otherwise expressionless. "Can we continue this tonight? Please? Can you promise to stay in the basement and not go anywhere?"

I nodded because I knew that was the best and easiest way to answer, even though I wasn't sure if that was what I was going to do. I didn't know what to make of what Paul said. My heart had begun pounding furiously but I couldn't tell if it was because I was happy about what she said or just afraid she was lying in order to keep me with her.

"We don't have all day," Dustin shouted irritably from behind.

"I mean everything I said," Paul said to me. Firmly. She held her eyes on mine for a good few seconds before taking a long deep breath and jumping off the stack of bricks.

She never looked back after that.

It was me who watched her go.

With electrified nerves and a heart that felt as if it were going to beat through the bones that kept it in.

"Lane, wake up," I heard Gemma say hours later. "Soldiers are here."

Soldiers? I opened my eyes and saw the silhouette of a woman peering down at me, shaking me.

The silhouette became Gemma when my eyes adjusted to the blinding light behind her. Gemma with her eyes wide and afraid.

I sat up and looked around at once.

I was still on the stack of bricks I had been sitting on since morning. Nobody but Gemma was on the second floor of the construction site with me. The environment was much brighter and hotter than I remembered it to be though.

"They're in the basement," Gemma whispered. "Ten or twenty of them. I saw them come in through the gate. They went right for the basement. They have guns like the ones the guards at Wonderdrug had the day we escaped."

Rifles? That didn't sound good at all. I looked at the sky around us and decided it was probably mid-day.

Only mid-day. We hadn't even had lunch yet!

Paul told Gemma we could each have a can of tuna for lunch which meant she wasn't going to be back anytime soon; we were on our own with the soldiers! *Was that a good thing or a bad thing?* Would they take us back to Wonderdrug if I told them we needed help or would they just jail us for trespassing right away, I wondered.

"How are we going to get away?" Gemma asked.

I didn't know. But that wasn't my concern at that point. The more pressing question was... *Did I want to get away?* I really should have figured it out earlier, before I gave in to sleep, I realised.

There was no place to hide on the second floor or any of the floors above; no walls, no rooms, just wide open empty spaces with thick cement pillars running through the slabs of cement that made the floors. If the soldiers were already in the basement, they likely had the gate—our only route of escape—blocked as well, which meant the choice of whether to stay or go had already been decided for us. Perhaps a more constructive use of time would be to think of how we were going to convince the soldiers to send us back to the Wonderdrug Psychiatric Centre without legal prosecution?

"Why don't we try jumping over the fence from the third floor," Gemma suddenly said, to my surprise. There was seriousness and determination all over her face—something I never thought I'd ever see. "It's not all that far away, right? Come on, let's give it a try."

Before I could decide whether or not to agree, Gemma was already climbing the cement stairs that led to the third floor two at a time, on the tips of her toes. She seemed way more desperate to get away than I was and I didn't understand why. How was it that the Wonderdrug Psychiatric Centre, with all its security and comforts, could be less appealing to her than living in a dusty construction site?

The third floor was much higher and windier than I remembered it to be but Gemma hadn't been wrong.

At one corner, the slab of cement that was the floor stuck out more than it did anywhere else and was really close to the wooden, barb wired fence surrounding our construction site. The gap between that part of the floor and the fence was approximately seven feet wide—not impossible to cross—but the drop after the fence certainly wasn't for the faint of heart. Down below, there was a hard concrete pavement.

Bones would be broken if we fell on that, for sure. Not a problem for me if the whole CRO and superhuman regenerative abilities thing was real, but also possible death and permanent disability for me if it wasn't. I *could be* screwed if we jumped and Gemma *would be* screwed no matter what.

"Why don't we just explain our situation?" I said to her as we stood by the edge analysing the impossible. "Maybe they'll be sympathetic? I mean we *are* patients, right? Most people treat patients decently, don't they?"

To my surprise, Gemma frowned and said, "No." A spark of fire that had never been in her eyes before suddenly appeared. "It'll be really hard to get out again if we go back now, Lane. I haven't gotten sick yet so I'm not wasting this chance. Let's do this, come on!"

"Are you sure?" I said, but she never heard me because she had already taken many steps backwards and was staring at the edge with her hands flat, knees rocking and eyes intensely determined.

The drop would kill her, that was all I knew. *She doesn't realise how dangerous the world really is! She doesn't know how the world really works!* I watched her lift her knees high and sprint towards the edge. I felt a gust of wind swoosh across my face as a blur of black, grey and yellow passed me and I screamed. "Gemma, no!"

She didn't listen. I picked my feet up and sprinted after her like a competitor in a race. I managed to grab her just as she reached the edge and pushed my feet off the floor just seconds after she pushed off too.

We sailed through the air, arm in arm, with our legs wide open like ballerinas leaping in a dance. We floated two feet away from the protruding cement floor, then four feet, then six feet and at last, eight feet, right across the barb wired wooden fence under us. I swung my body towards Gemma's as gravity wrenched us towards the hard-looking grey ground and did my best to stay under her.

I heard a loud thud and many cracks when my body made contact with the unforgiving concrete pavement. Familiar hot pain shot through my back, left arm and both feet. I heard Gemma cry out in pain—and perhaps, surprise—too.

A woman screamed in the distance. A man shouted, "West side! Targets escaping!"

I craned my neck back and saw, upside down, a tiny man in a dark blue armoured uniform, with a black helmet on, running towards us with a rifle in his hands. I looked to my right and saw Gemma holding on to her wrist with her face scrunched up in pain. I tried to sit up but realised I no longer could. I had lost all feeling in my legs, yet again.

This was it for me. "Gemma, if you can, run. Now!"

Gemma opened her eyes, saw both me and the man in uniform, and jumped up at once. She looked terribly confused. "What are we going to do, Lane?" she asked. Other than her limp-looking hand, the rest of her body looked fine. She was standing like any other normal, healthy human being would and could even pick up the muesli bar which had fallen out from my pocket onto the ground.

I grinned because I knew I was the reason Gemma was fine and it felt kinda good. Somehow. I have no idea why.

"Forget me. Go! Run! See the world! Have the time of your life!"

The man in the dark blue armoured uniform yelled at us to stay where we were.

Gemma looked up at him then down at me and nodded. "Sorry, Lane, and thank you!" She picked her knees up and ran like her life depended on it.

And I guess, maybe, it really did.

The man in uniform didn't go after her. He jumped right over me and shot me in the arm. "P-eight-seven acquired," he said as if talking to a radio somewhere on his person.

I didn't feel anything hit me. The excruciating pain in my back was all I knew as those familiar patches of black began creeping in front of my eyes all over again.

Before I passed out fully, I dug out the piece of yellow chalk I had been carrying in my pocket and drew a small heart on the pavement when the man in uniform wasn't looking. I added a 'd2' right behind the heart too.

I did it for Paul. After everything we had been through together, I thought she deserved a proper goodbye.

CHAPTER 27
6 AUGUST 2033

When I opened my eyes again, I found myself staring at familiar blue skies, white fluffy clouds and green hills. One closer look, one sniff and I knew exactly where I was.

I was where I didn't mind being. At last. Best of all, nothing had changed. The paintings were the exact same ones I remembered. The bed and pillows under me felt and smelled just as clean as I remembered. The VRM entertainment system and its virtual reality headset were both in the exact same places I last left them. The layout of the room—treadmill built into the floor, the bar table with its lone stool, two white armchairs around a side table in front of a floor-to-ceiling bookshelf full of books—was completely the same.

A familiar creak sounded on my left.

I knew where to look and what to expect the moment I heard it. I knew the door on the left would open and a doctor would walk in. I couldn't help but wonder if Dr Clark would be the one walking in. If I could see his face again, see him move again in the flesh, it would mean everything was still fine and dandy, wouldn't it?

The door opened. A man in a white lab coat, shirt and tie walked in but he wasn't Dr Clark or even anything like him. The man who walked in was much older—he had a full head of white hair—and he was African-American. Other than the thin-framed metal glasses he wore over his large black eyes and the black tablet he held in his hand—exactly like the one Dr Clark used to hold—he had nothing in common with the man I had been praying I would see.

"Good afternoon, Miss Thompson," the elderly African-American doctor said with a smile that suggested a church-going habit and general decency. "It's time for therapy."

I stared at the wrinkles on the sides of his kind black eyes and felt a thick wave of wistfulness wash through me. *Those words, Dr Clark used to say as well, but he never would be saying them again, would he? He was dead and it was all because of me. The fourth person dead with me in the vicinity. How often did that happen to other people?*

"How are you feeling, Miss Thompson?" the African-American doctor asked. His voice was full of bass—way deeper than Dr Clark's—and his accent sounded Southern.

A little sad, I thought but I didn't want to say it. I checked my body—wriggled my limbs, stretched my back and tilted my neck all ways—so that I would have something else to talk about. I watched my legs move and realised the excruciating pain I remembered feeling in my back was now gone. I could move just fine and felt just fine. *What did that mean?* Had Paul been right about me having superhuman regenerative abilities? Or had another long recovery period simply passed without me knowing?

I sat up and stared, first at the blue gown I was in, then at the African-American doctor who was waiting patiently for an answer. "How long was I out for?" I asked. My voice started out a little croaked but smoothened itself out by the time I was done with the sentence.

The African-American doctor cocked his head to the side and frowned a little. "What do you mean?"

I frowned in return. "What year is it? What date?"

"2033. 6 August."

God, really? For sure? "What happened to Dr Clark?"

The African-American doctor's white eyebrows jumped. "I don't understand your question."

"Did he stop coming to work one day? Was his body shipped back to elderly parents in a different state? What?"

The African-American doctor blinked a few times then looked away as if suddenly abstracted. "Who then do you think I am, Miss Thompson?" he said.

"I don't know. We've never met."

He looked up and right into my eyes and said, "Are you sure?"

"Yes." I didn't personally know a single person who was a doctor and was pretty sure none of my elderly African-American male acquaintances were anything like him. The only way I could have sort of known him was if he had been a member of The Gentlemen's Dinner Club whom I might have passed a few times without noticing. *Was he?*

"I am the only Dr Clark around here, Miss Thompson. I think I'd know if there was another."

Dread fizzled in the pits of my stomach then bubbled and rose up towards the rest of my body. I laughed in his face.

"You don't remember?" he said.

That question again? I kept on laughing. Louder this time.

Black Dr Clark made me sit in the white armchair white Dr Clark used to get me to sit in during therapy. He brought me a glass of water from the bar table and held out a clear plastic box in front of my face—the very same plastic box white Dr Clark used to hold out to me, the very same plastic box I took four pink pills out of while at white Dr Clark's apartment. I saw that the compartment containing pink pills had been opened.

"Please, take two, Miss Thompson. I promise you'll find yourself thinking more clearly after you do."

Are you sure? The last time I took four, I woke up in a taxi, traumatised and confused as ever, and ended up chopping a stranger's hand off. "I think I'm fine."

"It's not a request," he said in a firm yet benevolent manner. "I need to make sure you get better and if you're not going to comply I'm going to have to use other means to get you medicated. So please, Miss Thompson, just take two."

Okay. It was clear I wasn't going to have much of a choice in the matter so I did as black Dr Clark ordered. The water went down my throat, cold and refreshing. I have to say, I did feel that little bit more alert once I downed the pink pills.

"Thank you." Black Dr Clark took the seat across me and fished out a stylus pen from his pocket. "Why don't you try describing the Dr Clark you remember? Maybe we can find out who he really is that way."

The stylus pen he had in his hand looked exactly like the modish one white Dr Clark used to hold, I realised.

I pursed my lips. "He was nothing like you. Spoke differently, smelled different." I took a deep breath and checked if any headache might be coming on. *Nope, none.* My head felt fine. Black Dr Clark smelled like freshly squeezed lemons. Comparatively pleasant. "He was just a totally different person. Not like anybody else I know."

"Hm. How then do you explain why he's not here now?"

A familiar crawly sensation came over my skin as I recalled Dr Clark's corpse, missing a hand, sitting on the white blood-stained carpet in his apartment. "Death," I mumbled.

Black Dr Clark raised his eyebrows so high, his entire forehead seemed to rise like a raised stage curtain. "Death? How did he die?"

"Paul shot him."

"Paul? Where from?"

"Here. Paul Rafferty. She was a patient the other Dr

Clark introduced me to."

"Paul Rafferty? You think Paul Rafferty's a woman?"

The stupefaction on black Dr Clark's face made me suddenly very uneasy. "Yes?" I thought about Paul's breasts, curves and soft skin, and the way she once made my heart jump. Only women ever did that to me so if I did feel that way around her that must mean she was really a woman, right?

"Isn't Paul a male name?"

"Yes. But her mom chose it." I shrugged because… what else could I do?

Black Dr Clark nodded, scribbled something into his tablet then scratched his temple. "What if I told you, Miss Thompson, that the Paul Rafferty I know of is… male. Would you believe me?"

I laughed and began to feel a little sick. "I don't… I don't know. She bought female clothing when we were out there so, seems very female to me."

"Out where?"

I stared at him, felt my heart bang against my ribs, felt my nausea grow, and decided not to say another word.

"Hm." Black Dr Clark turned his attention to his tablet and scribbled furiously in it. "Did Paul have curly red hair, brown eyes, a large frame?"

"Yes… and no. She didn't have—" I frowned. "—a large frame."

Black Dr Clark looked up and smiled. Sympathetically. As if I deserved a smile as sympathetic as that. He clasped his huge black hands together and said, "I hate to tell you this, Miss Thompson, but the Paul Rafferty I know, the one who matches that description, is most certainly male. And… he's a convicted murderer. He came by Wonderdrug once for a psychiatric assessment and whistled at every single woman he passed. Even the ones being wheeled in on stretchers. That could have been how you came into contact with him."

My frown grew tighter and I found myself without

words.

"And, there's something else…"

What? I thought but said nothing.

"We don't have evidence of you going out with him, ever. He lives in jail so I doubt he would have been able to go shopping with you. Especially for women's clothing." Black Dr Clark chortled heartily, as if he found his last sentence the funniest thing in the world, but I didn't find it funny at all.

"It's what I remember," I said in the gravest of tones.

Black Dr Clark cleared his throat, wiped his grin off his face and nodded at once. He instantly looked a whole lot more professional. "I know, I'm sorry. Look, Miss Thompson, this is precisely why you should never stop taking your medication. This might come as a shock but you need to understand that you've just come out of a long and, clearly, very vivid psychotic episode. Frankly, you haven't been anywhere since you got here. You were right here yesterday and the day before that and all those days before that too. You were never out shopping with Paul Rafferty or anybody else and I'm absolutely certain you never shot me in the head."

Oh? Suddenly, I found myself wondering why I even thought Wonderdrug would ever make me feel better. It seemed every time I spoke with any one of their doctors, I found myself sicker than I ever imagined I could be.

"Are you okay?"

"Arden Villeneuve," I heard myself say. "Is she alive?" White Dr Clark said I did something 'terrible' to her, didn't he? If she were dead or injured, that would mean Room 103 really happened, wouldn't it?

"The movie star? Yeah, why wouldn't she be? I saw her in the news yesterday, opening a new mall in Africa with her husband. She looked more alive than either of us do now, I think." He chortled again but quickly stopped himself when he caught sight of the look on my face.

I stared at him. "What's my name?" I asked.

"I beg your pardon?"

"My first name. What is it?"

Black Dr Clark cleared his throat and looked a little uncomfortable. "Your name is Blaine, Miss Thompson. You are Blaine Thompson. Why do you ask?"

"Is Lane Thompson dead?"

He inhaled sharply. "Yes. Do you miss her?"

"Was there a diary? Did she leave me her diary?"

"Yes."

"I want to see it. Show it to me."

He didn't move. "You don't remember?"

"No, and stop with that phrase." My voice came out low and dangerous. "Just tell me where her darned diary is. Please."

Black Dr Clark took in a long, deep breath and scratched his eyebrow for a good few seconds before speaking. "Lane's diary is gone forever, Miss Thompson. After I told you she killed herself, you ripped all the pages apart with your bare hands and flushed every last piece down the toilet."

Ah. So I was nothing but a book-flushing twin who went on a vivid psychotic trip as her own dead sister? Was that what everything I had been through really was? It would explain the flying objects and super speed and all, wouldn't it?

Great. I sank down into the comfortable white armchair and felt my muscles properly relax for the first time in a very long time.

At least I now had a logical answer to the question of who I really was. At least now, everything made sense, I thought.

CHAPTER 28
DATES UNKNOWN

Three days after I snapped out of my vivid psychotic episode, I began self-mutilating again. I found myself screaming my lungs out within seconds of waking because my left forearm had been thoroughly burnt to a crisp.

The real Dr Clark revoked my in-room cigarette privileges and removed the lighter I burned myself with but a week later, I managed to dig a hole in my right calf with just my nails and in the two weeks that followed, I dislocated every last one of my fingers on both my left and right hands.

One month on, I was covered in bandages again and had hands that were so tightly bound, they became no different from unusable blocks of wood. I never remembered having done any of those awful things to myself but Dr Clark said the CCTV cameras in my ward caught me red-handed. Every single time. Apparently, I was sleepwalking and physically enacting my dreams in a very agitated manner every single night. I had nothing to say against that because I did remember the nightmares. I had many nightmares in those days. More nightmares than I ever had in my life. I dreamt a lot about the injured and dead individuals from my vivid psychotic episode—the raging security guard with only one hand, Arden

Villeneuve unconscious with that ginormous red bump on her head, Gemma and her body full of misshapen skin, and of course, always, the other, imaginary and very much dead, Dr Clark sitting in a patch of his own dried blood. In my dreams, I was always screaming and trying to fly away from those people but it would never be possible to get away from them. They were always *just there*. As was Paul, the woman. I dreamt of us kissing and sleeping together a couple of times but at the end of every sexual encounter, she would always tell me she was really a man with superpowers and I would run from her, screaming at the top of my lungs.

One day, Dr Clark got me taking a single pastel yellow pill with breakfast. Subsequently, a yellow pill always appeared in the little plastic cup of pills that came with breakfast. The yellow pill should sedate enough to stop the sleepwalking at night which should consequently stop the self-mutilation, he said.

He was right. Once I began taking the yellow pills religiously, I stopped self-mutilating. I woke up perfectly fine every single morning and as a result, slept better and had fewer nightmares at night too.

The only problem I had with the yellow pill was its one side effect—it would make me violently sick within the hour. Every morning, after taking the pill, I would throw up four or five times in quick succession, always while shaking uncontrollably. I always felt horrendous during that hour and to this day, haven't yet experienced anything quite as awful as those stomach-churning shakes had been.

Dr Clark and I weighed the pros and cons together. Was not self-mutilating worth the daily sickness? I decided 'yes'. I hated being bandaged—hated the way bandages restricted my scope of movement; hated the way I looked with bandages—and decided I would do whatever it took to save myself from having to be bandaged ever again.

As before, Dr Clark would come in once in the morning on weekdays to do physical tests and again after lunch for an hour of therapy. During therapy, we would talk about my memory of my vivid psychotic episode—where Paul and I went, what we did, how we moved about, how we got money and food—and Dr Clark would make me tell him my thoughts on everything that happened in great detail.

The real Dr Clark was way more of a joker than the imaginary Dr Clark had ever been. He often cracked jokes in the most inappropriate of circumstances so I grew to like and enjoy his company. When he told me talking would help me heal, help me see my psychosis for the vivid hallucinations they really were, I told him everything. I told him what Paul said about CRO and shared what she could and couldn't do. I told him everything that happened with Arden Villeneuve and gave him all the details concerning the murder of the imaginary Dr Clark. I told him all about the 'secret' places we lived in and shared all the fun moments we had. I told him all about Gemma and Dustin. I told him everything because I wanted very much to heal. I wanted to put the whole vivid psychotic episode behind me and feel like the person I truly was again. I wanted to genuinely feel like Blaine and not keep thinking I was Lane.

Days turned into months. More time passed than I have things to say about it.

I grew bored of the VRM entertainment system eventually—yes, bored of the billion movies, games and music tracks—and actually began reading some of the books on the shelves. When I grew bored of those too, life became a blur of activity that wasn't really happy or sad or remarkable in any way. I developed the habit of going about my day without thinking—food, vomit, vomit, vomit, shakes, vomit, vomit, tests, space out, food, therapy, space out, food, space out, sleep, space out; repeat, repeat, repeat and repeat—and stopped feeling all that excited about all the fancy items and services my Wonderdrug ward had to offer.

I worked really hard on becoming Blaine—told myself I was Blaine every single morning and tried to recall Blaine memories every night—but yet... I remembered nothing of being Blaine. I remained with Lane's mind, with Lane's thoughts, with Lane's memories.

No amount of talking or pills ever changed that.

CHAPTER 29
DATE UNKNOWN

"Lane, wait!"

I froze while seated at my ward's bar table, with my little plastic cup of pink and blue pills propped between my two bandaged hands. I turned and checked behind me.

There was no one there; no one in the ward but me.

Yet the voice had sounded like it had been right behind me, and it was very familiar too.

"Don't take the pills. Pretend like you're taking them of course but find a way to get rid of them without the cameras noticing. Shit! I've got to go! I'll see you tonight—don't take the pink pills! I won't be able to wake you if you do." It was Paul's voice.

I gasped. It was Paul the woman's female voice! Back in my head right after dinner, even though I had been taking all pink, blue and yellow pills just as my doctor instructed! *What was this? A relapse? And what the hell did 'I'll see you tonight' mean? Was the voice I heard a prodrome? A sign that another long, vivid psychotic episode was to come?*

"Paul, where are you?" I asked in my mind. I stared at the little plastic cup still between my hands and couldn't help but wonder if eating the pills in them would make the voice stop.

In the end, I found out I didn't even have to eat the

pills to make the voice go away. Paul's voice never appeared again that day.

Not even when I willed it to.

I got the two pink pills down the toilet by holding them in my mouth for a good ten minutes before pretending to vomit and pulling on the flush before removing my head from the toilet bowl. It wasn't pleasant to do but it got the job done.

That night, for the first time since snapping out of my vivid psychotic episode, I found myself unable to sleep. I tossed and turned for hours in the darkened ward, waiting for Paul to appear in my head or in front of me and eventually got frustrated when she didn't. I had been convinced her voice had been nothing but a hallucination and had been about to try to get to sleep when something warm and heavy materialised next to my legs, above my blanket.

I sat up at once.

It *was* Paul. The woman. In my ward. On my bed. Next to me. She was in the same blue gown I was in and looked almost as I remembered she did, except maybe a little sadder. There was also a couple of inches of red at the roots of her mostly-brown, long, curly hair. She was still slim and her frame could not be considered large by any definition.

"Hi, Lane," she said.

Lane. With Paul, I was always Lane and never Blaine, wasn't I? My hands were incapacitated so I used my forearms to touch her instead. I ran my forearms over her cheekbones, ears and chin, just to make sure she really was there.

She felt like flesh against my bare skin. Warm, solid, human flesh.

"Again, yes I'm real," she said. Her lips moved in sync with the words I heard. "And yes, I really am female." Her eyes twinkled as she took in mine, in the same way they used to do all those times before. "There's a good reason my mother gave me a male name but we don't have time for that now, we've got only four minutes so... Are you okay? How do you feel?" She took my bandaged hands into hers and stared at them as if trying to see through all the layers of cloth.

I took a deep breath and tried to calm my nerves. I felt shame when I saw how funny my bandaged hands looked next to Paul's perfect ones. "Why four minutes?"

"Security reboot. Wouldn't have been able to get in here otherwise."

Those words—'security' and 'reboot' together—triggered a surge of energy within my muscles. I felt as if I were Frankenstein's monster in the very moment of being electrified into life; eager all of a sudden and a tad reckless. The thought of jumping out of a stairwell window now sounded like a great idea to me. I thought about getting to do things out in the real world—actual tasks and activities—and found myself more thrilled than I remembered I could be. I didn't even care whether or not it would all be real. I finally understood, there and then, why Gemma had run with every ounce of energy she had that day. She had been bored. She had been empty. She needed more once she realised there *actually was more*. I felt the same way that night. "Let's do it," I said. "Why not?" I flipped my blanket off my legs and tried to jump out of bed but Paul put both hands on my shoulders and held me down.

"We can't today," she said with a smile that was most definitely sad. "CRO fixed all security loopholes after all those things we did. I haven't figured out how we're going to get out yet but I just... I just wanted to see you. See if the yellow pills they've been giving you caused any damage? Those pills are poison, you know? CRO's trying to see how long your body can defend itself from poison. Their plan is to keep at it till your body breaks down, you know." She looked like she was about to cry after she said that, even though her smile never once went away.

The superhuman energy I had been feeling just seconds ago fizzled out and mutated into a dull ache of disappointment when I took in the look on her face. There was something different about Paul's demeanour that night and on top of that—

—on her temples, under her hair, there were two circular reddish and bumpy splotches. It looked like skin had been ripped or burnt off in those places.

"What's that?" I reached out and pushed her hair aside to get a better look but Paul flinched and backed away at once.

"Don't. It... hurts."

"Where did you get those?"

"From here." She pursed her lips, looked away and shrugged. "'Brain tests.' They found out about my telepathy somehow and now they really, really, really want to know how my brain does it. I don't know how they figured it out. Maybe Mr Anderson's home was bugged and he didn't even know about it? Maybe I should have just kept my mouth shut? I don't know."

But I did. And I knew it would be best for everyone if I said nothing. A heaviness came over my heart and I felt it sink and swirl amidst the most awful of sentiments—guilt. Suffocating, all-consuming guilt. With a touch of fear.

Paul turned to face me and turned to stone the moment she caught sight of the look on my face. Her eyes became wide and I saw her shoulders rising and falling faster than they had been doing before. She turned away a few seconds later and the sadness on her face changed into a look of sudden realisation.

"I'm so sorry," I whispered right away. I got the feeling I was going to be in danger. Paul would kill me now that she knew I had betrayed her, wouldn't she? There were consequences to everything—I got kicked out of Aunt Mary's home because I hadn't woken up in time to save

Uncle Tim from dying, I got a lifetime of hardship because of my poor grades in high school, I got no love because all I ever wanted were women I was in no way good enough for—and my betrayal of Paul would be no exception, I knew. I backed away and prepared myself for the worst.

I never expected Paul to let it go, but she did. Paul didn't follow up with rage. She simply sighed, showed me the body language of a woman defeated and eventually even smiled a little. "Don't worry, it's not your fault. CRO's just way too good at getting stuff done, I guess."

Her voice was gentle and her beautiful brown eyes remained more disappointed than murderous. She did not look psychopathic or dangerous in that moment, just... sad. So very, very sad. Seeing her that way, a wilted version of the woman whose tenacity I once admired, made me suddenly want to cry. What hope was there for the rest of us if even brave, fierce, invincible Paul could be broken like that? "What are you even doing here?" I whispered. "Did they catch you? Did you break in again? Or…?" *Am I hallucinating again?*

"They didn't catch me and no, you're not hallucinating. I chose to get myself admitted. To get you out. Until I realised I couldn't." She looked right at me and sighed again.

Paul, trapped in the tasteless world that was Wonderdrug all over again, all because of me? And me, guilty of screwing her over because I refused to believe she existed, even though she had been right in front of my face showing me kindness so many times before? I shook my head and felt like the most stupid and selfish horrible person in the world. My heart pounded furiously, I gulped and a cascade of tears came down both eyes. I found myself heaving, hot in the face and hating myself for not being smarter, more observant or more kind.

"Hey. Hey?" Paul took me into her arms. She pressed her chest up against mine and brought my head to rest against her shoulder. A shoulder which was warm and thoroughly solid. *Not imaginary at all.* "Don't blame yourself. You're just very confused because they want you to be. Anybody else in your situation would have done the exact same so stop beating yourself up over it."

I felt her heart beating fast against mine, got a whiff of her unique bodily scent and my face crumpled and poured forth even more tears.

"You're so stupid," I choked, in between sobs. "I'm nobody, I can't do shit, I'm so dumb and gullible, I screw up everything all of the time, you shouldn't have come back here for me! I'm not worth it."

Paul shook her head many times and tightened her hold of my body as if she wanted to make sure she was not going to drop me. "You are to me," she whispered. "It was my fault CRO found the 'safe house' anyway. I should have been paying attention to Dustin. I should have noticed how unhappy he was and realised he was planning on running back to Wonderdrug, ready to tell them everything. I should have been watching him but… I didn't. Because all I kept thinking about was…" She sighed. "You."

I pulled away from her at once, did my best to look for the truth in her eyes even though mine were blurred by tears, and found her smiling right at me. "Why didn't you just say so before?"

She shrugged and tears dropped right out of her eyes too. "Because you didn't love me back? I thought if I stopped myself from wanting you, it would pass, but, who knew? It didn't. I tried doing what you would do in the same situation—I tried to ignore you, pretend I didn't like you—but it didn't work either. And when I saw what you drew in the concrete, I just knew I had to—"

I took her cheeks into my bandaged hands and kissed her firmly on the mouth—a move I now realised I would have made many times before had I not been so preoccupied with Arden Villeneuve and all the crap Wonderdrug personnel had been shoving into my mind.

THE WOMAN WHO MADE ME FEEL STRANGE

My tongue found its way around hers and spoke how I felt with tender, ardent manoeuvres. My bosom came together with hers and our stomachs and thighs followed suit like magnets.

I heard Paul's breathing quicken and felt her tongue and hands reciprocate. I felt my body tingle and burn with excitement as we meshed like dancers doing the most perfect sensual dance but, as abruptly as we had begun, Paul pulled away.

"I have to go," she said, suddenly flustered and suddenly more beautiful than ever before. She looked all over my face as if trying to commit my features into memory while simultaneously trying to smile at me while looking into my eyes. "I'll come back and see you next month and I'll try to find us a way out of here, I promise."

"Paul, wait—"

"I love you," she said with that sad, sad smile that was now thoroughly hers and the next time I blinked, she was already gone.

I was all alone on my bed again; the only person in my ward in the dark. Nothing around me had moved or changed but, somehow, I felt as if I were no longer the same person.

I wasn't Lane trying hard to be Blaine any longer. I was just... Lane.

Lane who was in love with Paul, the woman.

CHAPTER 30
DATES UNKNOWN

Paul did not come back. I waited four whole months and willed her voice to appear in my head over a hundred times but it never did.

By the end of my first month of waiting, I was on edge. My mind went through all possibilities on loop. Had something bad happened to her? Had she changed her mind about being in love with me? Had she decided she never wanted to see me again? Had she gotten out without me? Or—the worst possibility of all—had her presence in my ward been nothing but a hallucination? A blip in my otherwise salvaged sanity?

Since I couldn't get the door Dr Clark always entered from open, (and believe me, I tried, many times) there was nothing else I could do but experiment with what I could do. I did the whole secretly-spitting-up-pills-down-the-toilet thing for three entire months to see if it would bring Paul back again and guess what?

It didn't. None of the horrid things Dr Clark said not taking my pills would make happen actually happened. I didn't find myself lost in another vivid psychotic episode, I didn't start self-mutilating again, and, best of all, the bandaged parts of my body never once hurt. Ironically, not taking any pills made me feel much better physically. I stopped getting sick after breakfast (though I kept on pretending to vomit after every meal) and I started feeling less foggy in the head. I felt more awake than ever before and even began noticing interesting patterns in my Wonderdrug routine.

For example, I noticed Dr Clark would always mention I was mentally ill at least three times during therapy. He would give me the exact same look of disbelief—face blank, eyebrows up for five seconds—if I told him my vivid psychotic episode felt real and would look away right before reminding me I was Blaine every single time. He would scribble significantly more on his tablet when I talked about the functional details of my vivid psychotic episode—how we did what we did, how we got to where we got to—and significantly less when I talked about my feelings, hopes and desires. He would want the most unnecessary of details—"Was there any weird energy in the air as the keycard flew? Did the temperature change? Were there any sounds?"—but would always be reminding me that none of those things 'ever happened' afterwards. He was always asking how I felt, with utmost concern on his face, yet never once did a thing to actually help me feel better. He was always telling me I was getting better but could never confirm when I was going to be cured. He was always warning me about the dangers of not taking medication but never actually noticed I wasn't even on them.

After three whole months without pills in my system, I eventually began seeing everything Paul had been saying about Wonderdrug myself.

Wonderdrug clearly did not care about my health.

Wonderdrug clearly did not function the way a real hospital would.

Dr Clark likely wasn't even a real doctor.

CHAPTER 31
DATE UNKNOWN

"I had a dream last night," I told Dr Clark, when I could stand being at the Wonderdrug Psychiatric Centre no longer. "Gemma was in it."

Dr Clark's large black eyes twinkled with interest—the way they always twinkled whenever I spoke of 'crazy things' that weren't my feelings. "Let's talk about it," he said.

I took a deep breath and nodded, covered my face with both palms and tried my best to blush like genuinely innocent girls probably would do in similar situations. "I dreamt she was in my ward, on my bed, asking how I was. She gave me a phone number, told me to call her if I wasn't dead. She said life on the outside hadn't been too good to her so if life was good in here, she would consider coming back here too."

Dr Clark's eyes remained twinkly as he observed me. I watched him tap the stylus pen against his tablet many, many times. "Do you think that would really happen?" he said eventually. "Would Gemma, an imaginary person, really come here if you called her?"

"Yes."

"Do you still remember the phone number?"

"By heart."

Dr Clark nodded and looked away in thought for a period. When he looked up at me again, his eyes were twinkling more than ever. "Alright. Normally, I wouldn't recommend acting on information obtained from dreams but since today is Moody Monday, what do you say we get up to a little mischief together, hm? Follow your dream? See what surprises happen?"

My cheeks rose by themselves and I found myself not even having to feign being delighted. "I say yeah. Just to see what surprises happen."

He smiled, reached into his lab coat, took out a phone—the latest Android model, the one which could do holographic video calls—and handed it to me. "Go ahead. Who knows? You might learn a thing or two about yourself in the process?"

Or I might learn a thing or two about you? I smiled like a sweet young thing would, took the phone, admired and breathed in its plastic-scented newness then keyed in the number a little Asian child once told me about.

The number she said I was to call if I ever found myself stuck at Wonderdrug. I had thought long and hard for a way out and every time, that phone number turned out to be the only option I had. There was no way I was getting out of my ward on my own. If the number didn't work, if nobody picked up, I would find out I was permanently screwed but that was a risk I was now willing to take. I was sick of being at Wonderdrug. I was sick of being pushed around any which way life dictated.

My fingers trembled. My palm stained the phone's gratifyingly smooth backing with sweat. I put the phone to my ear. It rang. Once, twice, three times, then...

"Hello?" a woman said. Not Gemma. The voice on the line was much deeper and huskier; the voice of an older woman, likely a heavy smoker.

"Gemma? Is that you?" Paul once said all phone calls could be tracked by CRO and everything Paul ever said was word again so I kept the act up. "It's me, Lane. I mean... Blaine but, of course, yes, you know me as Lane. Anyway, I... I saw you in my dream last night. You wanted to know how I was doing so I thought I'd call and tell you I'm doing great. The Wonderdrug Psychiatric Centre in New York is really great. My doctor's great, the food is really great, the amenities are also great. I really think you should come join me. Soon."

"Ha ha," the woman on the other line said. She didn't sound amused though. "I ain't crazy like you are, psycho! And I ain't who you think I am so don't call again!" The line went dead.

My hope died along with it. The voice on the other line hadn't been one I recognised and whoever that was had been clearly unfriendly. I took a deep breath and handed the phone back to Dr Clark who wouldn't stop staring at me like I were some freak show.

"What did she say?"

I swallowed the lump in my throat and tried to keep disappointment from showing on my face by making sure my face stayed blank. "Wrong number," I said and realised the disappointment came out in my voice anyhow.

Dr Clark narrowed his eyes and gave me a few sympathetic nods but there was just something about his face that suggested he didn't quite believe me. One big breath and a few dramatic blinks later though, his face was as kind and friendly as it always was again, as if he had never been suspicious of me at all. "Well, that's why I call them Moody Monday and Touchy Tuesday. And that's why you need to keep taking your medication, Miss Thompson."

I agreed, and not just verbally.

That night, I swallowed all the pink and blue pills that came with dinner.

There was no point in knowing everything that was wrong if there was nothing I could do to change it, I decided. Might as well get with the programme and get the programme over and done with, I thought. If CRO didn't want me to be aware of what was really going on, perhaps it was best if I wasn't.

CHAPTER 32
THE DAY I BECAME A
WHOLE NEW PERSON

"You have to swallow," I heard someone say a couple of nights later. "Move your throat. Follow my fingertips." Something soft landed on my neck and pushed my skin up then down.

In that moment, I couldn't remember what 'swallow' meant. I knew I had known the word before and guessed it was likely an action of some sort but, for the life of me, couldn't recall how to physically make it happen. I felt my brain let go of my body and found myself drifting away into sweet nothingness; I found myself enjoying the lack of light, sound, sensations and emotions.

Something bit me in the arm. Or rather, that's what it felt like. My body jerked away from that sweet nothingness and moved back towards my brain where it remained somehow next to it yet not quite connected. I tried to open my eyes but they were as heavy as a wall of bricks and wouldn't budge.

"You'll be fine in a minute," the same person said. "The counteragent's working. Just give it some time."

What in the world was a counteragent? I tried to ask but my lips simply wouldn't move, so I gave up. I stopped caring and let myself float back towards sweet nothingness where

I much preferred to be and was absolutely content.

Something grabbed my arm and shook it vigorously a second later. "Okay, Lane, enough sleeping. You have to wake up now!"

Who in the world...? I wrenched my eyelids open and was surprised to find it was now easy to do so. But that became the least of my concerns the moment I caught sight of what was in front of me.

Someone, or some *thing*, was in my ward, on my bed, peering down at me in the dark. Her—it was most definitely a her—face was attractive but not entirely human. Her eyes and hair, worn in a loose ponytail, were normal and human in appearance—both brown—but her skin wasn't. Her skin was grey like light-coloured cement and just as patchy. I thought she looked very much like a statue with fake hair and eyes plastered on. Her features—strong nose and sharp eyes—were vaguely exotic. She wore a black jacket with a hood at the back and had a small black gym bag slung across her torso.

I gasped, sat up and backed away from her at once. *I recognised her! She was the odd-coloured woman I ran into at the alleyway behind The Canned Food Factory Hotel! The one who killed a CRO agent right in front of me!*

"Great, you're moving," she said. She grinned like we were old friends and threw a bundle of black clothes into my hands. "Get changed now. We're leaving. I already got your tracker out so don't worry about that."

I unravelled the bundle of clothes but got sidetracked when I realised I had hands in place of bandaged stumps. Perfectly functional, smooth and tanned hands. No fingers dislocated whatsoever. I could wriggle all my fingers without any pain.

Used bandages lay like pencil shavings all over the sheets. I realised the bandages over my left forearm and right calf had been removed too. Both parts looked normal again, as if they had never even been injured before.

"Yes," the odd-coloured woman said. "I got them out

while you were waking up to save time. Now come on, move. The clothes are the closest I could find in your style so I hope you like them."

I held up the black t-shirt I had in my hands and saw the print of a raised middle finger down its front. I glanced at the skinny black jeans under the t-shirt and realised the odd-coloured woman did actually understand me pretty well. "Wait," I said. "So you're the blue woman I called? The woman from my past?"

The odd-coloured woman put an odd-coloured hand on her throat and bent her chin down so low, a double chin appeared over her slender neck. "Ha ha. Don't call again!" she said in a suddenly low, husky voice that sounded like it belonged to an old woman. She lifted her chin and removed the theatrical voice and instantly looked young—about as old as I was—again. "Yes, I'm pretty good at playing pretend, though I have to say, you're pretty good at it yourself. Good job in getting the call made, I never would have known you were back here otherwise. They made it look like you were out on the streets in Mexico so that's where I had been searching for months. Anyway, do change now please, we're on a tight schedule."

I didn't change. I couldn't move. Not when I knew who she was. "Did you kill my parents and uncle?" I asked with a frown.

"Yes, but they're not really your parents so he's not really your uncle. Don't give me that look, that man was planning on raping you so he had to go. Your 'parents' I felt a little bad about because all they actually did was talk too much about your strange body but…" She shrugged. "I guess we all have to do what we all have to do sometimes. Even the hard stuff."

I gaped at her, speechless.

The odd-coloured woman observed my face and sighed. She put her hands—strange, stone-like hands—on my shoulders and looked me in the eyes. "Lane, I've been watching over you since you were a baby so trust me.

Come with me and you'll be safe from now on, I assure you."

Her words didn't make sense to me. She hardly looked old enough to have been mature when I was a baby, for one, but more importantly, I didn't understand why anybody would care to watch over me at all. "I'm just a nobody," I said. "I've done nothing extraordinary, nothing remarkable."

"I know, I made sure of that." She dragged me into a standing position and pulled the blue gown I was wearing up above my head in one swift move, to my horror. "Had you been outstanding, had you been Gemma Diaz, you would have spent your entire life in the clutches of the Office."

I watched, mortified, as she grabbed the rude t-shirt and pulled it over my head and naked torso. "Wait, are you saying I'm really Gemma Diaz?" I asked as she took my arms and pulled them out through the sleeves of the t-shirt. I flinched the moment she touched me for her hands were icy cold. As cold as hands would be if you submerged them in a bucket of ice for longer than a minute.

"Yes." She put the pair of jeans at my feet and ordered me to step in so I did, quickly, grateful I wouldn't have to be naked in front of her a minute longer. "The Office had their eyes on you way before you were born so we had to swap you. That was the only way we were going to get you away from them. We didn't think you'd end up getting pushed off a fifty storey building one day, of course." She shrugged again, grabbed me by the hand—and made me flinch again—and dragged me towards the door Dr Clark always entered from.

"Do you know who pushed me?"

"Yes, but let's talk about that later." The odd-coloured woman fished out a keycard made of rubber from her pocket, tapped it on the door the way Dr Clark always tapped his wrist before leaving my ward and opened the door without a hitch.

We went through that same small black-painted space I now recognised and went out through the door Paul brought me out of the first time we escaped Wonderdrug. That door had been locked when we approached it—red decorative line on the metal square above the handle instead of a green one—but the rubber keycard the odd-coloured woman had in her hand turned out to be as functional as any dismembered wrist. When we stepped out, I found myself back in that long corridor I once saw a hoard of patients in blue gowns standing around in.

The long corridor was empty this time. No swarm of patients in blue, no guards with rifles. Just me and the odd-coloured woman who peered cautiously around as if the corridor wasn't quite safe.

"This way," she said and led us towards the exit Paul and I had once dashed towards like record-breaking Olympians. "We'll take the stairs to the loading bay."

"Wait." I stopped in my tracks. "We need to get Paul out. And Gemma. Lend me your card."

The odd-coloured woman turned back to me and frowned. "Gemma's not here," she whispered. "And I didn't cater for Paul's escape. We'll have to leave her." She took me by the wrist with one icy hand and tried to drag me forward.

I held my ground and refused to budge. "We can't," I said in a volume that matched her whisper. "She came back here for me. I have to get her out too, no matter what."

"I didn't hack the cameras in her room, Lane. We'll be seen if we go in and all hell will break loose. This is not up for discussion."

I didn't bother arguing. Instead, I snatched up the rubber keycard she had sticking out of the front pocket of her black jeans and ran towards the door directly opposite the one we had stepped out from—Paul's ward, if her blueprint sketches had been anything to go by. I tapped the rubber keycard against the security panel on the door and pushed in the moment the line of red light above the handle turned green.

"Christ! Do you have any idea what you've just done?"

I didn't care. I ran through the small black-painted room I found within, tapped the security panel on the inner most door with the same rubber keycard and went right in.

I found myself in a ward that looked exactly like mine would through a mirror. Whilst my bed had been on the left of the entrance, this ward's bed was on the right. There was a woman in a blue gown asleep in the queen-sized bed in the middle. She had long, brown, curly hair which was also red at the roots. I ran towards her in relief and shook her right away.

"Paul, wake up!" I said but winced the moment I got to see her face up close.

There were two gigantic raw patches on both sides of her head. They went all the way up to the top of her forehead and down past her cheekbones as well as past the ends of her eyes and deep into her hair. They looked thick and protruded—a mix of dark brown scabs and bright red fresh wounds—but simultaneously seemed also immensely sunken, going way past the boundaries of her skull.

"Paul! Get up!" I grabbed her shoulders, pulled her into a sitting position and shook her more violently, suddenly full of rage. "We're getting the hell out of here now. For good!"

Paul didn't move. She didn't wake up. She didn't seem to hear me. She simply kept breathing in a calm, rhythmic way that suggested deep sleep and was practically as good as... dead.

Fuck. I wondered why briefly but stopped because I knew it was not a good time to ponder. I swung her arms around my shoulders, shoved my hip next to hers and dragged her motionless body off the bed, towards the door. She felt like she weighed a ton and the weight of her strained my back but I pushed on because I knew there was no way in hell I was leaving her there a minute longer.

I heard the alarm the moment I made it through the first door—the same loud and deafening alarm I heard the day Paul tried to break all curiosities out—and it only got louder when I opened the door that led to the main corridor.

To my relief, the odd-coloured woman was still outside, although clearly very cross with me. She took one look at Paul, swore and dug into the gym bag she had down her front.

The vial of copper-coloured liquid that came out of it, she shoved into my hands. "Pour this down her throat to neutralise the tranquilliser. When that's done, follow me! The guards are on their way! We need to hide!"

I did as she said right away; propped Paul's lifeless body up against the nearest wall for support and massaged her throat when the vial had been emptied into her mouth.

To my horror, the odd-coloured woman ripped out a handgun from the back of her jacket. She moved away from the exit door we had been heading towards before and ran towards the other end of the corridor instead.

Shit. The plan had changed, and it was all my fault. I realised I might have blown my only chance of getting out of the Wonderdrug Psychiatric Centre in that moment. All because I wanted to get Paul out with me? *But I couldn't have left her.* The odd-coloured woman would never have come back for her, I could tell. Getting Paul out was a risk I simply had to take.

"In here, Lane!" the odd-coloured woman shouted from afar. She had gotten a door at the far end of the corridor open and had already gone inside but stuck her head out just to wave at me. "Hurry!"

Paul was still unconscious so I propped her up on my shoulders and dragged her towards the odd-coloured woman. Sweat rose on my forehead and on the parts of my body under Paul's heavy warmth. I felt myself straining to breathe and move on, felt my muscles become wobbly and sore, but I kept on going.

I made it past the two elevators in the middle of the corridor right as the LED indicators on them started changing. '3'. '4'. '5'... I gathered all my strength and pushed myself into a run.

It was thoroughly difficult to run with Paul on me and I never thought it would be possible yet I made it happen. Door after door after door after door passed like lamp posts would if you saw them from a moving bus.

I made it to the door the odd-coloured woman was at just as both elevators chimed 'ding' and thrust Paul and myself through the door right in the nick of time. The odd-coloured woman shut the door behind us right away. Quietly.

We were in a storeroom full of floor-to-ceiling metal shelves filled with boxes of tissues, toilet paper, soap, toothpaste, sanitary pads, floor-cleaning detergent, dish washing liquid and other household items. The storeroom wasn't particularly big—only about twice the size of my former micro-apartment—and was lit by florescent lights that weren't particularly bright. I recognised most of the scents in the air—soap that had been in the bathroom in my ward, antiseptic that was always on the sheets—but there were unfamiliar smells in there too. Cleaning chemicals and paper, it seemed.

I was huffing furiously from the exertion of getting us in there but the odd-coloured woman did not give me a chance to rest. She dragged me—with Paul still as heavy as a bag of bricks on my back—towards the shelf furthest from the door and pulled us down into a crouch behind it. My knees crashed into the cement floor with huge thuds and hurt like a motherfucker but all I could do was grimace and let tears take over my vision because the odd-coloured woman warned me—through angry, sharp gestures—not to make a sound.

"You should not have done that," I heard her whisper as I wiped tears from my eyes and set Paul down. "Next time I tell you to do something, you do exactly as I say, are we clear?"

"I couldn't leave Paul," I whispered in return.

"Stop. You do exactly as I say from now on, are we clear?"

I nodded for she had the intensity of a military commander and made me feel very small and feeble, for some reason.

The odd-coloured woman pulled a huge, empty box out from a low shelf—the shelf closest to the ground—and put it between us. "Get in and lie down now."

"Into the box?"

"Yes. Do it, hurry."

I did as she said, halved my body and curled up into a foetal position to fit into the box which was only half my body's length.

"Lane?"

I sat up and turned at once. "Paul! Are you okay?"

"Great, just in time," the odd-coloured woman said. She directed her commanding gaze towards Paul—who looked like she was in a daze—and said, "Speed. Vent. You follow me and close up. We lead them away then tracker out. Tablets, go off radar. Got it?"

I did not get it but Paul seemed to. She stared intently as the odd-coloured woman spoke and by the time the odd-coloured woman was done with her instructions, the dazed look that had been on Paul's face was gone and she looked all ready for a fight.

The odd-coloured woman, who now actually did look a little blue under the whiteness of the florescent lights in the storeroom, shoved a brown tablet into my hand. "Swallow this now or they'll see you. And get your head down. Paul, help me get her box into the shelf."

Paul gave her a sharp, obedient nod and took one side of the box I was in. The odd-coloured woman took the other side. I sank down and tried to put the brown tablet into my mouth but, without warning, both Paul and the odd-coloured woman turned towards the door, jerked the box violently in the process, and shook the brown tablet out of my hands.

It fell somewhere at the base of the box where my feet were. I tried to sit up and reach for it but the odd-coloured woman pushed my head down and shoved the box I was in into the shelf. I couldn't move much afterwards. The box was too small and I was curled up too tightly.

Fuck. I wanted to say something about my lost brown tablet but, through the slit between the cardboard flaps over my head, I could see that the odd-coloured woman and Paul had already disappeared. A metallic clang—from the ceiling, I think—sounded a second later.

The door to the storeroom slammed open right after that. I heard heavy, hasty footsteps move in and appear really close to me.

Through the slit, I could see two tall, tanned and muscular men in dark blue, armoured uniforms, wearing black helmets, searching the room with huge, threatening rifles in hand. Both of them had binocular devices propped above their foreheads and black objects stuffed inside one ear.

They weren't dressed like the security guards at Wonderdrug; they were dressed like the man who shot me outside the construction site in Manhattan. They didn't look like they were hired to ramble the premises and issue verbal warnings—the way the guards seated in Wonderdrug's Security Office looked; they looked like physically-adept, tactically-advanced troopers with the ability to incapacitate and inflict serious damage.

"Clear!" one of them shouted to nobody in particular. He remained still for a moment then turned to look at the ceiling, where a black, globed security camera hung. "Must have been hacked, sir. Roger that." He turned to the other trooper and nodded. Both of them pushed the binocular devices on their foreheads down over their eyes and looked around the storeroom.

One of them stopped moving when he looked up at the ceiling while the other stopped when he looked right in the direction of me.

Fuck, he knows, I realised at once. *Those binoculars must be heat detectors and that brown tablet I dropped must have been a temperature regulator of sorts!* I ran my hands all over the base of the box as quickly as I could and felt my heart plunge when I felt nothing like a brown tablet within reach.

The trooper with his eyes on me began moving towards me slowly. The one with his eyes on the ceiling slung his rifle over his shoulder, took a handgun out from his holster, then climbed up the shelf that was right under the grill that covered an air duct.

I watched him yank the grill open almost effortlessly, flinched at the deafening clang its metal made when it hit the concrete ground, and saw him disappear into the air duct in the span of a few seconds. In the meantime, I got a whiff of male sweat and heard heavy, firm boot steps coming towards me. I clutched my legs tighter and tried to make my uneasy, rapid breath as quiet as was possible but that did nothing to help me. The box I was in swayed dramatically to the right, the cardboard flaps vanished from sight and before I knew it, there was no longer anything between me and the trooper—who had the thickest, most-muscular neck I had ever seen in real life—peering down at me through his high-tech, multi-coloured binoculars.

He grinned and said hi.

I jumped up and tried to punch him but he grabbed my wrist before my hand could even get anywhere near his face.

His grip of my wrist felt as solid as metal cuffs and I felt the tip of his rifle ram into my stomach, hard.

"Don't move," he said and flipped the binocular device back up onto his forehead. His eyes were mostly grey with a brownish or amber ring in the middle, somewhat like the eyes of a tiger.

I didn't move at all. "Paul, I'm caught," I said in my head. "And watch out, one of them's gone after you!" I prayed she would reply but she never did.

"P-eight-seven acquired, tenth floor store," the trooper in front of me said. "I repeat, P-eight-seven acquired, tenth—" Three loud claps cackled above and made us both look. *Gun shots!*

Fired at Paul and the odd-coloured woman or by them? I couldn't tell. Nothing had changed where I was.

"1073, report status," the trooper in front of me said. His eyes remained on the ceiling and he looked concerned. "1073, can you report status?"

1073 did not report status. The trooper in front of me removed his grip of my wrist, flipped his binocular device down over his eyes and turned his rifle and head up towards the ceiling.

I saw nothing but the opportunity to run and I grabbed it by the balls. I jumped out of the box and tried to make for the door but the trooper—much taller, much fitter—dashed towards me and got me in his arms before I could even get far.

He slammed me down onto the ground and knocked the wind out of my lungs in the process. I gasped and felt myself struggling to breathe again but the angry trooper could care less. He pulled me onto my feet and rammed my back up against a wall with his large, strong, partially-gloved hand pressed against my neck.

"Backup! Tenth floor store! Now!" he yelled.

I coughed uncontrollably, for his grip was restricting air to my lungs, and tried to push him away but he was too heavy and too strong.

"I said don't move!" he yelled again, his face close enough for me to see the large pores and glistening specks of sweat on it.

I didn't give a fuck about what he said because I knew I would pass out if I didn't get some air, fast. His whole body was covered in thick clothing and bulletproof padding so I lunged towards the only part of him I could touch—his cheek—and bit down with every last ounce of strength my jaws had.

The trooper screamed, grabbed me by the hair and wrenched me away from him like I were weightless. He threw me down on the floor and smashed the end of his rifle against the middle of my face with a ferocious amount of force.

I heard a loud crack and felt my nose burn as if acid or some corrosive liquid had been freshly poured onto it. Blood trickled onto the side of my chest in one steady stream and left my rude t-shirt damp.

As if that weren't bad enough, the trooper's finger twitched twice while on his rifle's trigger.

I felt sharp, burning sensations in both knees and thought I would soon pass out like before, but I didn't. Instead, I stayed awake and saw bloody holes in both my knees and also blood pooling on the floor underneath my legs. I tried to get up but it hurt too much to move either leg. That was when I realised the bullets the trooper's gun fired weren't tranquillisers no more.

"Why the fuck are you doing this?" I asked. All I ever did was try to get my freedom back. Surely that didn't warrant treatment as horrific as *that*?

The trooper wiped the little bits of blood my teeth had drawn from his cheek and raised his rifle to hit me again.

"Stop."

Both the trooper and I turned and found Paul suddenly standing next to us, pointing a rifle—the other trooper's rifle!—at his temple.

I became giddy with relief. Paul looked fully conscious and had that confident manner I once admired all over again.

"Hit her again and you're dead," Paul said to the trooper.

He flipped his rifle around and rammed the barrel against my neck at once. "Shoot me and she's dead," he replied. I saw him gulp.

"You know she can't die, right?"

"She might," he said. "If I sever her head from her neck? Hard to heal properly when your head's in a totally different place, right?"

"Your bosses wouldn't let you."

"Oh yeah they would. You've both used up the maximum amount of pardons, unfortunately. A dead specimen is always better than no specimen at all." He smiled a little, slightly nervously, but dropped the smile the moment something black and metallic appeared right next to his hand.

A handgun. The one his buddy had taken out of his holster right before climbing into an air duct. The odd-coloured woman was holding it and she was smiling. "Let them go. Please." She had her own handgun in her other hand pointed at him too.

For a good few seconds, the asshole of a trooper looked pale and downright afraid, but then, all of a sudden, he heaved sharply and began to smile again. "No thank you," he said with what sounded like relief.

Paul and the odd-coloured woman turned their heads to the storeroom's door even before it slammed open and froze when the hoard of, perhaps, fifty troopers, in dark blue uniforms similar to the trooper's in front of us, barged in with their rifles all aimed at us.

It was hard to imagine three civilian women would warrant a storeroom full of troopers but there they were, stuffed to the brim in the small storeroom, blocking any hope we might have had of ever getting out.

"Identify yourself!" one of them said to the odd-coloured woman.

She stared at him, her smile gone and looked more

thoughtful than she was afraid. "No," she said. With that, she turned her gun on him and shot him right in the middle of his forehead, faster than I could even gasp.

The last thing that trooper did before melting to the ground like Arden Villeneuve once did was stare at the three of us in absolute horror. When his head hit the ground with a loud thud, all hell broke loose.

All the troopers in the storeroom turned their rifles on us and fired with rapid speed. I felt Paul grab me and saw the world swoosh by as we dodged bullets together at breakneck, superhuman speeds. I saw the odd-coloured woman levitate—yes, she actually levitated—up towards the ceiling. She shot rapidly downward with the two handguns in her hands, hitting many a trooper square in the face.

"Code 33! Code 33!" one of the troopers at the back shouted. "Tenth floor store NOW!" Around him, troopers began collapsing with bloodied holes in the middle of their faces. Half the ones standing aimed their guns up at the odd-coloured woman who was flying—yes, flying!—around the ceiling like a supernatural being while the other half turned their guns on Paul and I.

I barely registered what was going on at first because the scene before my eyes changed faster than my brain could process but at some point, the rate of change began to slow and I began getting glimpses of Paul struggling to haul me away while the few remaining troopers sprayed bullets at us with eyes wide with hate. Only when the scene stopped changing did I notice the bullet holes in Paul's chest, limbs and cheek and see the volume of blood spurting out of a hole in her neck.

"Paul!" I grabbed her right before she collapsed and sank down onto the ground with her in my arms. I threw my body over her motionless one and felt a shower of pain burn into my back and the back of my head as the racket of unrelenting popping sounds continued to surround us. "Paul! Stay with me!"

"Lane, listen," Paul whispered in a voice that sounded like it was gurgling. Her eyes were large and scared in a way they had never been before. Her lips were deathly pale, her mouth wide like a fish's would be fresh out of water and every huge, desperate breath she struggled to take in through her mouth seemed to do nothing to make her feel better. "Stick with her... she knows... your real parents... why advantages exist..." Her face turned one shade paler after she said those words and her eyes rolled back into her head.

"Paul! No!" I shoved my hand over the hole in her neck and tried to plug the bleeding but all I felt was blood tickling my fingers as it continued rushing out of her body. "Look, you were right, I see that now. We need the numbers to survive, so we need you to hang in there! I'm going to get you out of here, get you help and you'll be fine! I promise! All you have to do is hang in there!" Tears poured down my face after I said those words because I knew I was lying. I could tell Paul was not going to make it and I knew it was all my fault. *I screwed up! Again!*

"Okay," Paul whispered, so softly I could barely hear. She gave me a small smile and stopped straining to breathe. "But just in case, I need you to know... you are more than your job and things... Lane... don't let people tell you who you are... you're not nobody... you're... beautiful... in your own... magical... little... way."

I blinked the thick tears in my eyes away so I could see her better but all I saw was the spark go out of her eyes and her smile fall as the muscles on her face went weak.

Paul never moved again after that.

Not even when I willed her to. Or shook her! Or yelled!

I took her into my arms and wept more than I had ever done for any person before her. I cried more for her than I ever did for my parents or Arden Villeneuve or any other lover. Paul was the one for me, I realised then, only I had been too distracted and ignorant to realise it before.

A trooper grabbed me from behind, did something to my neck that caused me a hell lot of pain and threw me face down onto the floor.

Only when I felt the violent throbbing in my neck and saw the blood streaming down into a puddle under my face did I understand the trooper had sliced my neck with the blood-covered dagger he was holding in his hand. He stared at me as if waiting for me to pass out but I refused to.

I knew then I had enough of blacking out and being toyed with by Wonderdrug Laboratories. I knew then I had to get Paul out of there, as I promised, even though she would no longer be able to see it happen. I got onto my knees and pushed myself into a standing position, even though my back felt as if it were on fire and my head was starting to spin.

When I did manage to steady myself on two feet and look the offensive trooper in the eye, all I could see was the stupefaction on his face. He kept staring at my back so I turned and looked and that was when I realised my back was so thoroughly covered in bullet holes, it had the texture of a blood-filled honey comb.

Yet, it did look somewhat beautiful, in its own magical little way, even though it burned and seemed congested with objects that didn't quite belong. I took a deep breath, squeezed my back hard and felt much better the moment a multitude of bullets dislodged themselves from my flesh and spattered onto the floor like rain, making little clanking sounds as they hit the hard concrete floor.

The trooper's mouth fell open and he began to back away with the dagger firmly held between us.

Watching him react that way made me finally realise who I really was and what I was really capable of. Despite everything I failed to achieve in life, I was most definitely not a nobody indeed. Nor was I crazy. *I was just more unique than most people could ever imagine possible!*

I grabbed the rifle Paul had dropped and aimed it at the

trooper who quickly dropped his dagger so that he could lift his rifle towards me instead. I fired a few times but couldn't get him, so I moved closer. As I marched forward, he shot me nine times in total. Six times in the legs, twice in the chest and once in the head but I never stopped moving.

I shot him point blank with a single bullet the moment I got close enough. He was down on the ground and dead less than a minute later. I, although awash with new pains, remained standing. My neck no longer bled either.

Once I realised that could happen, I became unstoppable.

With the rifle firmly in my hands, I joined the odd-coloured woman in her fight and downed every single one of the troopers I came across. They shot at me as I walked through them, possibly over a hundred bullets collectively, but I never once stopped marching forward and shooting them in the face.

I no longer cared that I was killing people because I could tell—from their faces and the way they ran bullets through me like I were a paper target—how much they wanted to kill me. I no longer cared if they were fathers or sons or mere wage slaves like I once was because I could tell—from the way they lunged towards me and tried to strangle me or saw my head off—that they saw me as nothing but a specimen to be acquired. I could see I was never going to get to be free if I didn't fight my hardest for it.

That day, the day Paul died in my arms, I ended the lives of more than ten perfect strangers and became a whole new person.

CHAPTER 33
THE MORNING AFTER

I watched it all happen this time; saw the polka dots of blood all over my body change in size and texture while lying at the back of a car with the world going by and sunlight in my eyes.

It wasn't pleasant. There were horrific pulling sensations and lots of pain at first—excruciating, wholly absorbing pain in my back, legs, arms and head. Every breath became a shot of agony. Every thought, equally so. At points, I considered willing myself to black out but each time, I found myself deciding otherwise. I had to see all this for myself, I knew. *I had to know what my own body could really do.*

It was surreal. My wounds were different each time I looked. Deep holes of fresh blood metamorphosed into crusty, dark brown scabs within two hours. By the end of the third hour, the scabs were dropping off like leaves of a tree in autumn, revealing the brownish, discoloured blotches underneath. By the end of the fourth hour, the brownish blotches had already faded into nonexistence.

I sat up on the damp, blood-stained car seat when those strange pains desisted and my skin looked almost as good as normal. The song playing on the radio in that moment was something old and slow, something I remembered having heard once or twice when just a child, constructed from electric notes, drums and lamentations of a saxophone. The pensive male singer sang about some playground love in time with the passing world outside the car window.

In the driver's seat, the odd-coloured woman sang along. She had shades on and gloves over her hands and she knew every word. She sang like she meant every phrase too.

I scooted forward and put my head between the two front seats. "Are you real?" I asked her.

She turned her greenish-blueish-greyish head to glance at me and smiled. "After all that happened, can't you tell?" Her voice was gentle. Patient. As if she understood perfectly why my mind would be, in spite of everything in front of me, full of doubt.

"Just double-checking. And triple-checking. Just in case."

She nodded, I think, as she bobbed her head to the beat of the song she seemed to enjoy very much. "I'm real. You're real. Your friend was real too."

Paul. In the boot, covered in ice, just an inanimate object I couldn't bear to get rid of now. A lump snowballed in my throat and the world around me turned into a blur. I couldn't help but think Paul was truly my playground love and yet... "I fucked everything up big time, didn't I?"

The odd-coloured woman glanced at me through the rear view mirror and shrugged. "We all do. At first. That's how we learn. Lucky for you, we have the option of getting your friend back, if that's what you want."

"How?"

"You'll see."

I frowned and it made fat, heavy drops of tears roll down my cheeks.

My world became distinct again. The interior of the car looked cheap and was full of specks of dirt and scratches as rented cars usually were. The windshield ahead was full of water stains and mud. I looked out the side window and saw trees and endless roads and not many signs of human life. It looked like spring.

New York was nowhere in sight. None of Wonderdrug Laboratories' services or products were anywhere in sight.

That was a relief. I had no idea where we were headed but then, it no longer mattered, did it? *The old me was gone. My old life was gone. I could start again anywhere, and this time, with full knowledge of what I really could do.* Knowing that made me feel a tad hopeful.

The odd-coloured woman hummed the chorus of the song as if driving around with a dead body in the boot was nothing to be bothered by. Her calm, and maybe the calm of the human-less world outside, infected me. I felt myself sink back into the car seat and loosen up despite knowing how wrong it was for me to do so after having only just killed people.

"Can we talk about who pushed me now?" I asked at some point.

"What's that?"

"The woman who pushed me. You said you know who she is? So tell me. I want to know why she did it. I want to know why she thought I deserved to die."

"Ah, that." The odd-coloured woman turned the volume of the radio down and shrugged. "You don't actually know her personally but she found out we were hiding you, somehow, and she figured pushing you off a building would be the best way to inform the Office of your existence."

"I don't understand."

"Until the Office got to know about you, your grandmother had been the last person they knew of with a body like yours. After she died, all research on superhuman regeneration came to a standstill. It's been over forty years since they last made progress so I guess the woman who pushed you decided it was high-time they got moving again."

"Wait, so you know her?"

"No, I just know of her. I never met her but... I've been hearing a lot. Enough to know we should all be staying as far away from her as is humanly possible."

I frowned again. "Okay. And... who are you? How do I know I can trust you?"

The odd-coloured woman laughed—a genuine, truly amused laugh. "I see you're learning fast," she said with a sly grin once she was no longer laughing. "Lane, my name is Fleur. You can trust me because I was... how should I put it... I was your mother's really good friend." She smiled, slyly again.

My eyebrows moved upwards. "Tell me everything."

ABOUT THE AUTHOR

Anna Ferrara is a mostly-closeted lesbian living in a mostly-conservative city where male homosexuality remains illegal and female homosexuals do not have legal rights. In early 2017, she decided to begin expressing the mostly-secret side of herself through fiction and published her first book, *Snow White and Her Queen: The Untold Affair*. *The Woman Who Made Me Feel Strange* is her second book and the first in the *Those Strange Women* series. You can find out more about her life and work at annaferrarabooks.com

If you enjoyed this book and would like to express your support for the author, please do leave her a review on Goodreads.

OTHER BOOKS BY
ANNA FERRARA

About the Those Strange Women series

Those Strange Women is a series of six books about the lives of six 'unusual' women over nine decades. Amidst changing attitudes towards women and homosexuality, the women grow, adapt and find their own ways of existing in a world in which they don't quite belong. A few of them learn to love but most learn to hate; a few of them fail to thrive but most survive and develop a taste for revenge.

The Woman Who Pretended To Love Men

(Those Strange Women #2)

Set 30 years before The Woman Who Made Me Feel Strange (Those Strange Women #1), The Woman Who Pretended To Love Men (Those Strange Women #2) is Fleur's story—a mystery/lesbian romance novel which is complete in itself and can be enjoyed even if you haven't read Those Strange Women #1.

In 1999, Fleur de Roller walked into a tea house in Hong Kong and introduced herself to Milla Milone, daughter of a New York mob boss. Sparks flew.

Despite the obvious chemistry, Fleur repeatedly denies having any feelings for Milla because she has secrets—another identity and a job she can't talk about—that might get her into big trouble if the possibly dangerous younger woman ever found out.

Trouble comes anyway when the frustrated Milla moves on, starts dating other women, and leaves Fleur all by herself amidst a fervour of loss and wanting.

Fleur has to decide if the career she worked so hard to establish is worth the lies she has to put on to get ahead or if the 'alternative lifestyle' she read so many negative things about is worth giving up her well-paying job for.

She also has to decide if Milla is safe to love because Milla seems to be hiding a whole assortment of secrets of her own.

The Woman Who Tried To Be Normal

(Those Strange Women #3)

In 1975, Helen Mendel married a widower and aircraft engineer, moved into his suburb in Los Angeles, 375 miles away from Area 51, and got herself merrily settled into a life of domestic bliss with nothing but her husband's pleasure on her mind.

Ethel Ashlock, wife of her husband's colleague, a depressed alcoholic addicted to Valium with unfulfilled dreams of becoming a pilot, hates her on sight. She thinks Helen's just another boring, brain-washed housewife and doesn't make any effort to hide how much she detests her.

She doesn't realise Helen is not as commonplace as she appears; that she has synaesthesia—the ability to see sounds, hear images and taste feelings—and a past she's not telling anyone, not even her husband, about.

Things change when Helen, having tolerated enough of Ethel's persistent hostility, lifts her veil of pretence. Ethel soon finds herself blackmailed, frightened, and also… irresistibly intrigued by her new neighbour.

She becomes obsessed with getting Helen to like her and soon discovers they have more in common than she previously thought. Neither of them believe their husbands are truly aircraft engineers, for one, and neither of them believe Helen's husband's former wife, Violet, actually killed herself in the year before…

Together, the two women work to uncover the truth about Violet's sudden death, until they discover the truth, not out there, but closer than either of them ever thought possible…

Snow White and Her Queen

Before there was Snow White and the Seven Dwarfs, there was another story some preferred not to tell.

"Mirror, mirror on the wall, who in this land is fairest of all?"

"You, my Queen, are fairest of all," the Princess had said, unravelling a nightmare of obsession and forbidden desire.

At an apple orchard in the dead of the night, Queen Katherine runs into her reclusive stepdaughter for the first time in 17 years. Surprised by her ravishing beauty and unconventional boldness, she pursues a friendship, only to find herself inescapably captivated by the Princess' charm and wanting more.

"The Princess is a thousand times fairer than me," she concludes in an inexplainable fever of despair that shocks her servants as much as it does herself.

But at a time when romance between women is unthinkable, the Queen has to put on all the pretence she can muster to keep her horrible secret from both her powerful husband and the smitten huntsman trying to win her heart.

To make matters worse, seven peasants and a handsome Prince threaten to snatch the Princess' affections and take her away from the castle for good.

The Queen has to decide once and for all what to do about her strange feelings for the Princess, before she misses her chance.

This intimate retelling of the popular Grimms' fairy tale will change your understanding of the wicked Queen's infamous jealousy forever.

THE WOMAN WHO PRETENDED TO LOVE MEN

(Sample)

Chapter 1
25 Jun 1999, Friday

Milla and I first touched on a stormy evening in the last year of the twentieth century, inside a packed tea house in Hong Kong, amidst a flurry of inescapable noise and movement that was the inevitable result of too many people trying to co-exist in too small a space.

I was just inches away from her face, shoved forward by the stream of waiters and dinner patrons trying to squeeze past me from behind, drenched below the knees, with hair and arms covered in droplets of rain, when I asked if I could share her two-seater table.

"If you don't mind?" I added, when she looked up at me with suspicion, even though there were zero empty tables around her, no other empty seats and a horde of umbrella-wielding locals right outside the tea house's window. Normally, I wouldn't even have asked—table-sharing was just the way dining worked in Hong Kong—but this wasn't a normal situation.

At the table next to hers, four gangster-like men had looked up from their bowls and were staring daggers at me. The message they were trying to send me was clear. *Mess with her and you're dead.* Though I stood my ground, I made a big show of being polite—took my earphones out of my ear, adjusted the glasses on my nose to make sure they noticed I was the bookish sort—and made a mental note to leave if she did say 'no'. It was, after all, the year Columbine happened, just two years after Hong Kong's handover to China and months before the turn of the new millennium; I was decidedly aware that anything, even the most unexpected, could happen at any point.

"Go ahead," she said, after sizing me up with her large blue eyes for a good half second. To my relief, when she smiled, tucked one side of her long, dirty blonde hair behind her ear, and turned back to her bowl, the four gangster-like men dropped their glares and went back to eating too.

"Thanks."

I took the seat opposite her, just seconds before a waiter dropped a plastic cup of pale brown tea in front of me and asked, in English, "You want English menu?"

"No," I said, in Cantonese, and promptly glanced at the hand-written Chinese words on the longish slips of paper pasted all over the walls and mirrors of the tea house. *"I'll have a French Toast and a Milk Tea, thanks."*

He glanced up from the pad of paper he was scrawling on and regarded me with surprise. *"You're a Hong Konger?"* he said in Cantonese. *"Thought you were a foreigner, like your friend."*

"No, I'm from here and she's not my friend. I don't know her."

"I see. In that case, I suggest you don't piss her off." He shot me a knowing look, right before he tore out the order chit he had been scrawling on and stuffed it into the plastic cup next to the box of utensils at the edge of the table. In the blink of an eye, he was gone and screaming my order loudly enough for the entire tea house to hear. When I turned my eyes from him, I found Milla staring at me.

She looked away the moment she saw me see her but I could tell from the slightly self-conscious way she looked at her noodles afterward that she had been watching me for a good while.

"I just need dinner. That's all," I said to her in English as I grabbed a fork and knife from the box of utensils and rinsed them in the plastic cup of tea in front of me. I wanted to sound steady and nonchalant but my voice came out nervous nonetheless. "I'll leave the moment I'm done," I mumbled.

She looked up at me, with eyes that appeared to be laughing, and shook her head slightly. "It's fine. Don't worry."

"Thanks."

Milla turned her eyes back on the soupy, springy 'doll' noodles she was having. I didn't know what else to do with myself so I adjusted the leather satchel bag I had on my lap and looked all around.

I looked past the tumult of human activity, at the colourful mosaic tiles all over the floor and walls, at the wooden and green-cushioned booths that gave the tea house its '70s vibe, at the haphazard placement of tables and chairs, at the cream cushioned chair I was seated on; I watched waiters in their bright yellow uniforms weaving through the congested space as quickly as their hips would take them, like their lives depended on it, and the diners in office attire, with oily faces and blank expressions, shovelling food into their mouths without stopping to reflect or comment on what they were tasting; I checked out the tattoos the four gangster-like men at the next table had over their bodies, at their black outfits and the way their hairstyles were either too long or too short to be considered decent... I looked everywhere and at everyone but *her*.

"Wet night, huh," Milla suddenly said.

I turned my eyes back on her and found her staring right at me. "Sorry, what was that?" I asked and realised, too late, that I sounded breathless.

"The weather... very rainy."

"Oh, oh yeah. It's always this way in summer but it eases up when the weather cools so, hang in there." I tried to smile warmly but my smile came out weak and way more shaky than it was warm, I think. Lucky for me, it did what I intended it to do anyhow.

It made Milla smile. "How is it you speak English so well?" she asked as her eyes lit up. "Did you grow up somewhere else or... I don't know, go to a really expensive school or something?"

I laughed. "No, no. I lived here all my life and went to normal schools. But my mum's British, which means I'm half English so... Anyway, what about you? I'm guessing you're from... America?"

"Excellent guess. I'm from New York—"

"New York? You wouldn't happen to know a guy named Danny Diaz would you?"

"Danny Diaz?" Her grin went away but her face remained the perfect picture of calm. "No. I've never heard of him, sorry. Who is he?"

"I'm not really sure myself. All I know is that he's a tourist from New York who went missing from the ICU of King George Hospital just a few days ago."

"Does that happen often here?"

"No, not at all. Strangest thing is, he was still in a coma the last time any of the hospital staff saw him."

"Wow. Did he wake up? Walk out by himself?"

"I have no idea. The hospital wouldn't tell me anything. Has he been in American news yet? Is there anyone who knows what's really going on?"

"No. Not that I know of."

"Damn. I'll just have to go snooping around again, I guess. Maybe break into the hospital and get their report or something?"

"You know how to do that?"

"Maybe? How hard can it be, right?" I smiled again.

In return, Milla laughed. "Why do you need to know anyway? Are you a private investigator or something?"

"No, worse. Journalist. Sandra Sum from the East Asian Morning Post." I extended a hand towards her. "It's a local newspaper. I write in Chinese."

"Milla Smith. Tourist." She took my hand.

"Nice to meet you, Milla Smith."

"Likewise, Sandra Sum."

We shook for what felt like forever, with our eyes fixed on each other and smiles plastered on our faces. I thought her hand, which was a little smaller than mine, felt exceptionally smooth and delicate. The texture of her palm reminded me of a silk-lined woollen blanket I used to hold to sleep as a child; the one I used to think I would never be able to live without. I found myself wondering if she moisturised on a daily basis and how the texture of my own seldom-moisturised hand must feel like to her. I could detect a twinge of surprise in her eyes as she held on to me and I was convinced it was a sign I really had to get back to moisturising regularly again.

A plate of french toast and a cup of steaming milk tea on a matching saucer landed between us and ended our handshake for good. The waiter who dropped it down (not the one who took my order) crossed out the other waiter's scrawl on the order chit in the plastic cup and darted away before I could even utter a word of thanks.

Milla didn't even look at him. Her eyes remained on the hefty slice of deep-fried bread I now had in front of me and she told me it was the most delicious piece of bread she had ever seen.

The bread had a mound of butter on its very top, syrup streaming down its sides and smelled as sweet as a pail of warm honey yet I shrugged. "I bet it won't be as good as the one at Luk Kee Tea House. Have you heard of that place? It's been around since the '50s, near the mountains, in New Territories."

"I haven't, but it sure sounds like a whole lot of fun."

"It is, I have so many good memories of that place. I could take you there for dinner this weekend if you want to go. Do you?"

I couldn't tell if she did for Milla seemed to freeze, with eyes widening like a blooming flower. She didn't say a thing but simply stared at me as if she had only just found out I were an alien or something.

"You don't have to if you don't want to," I said eventually, after swallowing the nerves that had been snowballing in my throat since the moment I began walking up to her table. "I'm just putting it—"

"No. I mean, yes! Yes, I do want to go to dinner with you. Tomorrow." She beamed at me and, all of a sudden, began looking as beautiful as those supermodels in fashion magazines.

Relief washed over every inch of my skin and I found myself beaming as well. "Okay. Great. Why don't you give me your address so I know where to go pick you up and I'll write my cell phone number down for you so you can always call me if you change your mind." I dug around the bag on my lap, pulled out a brand new pocket-sized spiral notebook and pen, and handed them both to her.

Milla's eyes widened and for a second, she looked a little frozen again, but she managed to do as I asked and handed the notebook back to me.

"Big City Hotel?" I said when I saw what she had written. "How is it? I heard the breakfast buffet's really good there."

"It's alright. What time should I meet you tomorrow?"

"Seven? I'll pick you up at your hotel's lobby?"

"Sure," she said. Then, she added, in a softer tone, "I can't wait."

"Me too," I said.

I really did mean it.

Chapter 2
18 Jun 1999, Friday

The week before, I didn't even know one Sandra Sum. I had known a Sandra—some girl I did a project with in university—but I hadn't seen her in years and wouldn't have been able to pick her face out from the crowd even if my life depended on it.

The week before Milla and I first touched, I had only one name and one identity: Fleur de Roller, right on the verge of turning thirty, single and stuck in a job that hadn't changed in six whole years.

My mother—a Hong Konger and pure Chinese through and through—never failed to remind me of the major milestones I hadn't yet met. Once a week, always between 7 and 8am, during which I would most certainly be making myself my daily cup of instant coffee, she would call me on my Motorola StarTAC to demand updates. *Are you dating yet? Any news of a promotion yet?* For years I had been telling her to stop asking the same boring questions but she never once listened.

"I'm only asking for your own good, Lola," she would always say in Cantonese, the language she used with me. *"I just want you to be as happy as Carla is."*

Carla was my mother's second husband's daughter and the person she mentioned most often when chatting with me. When I first met Carla at age thirteen, when my mother and I moved into her father's home where she lived, she had been a sweet-looking teenager with creamy, flawless skin. We were the same age and ended up going to the same school but she had more admirers than I had friends, started dating six years before I did and ended up with more boyfriends than I had first dates. Although my grades were consistently better than hers, she attained the more glamorous degree and ended up with every Hong

Kong parent's dream job—doctor. In our twenties, Carla did everything right by my mother's standards—never wore the same dress more than thrice; visited beauticians for facials once every month; always had her nails coloured; used sunblock so religiously, her skin was always about three shades fairer than mine even though I was, as far as genetics were concerned, supposed to be more 'white' than she. She remained close to the clique of female friends she had grown up with, got herself a long-term boyfriend by the age of twenty-four and was paid relatively well by the hospital she worked for. In short, she was on track to becoming rich, happy and successful in old age.

I, on the other hand, had been a pimply teenager with braces, who was, unfortunately, also more than a head taller than the average girl at school; Carla included. Because I enjoyed reading and playing games on my NES more than I enjoyed shopping or talking about boys, hair, skin, nails and fashion, I never really clicked with any of the girls at school the way Carla could do so effortlessly. I just never got their jokes the way they seemed to get each other's jokes and always ended up feeling odd and awkward as I faked giggles. I didn't click with the guys much either—they just never developed crushes on me the way they crushed on Carla and her friends; I eventually concluded they were either intimidated by my height and grades, or turned off by my A-cup chest. I did manage to meet a guy who liked me enough to want me as a girlfriend in university but by age twenty-nine, that guy was getting ready to propose to a woman he had been dating for twice as many years as he had me and I was not even playing the dating game anymore. I wasn't doing that much better in my career either, as far as my mother knew. To her knowledge, I was a statistician at a small, local enterprise, earning less than Carla or any of her friends, and it exasperated her to no end.

"You should ask your boss for a promotion," she barked one morning in the summer of '99. *"If he doesn't give you a*

promotion, find another job! Why the hell else did you get your Master's degree for? Your job doesn't even let you afford breast enhancement surgery for goodness sakes!"

"I don't want bigger breasts, and I kinda like my current job—"

"Jobs aren't for liking, Lola! They're for moneymaking. If you aren't making a little more every year, you need to leave. Immediately! And in the meantime, get some new clothes, go out more, meet some men! You're going to run into a lot of problems later on if you don't have a baby soon. I know you're shy, I know you're introverted, but frankly, you've had enough alone time to last you a lifetime. It's time to work on the adult stuff, start a family like everybody else your age!"

"Is this because Carla got promoted?"

"No. It's because she's getting married."

"Really?"

"Her boyfriend proposed two nights ago. She called Daddy and I to announce the news last night."

"That explains a lot."

"You don't even call. I'm always the one calling you, and you don't visit."

"I can't deal with this right now, I need to get to work."

"Lola, I'm not kidding. Go shopping then go to a party! I know you won't so, please, I'm begging you, do! Dress yourself up better and meet as many men as you can, while you're still young! Also, ask your boss for that promotion or else—"

"Alright, bye Mummy!"

I clammed up my StarTAC without waiting for a reply and found myself feeling a tad more annoyed than usual that morning.

My mother did know me. As she predicted, I didn't make any plans to go shopping or to parties after our phone call—I thought walking around scouring racks of fabric was just about the most boring activity ever and I loathed small talk with every inch of my soul. What I did do, however, was write my boss an email asking about the possibility of being considered for a promotion during the next round of appraisals in November. I concurred with my mother in that regard; six years was way too long to be staying at a job without a promotion of any sort.

What my mother didn't know, however, was that I wasn't a lowly-paid statistician like she thought I was. In fact, I wasn't even a statistician at all. The company I worked for, Everquest Incorporated, did offer data analysis services but that wasn't the job they hired me for. The job I got had been hard-won; I had to beat over a hundred other hopefuls in nine rounds of interviews and tests—both physical and intellectual—just to get the role. It paid extremely well too, way better than Carla's hospital or her friends' Japanese corporations or government offices. I never told my mother the truth about it, however, because there was a clause in the employment contract I signed that explicitly stated I wasn't allowed to let anyone but my official spouse—whom I was to declare by submitting a Spouse Declaration Form along with a copy of our marriage certificate and a recent photograph of my spouse—know how much I really earned or what I actually did at work. The title of 'Statistician' and the amount of money I was to say I got for doing the job wasn't my decision either; it was in that contract, explicitly stated in bold, black letters.

While I didn't understand why there would be such a clause when I accepted the job, over time, the reason for such secrecy became obvious. You see, my job wasn't the office-based nine-to-five sort. Not even close. After six months of intensive, one-on-one training with a trainer who told me to call him Benny, I worked round the clock, as and when, wherever and whenever, and mostly in the shadows.

For five and a half years, I stood behind curtained windows, crowds of people, pillars and walls and observed the daily activity of a woman my boss called C31. He never explained what the 'C' stood for and I never asked for there was another clause in my employment contract that stated I was never to be inquiring about my assignments, but in my own head, I concluded 'C' likely stood for 'Caution' or 'Cult'. 'Caution', because C31 was, my boss said, really a terrorist in hiding; 'Cult', because she was, I was told, a high-ranking member of the Japanese cult that carried out that deadly chemical gas attack on the Tokyo subway in 1995. Eight people died in that attack and more than two hundred were wounded; as a result, a client of Everquest (my boss was not allowed to disclose who) was not taking any chances with her. Intel was that she had been in constant contact with the cult right around the time they started doing assassination experiments on sheep and people. The client wanted somebody to watch her round the clock just so they could be sure she wasn't planning a similar attack on the train system in Hong Kong. For five and a half years, that somebody was me.

I rented a tatty one-bedroom, one-bathroom apartment opposite the dilapidated '50s building in which C31 and her family lived and turned it into my home and office. On week days, when C31 sat in the teeny, dusty palm-reading shop she and her husband, Mr Lam, ran on the first floor of the towering apartment block, I would attach a long lens to the video camera I had permanently on tripod in my living room and point it down towards the ground. When she went back up to her cramped, old-fashioned apartment on the sixth floor, I would put a shorter lens on the video camera and tilt it upwards to record the inside of her apartment instead.

On weekends, if C31 left her apartment, say for meals with her husband and fifteen-year-old son, or to meet friends and family, I would tail her and record who she met, where she went and what she did in one of the many pocket-sized spiral notebooks I bought with my office's approval. If I knew the entire family of three would be out of the house for more than an hour, say to go to a gathering or for a day out at the beach, I would sneak into her apartment to collect and replace the eight tiny cameras my boss made me install and keep hidden in her apartment at all times. My boss told me to buy an entire box of such cameras the day I finished my six months of training; they were state-of-the-art spy cameras with motion detection capabilities, only just the size of an eraser, and they could record video on removable MultiMediaCards for at least a week before running out of battery or card space. By attaching them to a wad of plasticine and climbing onto whichever chair or table I could get my hands on, I could hide the tiny cameras in high places C31 and her family would never touch—inside ceiling lamps, on the tops of cupboards, above the hood of their stove and on their prayer shelf, on a plastic fan that was mounted on a wall. It helped that C31's apartment was filled with mismatched furniture and cluttered—clothes and bags of plastic hanging from cupboards and doors; shoes, boxes and storage bags stuffed under beds and chairs or wherever possible; for five whole years, the family of three lived with cameras all around their two-bedroom, one-bathroom apartment and not one of them noticed.

I came to know C31 more intimately than I did my own mother. I knew exactly how long she took to shower and eat, how often she let her husband make love to her, how often she spent helping her only son with his homework. I knew her palm-reading business was doing well, that they had a loyal following who believed she was practically psychic, who came for readings at least once a year or whenever they needed someone to help them make big life decisions. I knew C31 and family had way more savings than the decrepit, shambolic home they lived in implied; that the whole family had even gotten American citizenships by investment approved and were planning to move away from Hong Kong at the end of 1999.

That was the other reason I decided to ask for a promotion. For five and a half years, all I had ever done was watch, record and write weekly reports on C31; I had no idea what my job would be like if she left the country. My boss had been aware of her move to America for months yet he never once mentioned a transfer to America or a new assignment for me. It didn't feel like there was anything in the cards just yet and that worried me. I liked my job; I didn't want to lose it because of sheer bad luck. And hell, if I couldn't get wed or a boyfriend like other women my age, the least I could do was get my career sorted, right? I had been 'Fleur de Roller, *Junior* Security Agent' for way too long.

I got lucky. My boss replied my email that very day.

'Let's discuss. Meet me at the office on Monday, 3pm.'

I was beyond excited.

Chapter 3
21 Jun 1999, Monday

Everquest Incorporated had its headquarters in a tower of many small and medium businesses within the Central Business District. The tower wasn't the most modern or stylish of the towers in the area but it wasn't the shabbiest either.

Whenever I went over to the office, usually only once every six months for my compulsory appraisals, I would wear a black business suit over a crisp white blouse and pull my long black hair back into a tight, neat bun to blend in with the office crowd on the streets below and within the building.

After going through the glass door with the Everquest Incorporated logo on it, I would go right to the corridor of doors on the left of the reception counter, to the first bright blue door on the left, behind which I knew my boss and the smell of stale, bitter coffee would be waiting for me.

On the rare occasion I ran into another office-attired person when making that short journey, I would simply smile and walk on without saying a word like my boss had told me to do very early on. He never explained why but since nobody I ran into at the Everquest office, not even the receptionist, ever made conversation with me, I presumed it was because we all had projects we weren't allowed to talk about.

"Hello, de Roller," my boss said the moment I stepped into his room that Monday, right on the dot at 3pm. His name was Mr Yamamoto. He was Japanese, in his early fifties, with a greying moustache, perpetually neat side-combed hair and a preference for short-sleeved shirts in pale blue, which he usually wore with a black tie. "Nice to see you again. You look prettier than ever."

"Thank you," I said, even though I could see his beady black eyes running over my chest from behind his thick glasses and feel my cheeks go hot. (My blouse was buttoned all the way up to my neck and the jacket above it covered three-quarters of my chest, mind you.) I made myself smile anyhow because I knew that was expected of me. Mr Yamamoto was not the owner of Everquest, just a salaried employee who made it up the ranks over the years, but he had been my boss from day one; he was the one who appraised my work once every six months and also the only person from Everquest with whom I interacted on a regular basis. So even though I had nothing nice to say about his appearance in return—I honestly thought he looked much older and more worn since the last time I saw him, with eye bags that were double the size they had been and creases on his forehead and eyes that were now more visible than ever—I saw no sense in making him dislike me. I kept my thoughts to myself because I knew I needed him more than he needed me.

"Please, sit." His tanned hand sprung up from behind the mountains of files, envelopes and paper that buried his desk and he gestured at the cushioned office chair that sat between his desk and me. "Make yourself comfortable."

I sat but found it hard to be comfortable in the presence of a man who could determine the future of my career with mere words and numbers; who also seemed to prefer keeping his eyes fixed below my neck most of the time.

"I called you in today, de Roller, because I want to know why it is you think you deserve a promotion right now," he said.

"I've been accomplishing my assignment on time and without any problems for six whole years, sir. I would like to progress in my career at some point and, I think, now that I have shown myself capable, I would like to do more."

"Fair enough. Unfortunately, de Roller, at Everquest,

due to the difficult nature of our business, we don't give out promotions that easily." He looked up and into my eyes at last. "We require our employees to pass a test, so to speak, to prove themselves capable of handling the next level of duties before we promote them."

I held my head high, held his gaze with confidence and nodded. "I would be happy to give the test a go, sir. If you think I'm ready."

"The test won't be easy, I'm afraid. It will require a lot more of your wits and skills than your previous assignment ever did. So, de Roller, what I want to know is... how badly do you want a promotion? Will you be willing to take on an assignment that will take up the whole of your existence for an indefinite amount of time and challenge you in ways you cannot yet imagine or would you prefer to remain on C31, doing what I personally think you've been doing a fantastic job on?"

I noticed he didn't once mention C31's move to the U.S. and it made me apprehensive all over again. *A sign he was getting ready to remove me from the organisation?* "I'd like to take the test, sir," I said.

"Are you sure?" He narrowed his already relatively narrow eyes and leaned forward, his brown crinkled cheek almost touching the formerly white, now yellowish, boxy computer monitor that stuck out from behind his stacks of papers. "Because there's no backing out once you choose to accept the new assignment and any screw up you make will have repercussions. It's written in your contract. You might want to read it again before coming to a decision."

I saw myself in the reflection of his glasses and saw myself looking tense so I took a deep breath and tried my best to present myself as a competent and intrepid individual. "I am aware, sir, and I know I'm ready to take it on. If you're ready for me to take it on, that is."

Mr Yamamoto smiled and dropped backwards into his chair—a chair that looked exactly like the one I was sitting on—and dropped his eyes below my neck yet again.

"Good. In that case, de Roller, clean up C31's apartment and be done with that. Don't ever monitor her, talk to her or go anywhere near her ever again. The consequences of doing so will be severe. Check your contract if you don't remember the details."

I nodded.

"Great. Now that that's done, I'm going to give you your new assignment." He spun around in his chair, pulled open a drawer on the metallic shelf that was next to him, dug around and pulled out a brown and sealed A3-sized envelope that was puffed out, oddly shaped and full of bulky items. He tossed it over to me and when the envelope landed on my lap, I saw it had the photograph of a young man stapled on its front.

"Your test will be C39, Danny Diaz from New York. He arrived in Hong Kong two weeks ago under a tourist VISA and our client received intel he's planning a big terror event in the region. Oddly enough, he's now, apparently, in a coma at King George Hospital. Your job is to monitor all of his activity, if any, and find out who he's been in contact with. Send weekly reports and footage back to me, the same way you did with C31. Don't leave anything out."

The young man in the photograph was an extraordinarily good-looking pretty boy who looked younger than twenty-five. His face was like a model's—perfectly contoured, with dark brown hair shaved close to his scalp, thick eyebrows, dark brown eyes, no stubble and a healthy-looking golden tan. He looked happier than most and possessed the sort of smiley, boyish charm I knew Carla and her friends, and maybe even my mother, would swoon over. He had none of the brooding disgruntlement you'd expect to see on a terrorist's face, but then, I remembered C31—she looked nothing like a terrorist either; she looked exactly like the average Hong Kong woman would when just a few years short of fifty, with the same innocuous demeanour, the same tight curls in her short hair, the same barely visible makeup, and the same floral blouses worn over loosely-fitted mono-coloured pants. I decided appearances were most certainly deceiving.

"Do you see the importance of your role here? If you succeed, that promotion you seek is yours, of course, but you will also have contributed to something so much bigger."

"I see it, sir, and I'd be more than happy to take on the challenge." I looked up at him and smiled in a way that would suggest I was both friendly and helpful.

He smiled back, to my relief. "Good. In that envelope are tools you will use to get the job done. You will assume a new identity and wear the glasses within at all times. You will keep those glasses in the case they now sit in for at least five hours every night when you sleep, without fail, and put on the other devices within when instructed. You will carry the phone within everywhere and pick up every call you get on it as soon as you can. Are we clear?"

"Yes, sir. We are very clear."

"Good. In that case, take that envelope, internalise your new identity and wait for the call that will instruct you on how you're going to get started."

"Yes, sir."

"I look forward to seeing you succeed, de Roller. Just between us, I must say I think you've been one of the most capable junior hires we've had in a while. I have a feeling you'll find a way to pass this test, just as you've always passed all of mine." His eyes fell back down onto my chest and this time remained right there.

I swallowed my discomfort, kept my smile on and stood up from the chair to bring my chest away from his eyes. "I will. I won't disappoint you, sir."

He looked a tad disappointed anyway. "Good," he said to my crotch. "Now get out of here, I've got another meeting in five."

I did exactly as he ordered.

My mother, my teachers, career coaches, self-help books, they always said it was to my benefit to obey everything the boss said.

(End of Sample)

Find out where you can buy

The Woman Who Pretended To Love Men at

annaferrarabooks.com